KT-468-240

The Summer We Ran Away

Jenny Oliver

ONE PLACE. MANY STORIES

This novel is entirely a work of fiction. The names, characters and incidents portrayed in it are the work of the author's imagination. Any resemblance to actual persons, living or dead, events or localities is entirely coincidental.

HQ
An imprint of HarperCollins*Publishers* Ltd
1 London Bridge Street
London SE1 9GF

1
First published in Great Britain by
HQ, an imprint of HarperCollins*Publishers* Ltd 2020

Copyright © Jenny Oliver 2020

Jenny Oliver asserts the moral right to be
identified as the author of this work.
A catalogue record for this book is
available from the British Library.

ISBN: 9780008297541

MIX
Paper from
responsible sources
FSC™ C007454

FSC
www.fsc.org

This book is produced from independently certified FSC™ paper
to ensure responsible forest management.

For more information visit: www.harpercollins.co.uk/green

This book is set in 10,9/15,5 pt. Sabon by Type-it AS, Norway

Printed and bound in Great Britain by
CPI Group (UK) Ltd, Croydon, CR0 4YY

All rights reserved. No part of this publication may be reproduced,
stored in a retrieval system, or transmitted, in any form or by any means,
electronic, mechanical, photocopying, recording or otherwise,
without the prior permission of the publishers.

This book is sold subject to the condition that it shall not, by way of trade
or otherwise, be lent, re-sold, hired out or otherwise circulated without
the publisher's prior consent in any form of binding or cover other than
that in which it is published and without a similar condition including this
condition being imposed on the subsequent purchaser.

For Kate and Becky, thank you.

CHAPTER ONE

It was the start of the bank holiday weekend and the air was abuzz with Lexi and Hamish Warrington's summer party. Music was already drifting over the street to announce the lavish annual event.

The weather was steaming. Clouds had been holding in the heat like a pressure cooker for days. Everyone with their own theory on when it might break, whispering about who was using their hose even though there was a ban. On Thursday's bin night all the blue recycling crates up the street were full of Dyson fan boxes and paddling pool packaging.

Across the road at number nine Cedar Lane, Julia Fletcher was busy icing fifty-five vanilla cupcakes, baked at Lexi Warrington's behest, before the party started. There was white frosting and white sugar stars everywhere to fit with this year's white-hot theme. Last year it had been unicorns. Lexi had dyed her hair like a rainbow and worn a tail which Julia, who had moved in last autumn, only knew because she'd found the picture on Instagram.

The party was all anyone had been talking about for months. Lexi had sent a save the date to the Cedar Lane WhatsApp group in mid-January when there was still frost on the pavements: Guys, so sick of this weather!! Only thing keeping me sane is SUMMER PARTY–yay!! Lxxx Everyone marking it in the diary months in advance so the date wouldn't be double-booked.

Now the party was due to start in half an hour and Julia was nowhere near ready. There was icing everywhere. The crappy oven had burnt half the cakes and under-baked the other half. There was a wasp buzzing furiously against the window. Inside the house it was like an oven. The red-brick Victorian houses on Lexi's side of the street kept naturally cool, whereas the pebble-dashed post-war terraced houses on Julia's side were built with walls as thin as bible pages so they heated up like furnaces in the summer and turned to ice in winter.

Julia's husband, Charlie, strolled casually into the kitchen. 'God, I love a bank holiday,' he sighed, the relief of the extra day off lifting his whole being as if at all other times he wore the job he hated heavy on his shoulders. He'd been for a cycle already that morning and changed out of his sweaty cycling kit into an old pair of turquoise shorts and a green T-shirt. 'Does Lexi know you've gone to this much effort?' he asked, watching Julia frantically trying to finish the cakes.

Julia looked up, pushing her hair out her eyes with the back of her hand, she was not in the mood for chat. The mid-morning almost tropical heat was making the frosting curdle. 'Try this,' she said, handing him one of the cupcakes that had caught in the oven. 'Can you tell it's burnt?'

Charlie examined the little cake, then popped it into his mouth whole. 'Nice,' he said, voice muffled with cake, nodding with approval.

Julia wasn't so sure and took a bite of one herself. It definitely tasted burnt, but there wasn't time to do anything about it now. If she covered them with enough silver balls and sugared white stars, hopefully no one would notice.

Charlie might very well be shaking his head at Julia's clear distress re the cakes, but the thing about Lexi Warrington was that she made you want to impress her. She was Queen Bee of the road with the perfect house and the perfect children – little blonde twin girls. Everyone loved Lexi. She had a buoyancy. A story to tell for every situation, an emoji reply for every one of the hundred Instagram comments she receives, an effortlessly understated outfit for every barbecue or Cedar Lane WhatsApp group drinks.

Since moving in, Lexi had taken Julia under her wing – inviting her round for a coffee and to do yoga in the living room, including her in the cocktail nights with the girls – and because of that, Julia didn't mind doing things for her, like making the cakes or, as was Lexi's current bugbear, helping campaign against the new Sainsbury's planned for development at the end of the street: Julia, you're in marketing aren't you? Could you knock up a good template letter of complaint for the whole street to use? Thanks, sweetie! L xxx

Julia wasn't stupid, she knew that in some ways Lexi was using her – she made you feel special so you'd do things for her – but it didn't matter. That was the thing about Lexi, there was something magnetic about her, something powerful. She made you *want* to do things for her.

Charlie had gone over to the window to let the wasp out and was now standing by the kitchen table that was stacked high with paint charts, decorating catalogues and tile samples, leafing through the mess to find something. 'Do we need all this stuff?' he asked, gesturing to the decorating paraphernalia.

Julia shook her head. 'I have no idea. Probably not.' Renovations on their property had somewhat stalled recently with the depletion of their bank balance.

Charlie said, 'Do you know where my seed catalogue is?' nosing his way through the stack.

Julia looked over at him in disbelief. How could Charlie be thinking about seeds when they were about to head out to the party of the year? She checked the time on the oven clock. 'Oh God, it starts soon. Shit, I haven't even got changed. You've got to get changed.'

'I am changed,' Charlie said without looking up. 'I think my tomatoes might have blight,' he mused, nudging paint charts out of the way with his finger to find the seed catalogue, 'but I'm pretty sure I ordered Mountain Magic which are blight-resistant.'

Julia paused her icing, wondering if she could somehow subtly ask him to please not talk solely about his vegetable patch while they were at the party, but she knew if she did that then she'd offend him because it was his current pride and joy and they'd have a row. But really, no one wanted to talk about tomatoes. Especially no one at Lexi and Hamish's.

She iced the last cupcake. 'Charlie, you can't go wearing that,' she said, gesturing to his turquoise and green colour combination. 'It's a white-hot theme. You need to wear white. Haven't you got a white shirt?'

'I hate white shirts. I look stupid in white,' he said, 'like I'm going to school.'

4

'You don't,' Julia replied. He did. But she didn't want him to stand out in his green T-shirt. She wanted them to blend seamlessly in. Julia had been immersed in Lexi's all-consuming outfit planning for weeks and as a result had found herself panic scrolling for outfits during work meetings, shopping in her lunch break and scouring Pinterest for good hair ideas, all especially for today.

She looked over at Charlie, trying to ignore the mess on the table and the cracked bare plaster wall behind him. 'You must have a white T-shirt, surely? Don't you have a polo shirt?'

'It's really old.' Charlie came over to the kitchen counter, picking an apple from the fruit bowl and taking a bite. 'This is fine,' he said, pulling at his T-shirt. 'Honestly, I just want to relax this weekend.'

Julia sprinkled tiny white sugar stars all over the cakes. 'Please, Charlie, please go and put the polo shirt on. For me.'

Charlie sighed. 'OK, fine, whatever.' Munching on his apple, he skulked out of the room.

'And you need your swimming trunks!' Julia called after him. 'They've hired a hot tub.'

From the hallway Charlie shouted back, 'There is absolutely no way I am taking my top off at this party.'

Julia went back to her cakes, pincering silver balls into the centre of each one. It was hypocritical of her to roll her eyes at Charlie because he was just reflecting back her own insecurities. She wasn't thrilled at the idea of being in just her swimming costume at the party either, but she didn't want to be *that* couple. Hamish and Lexi wouldn't have any qualms about stripping off; they'd probably get naked given half the chance.

Julia's phone beeped on the kitchen counter. It was a WhatsApp from her work friend Meryl. She reached over with icing-covered hands to read it.

Meryl: Had any more Hot Hamish fantasies?

Oh God. Julia leant over the counter to see that Charlie was definitely no longer around, her heart racing.

On Thursday night, Julia had gone for after-work drinks to celebrate Meryl's new job in Hong Kong. A bit pissed on countless glasses of Pinot Grigio Blush in the boiling sunshine, and sad that Meryl was off on a new adventure, Julia had admitted to the fact that, over the last few weeks, she'd been having erotic dreams about Lexi's husband, Hamish Warrington. Julia had never had erotic dreams before. Even the fact she used the word erotic suggested to her that this was not her normal territory. As she'd told Meryl, dimly aware of her uninhibited insobriety, 'I'm not an erotic sex-dream person. I have quiet, nice sex. I can't even believe I've said the word sex so many times in this conversation, I've never talked about sex this much in my life.'

Meryl, who talked about sex a lot, had guffawed. Congratulated her even for this unexpected candidness. Then insisted on seeing Hamish's Instagram page which was all pictures of him with his top off; six-foot-two, washboard-stomached, dirty-blond hair, on holiday in the Maldives or sweating through a HIIT workout. Meryl had highly approved and the sex-dream conversation had segued into Meryl disappearing down a Hamish Warrington Instagram wormhole.

Later that night Meryl had WhatsApped Julia with a drunken diagnosis:

I think the problem is that you're trapped in normality. On paper you have everything but maybe you're feeling constrained by convention. Your bored brain is seeking excitement, Mx P.S. Never let me drink Blush again

Julia had pondered the notion. When she and Charlie had bought the house on Cedar Lane last year it had all seemed very exciting. Charlie's granny had died and left him enough money, along with their savings, to make up the deposit. They had attained what had been deemed unattainable, a rung on the housing ladder. Even her parents had been impressed. Julia had splodged each wall with Farrow & Ball tester pots and made a Pinterest board for every room. She had dreams of pale grey Scandinavian kitchen cupboards, high stools and a snazzy hot water tap.

But now, after spending out on a new boiler, a new bathroom because the shower leaked, having the Asbestolux all over the top floor removed, and experiencing the nauseous horror of being told they needed a new roof that they couldn't afford and paying to patch it up instead, they were at a cash flow standstill. They were having to hold out on further renovations till they could afford them. The Farrow & Ball paint had been immediately downgraded to Homebase own-brand, but even that was sidelined when it was revealed the bedroom wall needed replastering. It meant they were living in depressingly wallpaper-stripped rooms with orange swirly carpet throughout and a half-torn down kitchen with bare plaster walls. They had sucked every last pound of their savings and interest-free credit. Their joint income was now spreadsheeted and accounted for for the next three years, including adjustments for possible interest rate rises and a freeze on bonuses, so that with every eight to ten months came the possibility of decorating a room, bar any further disasters. Charlie had weighted the spreadsheet to include a baby next year but, looking at the figures, possibly the year after would be better financially.

Even thinking about it made Julia feel claustrophobic.

She thought about how when Meryl had announced she was going to Hong Kong for a year's secondment – essentially to escape from a vile, harrowing break-up – Julia had actually felt a stab of envy at the excitement of it, even the relationship turbulence and anguish that went with it.

It had made her conclude that Meryl's drunken WhatsApp diagnosis was probably correct.

Now, in the sweltering kitchen, Julia wiped the icing off her hands and typed a message back to Meryl:

> Don't! I'm being plagued by them! I had another Hamish dream last night. We did it in the middle of the day, in the bushes by the children's playground in the rain! I feel so bad. It's like my brain is having an affair that my body has to keep quiet. It's awful.
>
> Lol. Doesn't sound awful ;-)
>
> Meryl

Julia rolled her eyes at Meryl's reply. It *was* awful. Lately, she found herself night after night, lying in bed next to Charlie, feeling like a traitor.

Standing in the kitchen, she was suddenly jolted by a flash of the dream. Hamish all rain-slicked, pressing her tight to him with bulging muscles, eyes all lust and adoration, grinning down at her with his dazzling teeth.

From upstairs Charlie shouted, 'Have you seen my white polo shirt anywhere?'

Julia's cheeks immediately flamed with guilt. She fumbled her phone, dropping it onto one of the fairy cakes. 'Damn.' She hastily wiped the frosting off. 'Hang on, Charlie,' she called, trying to sound normal. 'I'm just coming up to get changed. I'll find it for you.'

CHAPTER TWO

Across the road in Lexi's front garden, the ancient olive tree was festooned with white fairy lights and white concertina lanterns. Faux tealights in white paper bags lined the garden path. And white bunting hung from window to window. They even had a light projector that made snowflakes dance over the front of the house.

The heat blazed down on Julia's Tupperware full of cakes, the white clouds a laughable barrier to the ferocity of the midday sun. Charlie was frowning at a battered yellow VW camper van parked in the space outside Lexi's house. On the windscreen was a sign that read: PLEASE DON'T PARK THIS VAN OUTSIDE OUR HOUSE!

'Did Lexi write that?' he asked, even though it was obvious she had.

Just the week before, Lexi had WhatsApped the Cedar Lane Group the message:

Sorry to do this, guys, but re parking. I know the space outside MY house is not technically mine but I think we should RESPECT people's right to park in front of their

OWN houses. In my last street we did this as an unwritten rule and it worked REALLY well!! ☺ Lexi xxxx

Charlie shook his head. 'She can't stick things on people's vans. She doesn't own the street.'

Normally Julia would agree, but she knew the effort Lexi had gone to for this party and she could forgive her for wanting it all to be perfect. As Julia's father would say, woe betide anyone who got in her way.

They walked up the path together, Julia wowed by the effort of the decorations, Charlie still shaking his head, incredulous about the van sticker.

Charlie had changed his top to the polo shirt and only after a massive row had conceded to wear his green shorts that doubled as swimming trunks, but still flatly refused to get in the tub. Julia had her new bikini on under a new white dress with a floaty skirt – both of which she'd bought in H&M but they were exact copies of more expensive ones she couldn't afford – and a new pair of white Superga plimsolls that she had stumbled upon in TK Maxx and almost wept for joy. She had tried to thread a white ribbon into her hair like she'd seen on Pinterest but she'd run out of time to do it properly and in the time she had it looked a shambles. As a result of being overworked, her hair had gone annoyingly flat.

'I've never seen that dress before,' said Charlie as they waited for the door to open.

Julia shrugged. 'Oh I've had it for ages,' aware that they weren't meant to be spending.

Charlie nodded, still studying her.

'What?' Julia asked, conscious that she was being watched.

'Nothing,' he said, then after a second's contemplation added, 'It's just not very you.'

Julia rolled her eyes. 'You're meant to say I look very nice.'

'You do look nice. Just not very you.' Charlie shrugged.

Julia was about to reply when the door was thrown open and suddenly Hamish Warrington was there, arms thrown wide as he called, 'Julia! Charlie! Come in! Come in!' And Julia found that she couldn't speak – all hot suddenly and flustered by the sight of him and the memory of her dreams – as he pulled her into a big warm hug.

Hamish was decked out completely in white linen – shorts and shirt – with white flip-flops. Charlie looked him up and down as he pumped Charlie's hand in greeting, and said dryly, 'That's a brave outfit choice.'

Hamish barked a laugh, bright white teeth chewing on something or nothing as he gave Charlie a hearty pat on the shoulder, 'Good to have you here, Charlie old boy.'

Julia was still all flustered, pulling awkwardly at her dress, trying to balance the Tupperware of cakes which had the effect of making her feel a bit frumpy and self-conscious in front of Hamish. At the same time, she steadfastly avoided Charlie's sideways mocking glance as he tried to get her on side with regards to Hamish's white linen ensemble.

They followed Hamish as he led them through the hallway with its hot pink walls and acid yellow staircase – 954 Instagram likes the day it was painted – and into the kitchen.

As they walked into the room, it was apparent that there had been no scrimping on the decorations. Puffballs of tissue paper hung from the ceiling like giant pompoms, vases of white lilies graced every table and surface, on the floor were big glass urns of coiled fairy lights. Impeccably dressed waiting staff and caterers were busy arranging platters of food and uncorking champagne.

In the centre of all the action was Lexi, in a spaghetti-strapped, figure-hugging, floor-length gown of shimmering white sequins that she'd had shipped over from the States. She was leaning up against the pale turquoise herringbone tiles of her kitchen island, selfieing with Alicia Fox from number twenty-four and Nicky Merryweather from number seventeen, their matching blonde hair intertwining as they all pressed their cheeks together.

Julia had to pause to take a courage-mustering breath. She was really regretting arriving with a giant Tupperware now. They were all so glamorous, so effortlessly cool. They made her feel like the awkward new girl at school, desperate to belong. Nicky Merryweather was nice enough, but Alicia Fox always made Julia uncomfortable. Like there was a joke she'd missed. Whenever she saw Lexi, Julia definitely preferred it when Alicia wasn't there.

'Julia, darling! You look gorgeous.' Lexi sprang forward from the embrace with the other two blondes, her dress catching the light like a glitter ball. 'Are those my cakes?'

Julia nodded, handing over the cakes, grateful to relinquish the Tupperware. 'You look amazing,' she said to Lexi.

'Ohh,' said Lexi, waving away the compliment with faux-modesty. 'Well I never get to dress up nowadays. Two kids will zap away that kind of sparkle!'

Everyone smiled and nodded even though they all knew it was a lie – Lexi had a wardrobe bursting with designer dresses and festival fancy dress, and never failed to wow with her Halloween costumes – but she had the power to make everyone happily complicit.

She lifted the lid off the plastic box of little cakes. 'These are divine, Julia. You're a superstar,' she said, immediately taking a photo of the dainty frosting, showing them to Nicky and Alicia, who both oohed politely, then passed them over to the caterer who was putting together canapés with an air of tautly controlled calm.

Julia watched as the harassed caterer shoved the cakes to one side.

'Now, drinks!' Lexi clapped her hands together. 'There's a gin bar outside where they are making negronis and the most divine gimlets. They serve them with little red peppercorns – out of this world. Or on the table in the other room there's champagne and rosé. And for the boys, beer in a barrel by the hot tub.'

Charlie was straight outside.

Nicky said, 'Oh I'd kill for some bubbles,' and drifted over to the champagne table in the lounge. Julia hovered in the kitchen by Alicia. Lexi had zoned out for a second, editing the pictures she'd just taken for Instagram. 'God I shouldn't be doing this now,' she said, still deep in her phone.

Leaning against the counter, Alicia was wearing white cut-off denim shorts, two thin gold necklaces, and a white silk vest top, looking perfectly, expensively, dishevelled. The simplicity of it made Julia feel instantly like she'd tried too hard in her flouncy dress and new trainers.

Alicia looked Julia up and down. 'Nice dress,' she said.

'Thanks,' said Julia, self-consciously straightening out the skirt.

'Is it new?' Alicia asked.

Julia shook her head, 'No I've had it for ages,' she said, trying to match Alicia's indifference, all blasé and like she hadn't spent every lunchtime for two weeks shopping for something white-hot. There was a bag of clothes under her desk ready to be returned after the bank holiday.

'Really?' said Alicia, mouth tilting up, that same expression that Julia dreaded. 'I'm sure I saw it in the window of Whistles the other day.'

Julia made a face like she was none the wiser, especially as this was the H&M rip-off of the Whistles version, but she doubted Alicia had ever set foot in an H&M, she was a Notting Hill boutique kind of shopper. 'Maybe one like it,' Julia said as casually as she could, cursing herself for lying.

'Maybe,' said Alicia with clear disbelief.

Julia could tell her cheeks had flushed.

Pushing languidly off the kitchen island Alicia said, 'Come on, Lexi, it's your party, you can't be on your phone all night.'

'I'm coming, I'm coming,' said Lexi, hurriedly finishing her post then clicking her phone off. 'Right, that's enough of that. No more time-wasting, a hot tub is calling,' she laughed. 'Oh Julia you got the trainers!' she said, noticing Julia's feet for the first time.

Julia blushed again. 'Yeah, I wanted to go for the other style, you know, so they weren't exactly the same as yours but,' she scrabbled for an excuse not to mention the bargain TK Maxx price, 'they didn't have my size.'

'Don't be silly,' Lexi grinned, looping her arm through Julia's and leading her out into the garden. 'They look fab!'

Alicia sauntered along behind, Julia sensing her hawk-like

judgement. They picked up Nicky on her way through who was flirting with a waiter as he topped up her champagne flute.

Outside was magical. Like the Snow Queen's palace. Strings of white outdoor bulbs crisscrossed the piercing blue sky from the corner of the house to the giant conifers at the far end of the garden. Between the firs, a whitewashed shack had been built to house the gin bar. The waiters outside were all sun-bleached surfer cool. They looked barely old enough to drink and were dressed in sleeveless white T-shirts, boardshorts and white bow-ties, working their magic with Sipsmith gin. Across from that, the hot tub bubbled under a giant white sailcloth stretched between scaffold poles for shade. A suckling pig was being roasted over a firepit by a burly hipster in a leather apron ready for a late lunch. The patio was a dance floor, there was a DJ in wraparound sunglasses, there were white helium balloons, flaming Tiki torches, and giant white floor cushions and shisha pipes next to a spray-painted sign that read, 'chill-out zone'.

Julia recognised all the faces from the Cedar Lane WhatsApp group. Practically the whole street was there, except for a few undesirables who had never been invited to join the group. And then dotted around were some of Lexi's friends who Julia didn't know.

Charlie was standing by himself with his beer. In his white polo shirt he did look like a lost schoolboy.

Lexi, Julia, Nicky and Alicia walked towards him, in the direction of the hot tub, and as they passed, Lexi said, 'Fancy a dip, Charlie?'

Charlie winced. 'Nah, I'm OK thanks.'

'Oh come on,' Lexi cajoled, grabbing his hand and dragging him a few steps.

Hamish came to join them, yanking his shirt off over his head to reveal the washboard abs that had featured so heavily in Julia's dreams. 'Don't know about you, but I am ready to get wet!' he laughed.

Lexi giggled.

Julia had to look away. She could feel heat rising up her neck making it go a blotchy red. She was torn between the prestige of being a part of Lexi's elusive inner-circle and the awkwardness of having to sit rigidly aware next to Hamish, in her swimsuit.

Alicia stepped out of her denim shorts. Nicky wriggled her white bodycon dress over her head.

Julia was next to Charlie. Both of them standing watching. 'Shall we just get in, Charlie?' she said, hovering on the cusp of indecision.

'No,' Charlie flatly refused. 'I told you, I have no interest in hot tubs.'

Hamish looked over. 'Come on, Charlie, old boy, everyone loves a hot tub.'

Charlie shook his head. 'Not me.'

Alicia had peeled off her top and was climbing into the frothy water, yelping as the bubbles touched her skin. Nicky splashed her. 'You bitch,' Alicia laughed.

'Hamish, honey, can you just unzip my dress,' Lexi called, holding her hair up from her back to reveal the zip.

'Come on, Charlie,' Lexi ordered, tying her hair into a big bun on top of her head, 'don't be a spoilsport.'

Charlie made a face. 'I don't mind being a spoilsport.'

Julia found herself being drawn to the water, to the fun. 'Come on,' she said, inching closer.

'Why?' asked Charlie, expression bemused.

Something about Charlie's refusal was egging Julia on. 'To get you out of your comfort zone,' she suggested.

Charlie made a face. 'I like my comfort zone. It's comfortable,' he said. 'Why would I want to be uncomfortable?'

Julia stared at him for a second, then back at the water where everyone was frolicking with giggling abandon. Getting into the hot tub felt suddenly like a statement against being trapped by convention, it felt like it stuck two fingers up to their spreadsheet and Meryl's diagnosis of Julia's bored brain. It felt like living in the moment.

Julia took a step towards the pool, unzipping her dress. And while she hated standing in just swimwear in front of all the lithe Body Pump-toned figures of Lexi, Nicky and Alicia, she was quite proud of her pale-yellow and white striped bikini that was a near identical copy of one she'd seen in Lululemon. Understated but flattering. She'd never even stepped into a Lululemon before she'd heard Lexi and Alicia talking about how it was the only viable place to buy gym leggings.

'Oh my God, we have the same bikini,' said Lexi as she let her white sequins pool to the floor to reveal a two-piece in almost the same pale-yellow deckchair stripes as Julia's. Hers however was clearly the expensive version. 'Twins!' Lexi clapped, bounding over to stand next to Julia. It looked much better on pocket-sized Lexi and Julia immediately curled in on herself, loath to be compared.

Alicia leant over the hot tub, resting her chin on her crossed arms, and drawled, 'Well look at that,' in a tone that implied Julia had purposely tried to copy Lexi.

Thankfully Lexi didn't hear because she was too busy vaulting into the frothy tub in a move that made everyone whistle and clap, while Julia climbed in via the steps, head down to avoid meeting Alicia's watchful eye.

Hamish, who had no interest in swimming costume chat, stood in the centre of the tub and shouted, 'Charlie, get involved or see that off,' gesturing to the full pint in Charlie's hand.

All eyes were on Charlie. He looked like the small ounce of enjoyment he'd summoned up for this party had just been successfully squeezed out of him.

Julia was willing him to agree to Hamish's challenge, to just get over it and get in the pool.

Hamish started chanting, 'Down it, down it.'

Alicia, Nicky and Lexi joined in, clapping with glee. Another couple, strangers to Julia and Charlie, who were already lounging in the tub sat up to join. A group of grinning dads who lived up the street chipped in as the chant spread, as Hamish raised his hands high like a conductor and the bow-tied waiters over by the big trees paused to grin and whistle.

Julia sank down into the warm water, wincing in sympathy as Charlie looked momentarily startled by the onslaught. She hated herself for wanting to see him pushed out of his comfort zone. For craving any reaction outside of apathy. Anything to disrupt the status quo.

When she saw him start to raise his glass to see off Hamish's challenge, she sat up a little straighter. Then almost as quickly he stopped. Julia watched as an expression of pity crossed his face and with a narrow-eyed glance aimed at Julia specifically for being complicit, Charlie turned on the spot and walked away.

There was a collective, disapproving sigh.

'Spoilsport,' Lexi catcalled, semi-joking.

Hamish looked completely agog that someone could defy the rules of a challenge. 'He can't walk away. That's cheating. Julia,' Hamish said, nudging her on the bare arm, 'sort your husband out.'

The touch of Hamish's skin on her own made Julia almost flinch in fright. Immediately hyperaware of their contact, images from her dreams flashing before her eyes, his big hands roaming over her rain-soaked clothes, the crush of his mouth hot on hers. His smell. His taste. Julia had to press her fingers momentarily over her eyes to make the memories go away. And then, just to divert Hamish's attention from her, she shouted, 'Come on, Charlie, it's a game. Come back.' But she knew he wouldn't come back. He kept going towards the house without so much as a backwards glance.

'Shame on him,' muttered Hamish, lolling back so his honey-tanned shoulders were mere inches from Julia's.

She shrugged as if her husband were a lost cause, while gearing up to apologise to him later in private. Her skin alive at the proximity to Hamish. Her guilty heart thumping.

CHAPTER THREE

In the end, no one stayed in the hot tub for long, there was too much to do and see. The suckling pig was charring over the firepit in the centre of the lawn, the flames licking high up to a sky so blue it was almost white. The DJ was trying to corral people onto the dance floor with some thumping tunes that shook the garden. The surf-dude waiters were showing off their mixology skills with a Tom-Cruise-in-*Cocktail* inspired routine while a crowd whooped and clapped.

It being her party, Lexi was too flighty to be pinned in one place. When some new guests arrived, she jumped out of the hot tub to greet them with a squeal and stood chatting in just her bikini, freshly poured flute of champagne in hand. The couple Julia hadn't known got out as well after their polite small talk with her fizzled out quite quickly. Nicky was beckoned to the chill-out zone by her husband to delight in the fact that by chance he'd bumped into an old pal from boarding school.

On the other side of the hot tub, Alicia was on her phone. Julia found herself on the sidelines of a chat between Hamish and a couple of other guys from the street, the fellow dads who'd sidled over with their beers, about a possible men-only cycling trip in the summer. Hamish was stretched out, arms wide, his hand resting just behind Julia's neck. She was uber-aware that if she leant back they would be touching, so she was sitting slightly forward, a touch uncomfortable, as she tried to shuffle imperceptibly along so she was out of reach. Really she wanted to get out of the hot tub, but she hadn't yet been able to locate a towel. Hamish was busy expounding on the merits of cycle routes around Croatia. As she listened, Julia found herself wishing that Charlie could be part of this inner-circle trip. Part of all the in-jokes and the antics. But she knew that Charlie thought groups of weekend cyclists like Hamish and co. were idiots who just cycled round the park and showed off expensive kit. He liked to cycle solo. So even if he was invited, and somehow they conjured up the money for him to go, he'd probably turn it down anyway.

'And what are we supposed to do while you're bombing round Zagreb?' Alicia asked, glancing up from her phone, one perfect brow raised. Her husband was one of the other dads, a clean-cut city banker who looked like he could still be in the office even in casual clothes, leaning against the edge of the tub.

Hamish looked nonplussed. 'Go to a spa? Like you always do.'

Alicia grinned. Her husband rolled his eyes.

Julia found herself wanting to be invited to the spa. They made life seem so effortlessly exciting. But she knew Alicia would never include her. If Lexi had still been in the hot tub she would have done. Since it was now just Julia, Hamish and Alicia in the pool, the lack of invitation made her feel even more awkward so she made the excuse of needing another drink and climbed out.

She hunted for a towel but realised there were none. And since there was no chance she was going to stand around in just her swimsuit, the only option was to pull her dress on over her soaking wet costume. Her fingers were shrivelled like prunes. The material went immediately damp and see-through. Hamish and Alicia were still talking about the holiday. Julia felt invisible. She suddenly envied Charlie his forsaking of the whole hot tub malarkey.

The afternoon was getting hotter. Clammy and close. The music had got louder. More and more people had arrived. To get anywhere was a squeeze. There was a queue for the cocktails. The sun poured through the wispy clouds giving everything a hazy edge. Julia looked around for Charlie but saw just a sea of faces, some of them she recognised from the street, she waved a few hellos but the groups were so tightly packed it was hard to get involved in the chats as she squeezed through the gaps.

Finally, in the far corner, sitting on a low children's picnic table, she saw Charlie. He was animatedly chatting with Lexi's weird old neighbour who had clearly only been invited to fend off any complaints about the noise.

'Hey, Julia,' Charlie said as she approached. 'You know Harry?'

Julia nodded as the old man in the flat cap sitting by Charlie smiled his gappy grin at her. He looked like he'd dressed up for the occasion in his tweed trousers, old cream shirt and threadbare waistcoat.

'She always lets me go ahead in the Costcutter,' said Harry, taking his cap off and nodding his head at Julia.

'Well it's just you're only ever buying a paper,' Julia replied, itching to get Charlie away, to go and socialise with – she cringed with shame at herself for thinking it – better people on the street.

Charlie took a swig of his almost full pint. 'Harry says Mountain Magics always get blight.'

Julia frowned. 'I don't know what you're talking about.'

'Tomatoes,' said Charlie, bemused that she hadn't remembered.

'Oh.'

'Dixie Golden Giants,' said Harry, waving a shaky wrinkled hand, 'they're the best tomatoes on the market. You can pop round whenever you want to see mine.'

Julia smiled politely, but had to back away when Charlie turned his attention once again to Harry and said, 'And what was it, never beetroots and carrots together?'

Julia left them to it, feigning interest in a limbo competition that was just starting, not that Charlie noticed she'd gone.

The bow-tie wearing waiters were in charge of the limbo pole. Alicia had hopped out of the hot tub to have a go and was currently contorting herself with ease, dressed in just her bikini while sipping a martini, to the heckling cheers of the semi-naked waiters.

Julia's phone beeped. It was a WhatsApp from Meryl. It was quite a relief to look away from the spectacle to read it.

Meryl: How's the party?

Julia: There's semi-naked limbo-ing and Charlie's talking to an octogenarian about tomatoes!

Meryl: Time to run off with Hot Hamish then ;-)

Julia: I never wanted to RUN off with him!! I just wanted to have SEX with him!!

Meryl: Haha, my mistake!

Julia put her phone away, first laughing, then immediately feeling bad for making out that Charlie was a disappointment. Then she suddenly panicked that she'd sent the WhatsApp reply to the right person and got her phone out to double-check it had been to Meryl. Christ, that could have been embarrassing.

After that, Julia went in search of Lexi who she found in the kitchen dealing with a canapé crisis still wearing just her bikini.

'Oh Julia, darling, I was just going to come and find you. Could you do me a massive favour?' Lexi took hold of Julia's arm and gave it a squeeze. 'One of Vanya's waitresses has just sliced her finger open and has had to be taken to the walk-in clinic to get a stitch. We're down two of the waiting staff. Is there any chance you could just hand a tray or two around? I'd do it myself but I've had a complete blonde moment and lost my dress,' she tittered. 'God knows where it is. I'm going to pop upstairs to find something else to wear and then I'll take over.'

'That's fine,' said Julia, ashamed that she was secretly pleased that she was one of the friends Lexi would be comfortable enough to ask for help. 'Absolutely, no problem.'

'Oh you're a lifesaver!' Lexi sighed. 'Here, this tray of

smoked salmon blinis needs to go out before the fish starts to stink in the heat.'

Julia put her phone down on the counter and took the tray.

Lexi looked a touch less flustered. 'Right. Now to find something to wear.'

Julia held the silver platter. 'Are you sure your dress isn't over by the hot tub?'

'Well I thought it was,' said Lexi, 'but I just WhatsApped Alicia to have a look and she said it's not there. I think someone might have picked it up for me, I don't know.' She shook her head, and grinned. 'Only I'd be able to lose my dress at a party.'

Julia laughed. A couple of people trouped through the kitchen, one of them, a chiselled guy with a beanie hat, aviators and a white vest top on, plucked a salmon blini from the tray with a vague nod of thanks to Julia as he chewed it whole. 'Kitchen's looking good, Lexi,' he said, mouth full, as he carried on out the front door where a break-away party had started round the olive tree.

'Thanks hun!' Lexi called.

Julia recognised the guy from an Instagram story of Lexi's at Christmas. She'd taken a screenshot of it and studied it intently, amazed that someone could have such a good-looking, picture-perfect Christmas. He was Lexi's cousin, she'd deduced. They'd all posed wearing matching Christmas jumpers and pulled it off with ironic cool.

As he was walking out, however, someone else was sauntering in with no regard for his status, brushing him to one side without a care. The guy stood back against the wall, confused by the dismissal. 'Hey,' he said, clearly annoyed.

Lexi looked up. As did Julia.

Walking into the party was Julia's next-door neighbour, Amber Beddington. All cool with her pitch-black hair, maroon lacy bra showing through her snakeskin silk vest, skin-tight leather leggings and buckled boots, complete disregard for the heatwave. She always looked like she'd just rolled out of bed, smelling of cigarettes and heavy Chanel. Her kohl-rimmed eyes were all-knowing and her skin was lined like she'd seen what the world had to offer and sampled the majority of it.

Lexi visibly acquiesced in her presence. 'Amber, hi. You made it. I didn't think you were going to come.'

Amber strolled casually towards them, eyeing the decorations, expressionless.

'Can I get you a drink?' Lexi gushed. 'We've got killer negronis.'

Amber huffed a laugh. 'No, you're OK.' She paused when she got to them, reaching into her back pocket to get something out. 'I just came to return this,' and she handed Lexi the note that had been sellotaped to the battered VW van out the front. 'I presume it's yours?'

Lexi took a step back, 'I'm so sorry. I didn't know it was your van. If I had I wouldn't have written anything.'

Amber shrugged. 'It's not my van. I'm borrowing it.'

The fact Lexi was apologising more for whose van it was than the fact she'd left a note in the first place wasn't lost on Amber, her expression openly mocking.

As Lexi's pettiness seemed to grow in the silence, the note crumpled in her hand, Lexi got more flustered, retying her hair, shaking out her bracelets, trying to compose herself as best she could standing in just her bikini. 'Seriously, Amber, I'm so sorry,' she said. 'I shouldn't have done anything. God, what a psycho!' she berated herself. 'Please, have a drink, let me make up for it.'

Amber shook her head, 'No thanks.' Then she gave the kitchen one last glance, did a little laugh that seemed to undercut all the effort that had gone into the party in one fell swoop, said, 'Enjoy,' then turned and disappeared outside.

'Oh God.' Lexi put her head in her hand. 'How embarrassing. Amber of all people.' She looked at Julia. 'You know she's a buyer for Emerald House? The private members' club?'

Julia did know that.

'I've been hoping she'll get me in one day. Now it'll never happen. Shit, why did I have to write that bloody note?' Lexi tipped her head back at the ceiling. 'Damn.' There was a pause. Julia didn't know what to say. Then taking a deep breath, holding it for five and exhaling, like something she'd learnt on a relaxation podcast, Lexi clapped her hands together and said, 'OK, it's OK. Right, where was I? What are we doing? Oh yes, you're doing canapés. I'm finding something to wear.' With that, she nipped off up the acid yellow staircase.

The caterer was ushering one of the young waitresses outside with her silver platter of miniature roast beef and Yorkshire puddings, then she turned to Julia and said, 'You need to get going with that salmon!'

Julia turned to follow when she saw her phone ping on the kitchen island. She glanced at the screen, it was a message from Alicia: Found dress, hun.

Immediately Julia realised it wasn't her phone. That

Lexi had picked up hers instead and this was Lexi's. She grabbed it and called out, 'Lexi, I've got your phone. Alicia's found your dress.' But there was no answer. She put the tray of canapés down on the kitchen counter and went out into the hall. She was just about to call again when another message popped up, Yeah Julia will do it for you, she'd kiss your ass if you asked her to 😂

Julia paused.

The sound of laughter and the smell of cigarette smoke flooded in through the front door where the mini olive tree party was in full swing. She could hear Lexi upstairs, opening and shutting wardrobe doors. But mostly Julia could hear the sound of her heart thumping in her chest.

She knew Lexi's PIN code was a simple default 1243 – *'Two kids and a blonde brain… I can't remember anything more difficult than that!'* Julia had laughed that hers was exactly the same and with brown hair and no kids she had no excuse for the simplicity. A conversation about how they had always been able to remember the most convoluted phone numbers as kids had ensued and they'd blamed mobile phones for the demise of their memories while simultaneously scrolling through Instagram.

Now Julia's fingers hovered over the keypad of Lexi's phone. Did she even want to read any more? Of course she did. How could she not? Upstairs Lexi was singing along to the song the DJ was playing. There was the clatter of the caterers behind her. Julia was aware she was meant to be handing out canapés.

She turned to shield herself from any onlookers out the front and pressed the PIN code numbers.

It appeared that Lexi, Alicia and Nicky had a spin-off WhatsApp group called CEDAR LANE BLONDES.

Already Julia felt a stab that it didn't include her. She just had a bog-standard message thread with Lexi. The only Cedar Lane WhatsApp group Julia was on was the main one that campaigned against the new Sainsbury's and reminded them when bin day was going to be late.

Her eyes scanned the messages. Looking fast. Aware that Lexi was upstairs, that she was prying, that anyone could see her, but feeling a desperate, craving sickness to read:

Lexi: That dress Julia is wearing is DEFINITELY in Whistles. I saw it, too!

Alicia: Why lie? So weird. And was she ACTUALLY wearing the same shoes as you?

Lexi: *Sigh* Yeah. She does it all the time, totally copied the swimsuit, too.

Alicia: I knew it! Well what is it they say, imitation is sincerest form of flattery…

Lexi: Yeah but really f*cking annoying. Haha.

Nicky: The dress isn't Whistles. I saw an H&M label when she took it off.

Lexi: I never shop in H&M. The material is so cheap.

Nicky: Ditto. And what about that at the hot tub…

Lexi: Poor Charlie!😂

Alicia: 😂😂😂😂😂😂😂😂😂😂

Lexi: Shit!!!!! One of the bloody waitresses has cut her finger off. I NEED A WAITRESS.

Alicia: Actually cut her finger off?

Lexi: No. It was like a tiny sliver, TOTAL drama queen. Do you think it would be bad to ask Julia to waitress? BTW is my dress by the hot tub?

Julia was horrified. She felt sick. It was like seeing all her worst insecurities there in black and white. She didn't know what to do. Some guests barged past her on their way out the front. She looked up disoriented.

'The salmon needs to go, NOW!' Vanya, the caterer, called.

As if on autopilot, Julia went back into the kitchen. Closing WhatsApp, she turned Lexi's phone off and put it back where it came from, then she picked up the tray of salmon blinis that were waiting on the table.

She tried Lexi's trick of taking a deep breath and counting to five but it did nothing. She tucked her hair behind her ears, the tips still damp from the hot tub, and then she headed out with the tray of canapés, pushing through the crowd of people in the open plan living room, past the giant photo of Lexi and Hamish dancing at their wedding, past the custom neon wall light – a scrawl that read *Live, Love, Lexi* on the exposed brick wall – out into the oppressive heat of the garden.

In the far corner Alicia and Hamish were still in the hot tub, there was a big group in there now, all with champagne, bottles being tipped up and then chucked onto the grass. The music was really loud. The sky was a smothering duvet of cloud.

But as Julia stepped onto the patio, something happened to the atmosphere. The music was still thumping, there was still a hum of chatter, but it was coupled with the incessant beeping of multiple phone messages. And as people got their phones from their pockets their reactions seemed to mirror each other. Mouths opened, lips were bitten, eyes widened, and almost one after the other, like a Mexican wave, they paused, looked up and around and stared when they clocked Julia standing with her silver tray of smoked salmon.

Over by the hot tub, she saw Alicia gasp then almost splutter into a smirk of delight. What was going on?

The sweet new mum, Hazel, from number twenty-two had gone pink and wouldn't look Julia in the eye. Nicky's husband was in the chill-out zone snorting a laugh as he scrolled through his messages. The group of dads were silently, secretly cracking up.

Julia felt her heart rate rise.

She felt for her own phone but remembered she didn't have it. Lexi had it.

And then she remembered. She remembered the WhatsApps with Meryl. She remembered that Lexi knew her PIN code as she knew Lexi's.

Shit.

From the hot tub she heard Hamish go, 'What the hell?' Then bark a shocked laugh.

Julia stood frozen for a second. The party stilled. The children's picnic table where Charlie had been sitting with Old Harry was empty. People who weren't from Cedar Lane were looking around to see what had happened.

And then suddenly Lexi was there. Strutting through the bi-folds wearing a white beach kaftan, some day-glow tassel necklaces and a crown of white silk flowers. She stopped when she got to Julia, standing in front of her, arms crossed. Her expensively dyed hair was hanging tousled over aloof narrowed eyes.

The music dimmed.

Julia swallowed. Feeling the collective gaze of the party on her. People trying to look like they weren't staring but staring all the same.

Lexi held out Julia's phone.

Julia was still holding the huge bloody platter of smoked salmon canapés. She had nowhere to put it down so had to dig one edge of it into her front so she could hold it with one hand in order to take the casually proffered phone from Lexi.

Lexi shook out her hair, fluffing it up with her hands like she didn't have a care in the world. Then she said, 'I think you'd better leave, don't you?'

And Julia nodded. Feeling dazed and battered.

Lexi arched one perfect brow in pity, then turned to the DJ and shouted, 'Come on, people, let's get this party started!' Then whooped, arms raised as she shimmied through the crowd to the DJ's suddenly thumping Ibiza tunes.

Meanwhile, Julia was striding out of the house, shamefaced,

eyes downcast, smoked salmon shoved onto the coffee table in the living room, stalking fast through the kitchen, past the acid yellow staircase, out the front door, past the separate olive tree party, past Amber's VW van blocking the front of the house, her trembling fingers unlocking her phone, clicking on the six new messages to the Cedar Lane WhatsApp group, knowing without having to read them what she was going to find. Screenshot after screenshot of her conversation with Meryl. The words: '*Your bored brain is seeking excitement*' and '*I just wanted to have SEX with him!!*' dancing in front of her eyes. Having obviously retrieved her own phone from the kitchen, Lexi had then written: Wow. Seems Julia has been lusting after MY husband. That's friendship for you! Gives a whole new meaning to the phrase neighbourhood watch!!!

To Julia separately she'd written, Hands off, bitch.

CHAPTER FOUR

The house was furnace hot. Julia slumped against the brown wallpaper in the hall, kicking off her stupid Superga Lexi-inspired trainers. The orange flowery carpet was scratchy under her bare feet.

She closed her eyes. This was a nightmare.

To think about it made her stomach clench. The look on Lexi's face. Alicia's. Hamish's. It was all so humiliating. Not to mention the string of WhatsApps she'd read on Lexi's phone.

She pulled her hair off her face and tied it up with an elastic band on the sideboard, yanking out the stupid white ribbon. Then she walked into the kitchen. The still air enveloping her like candy floss.

Charlie was sitting at the table.

'Oh God, you gave me a shock!' Julia said, hand on her heart, recovering her breath.

Charlie glanced up. 'Me too,' he said, flipping his phone over where all the messages were clear to see.

The room was boiling. Suffocating. Julia went over to the tap and poured herself a glass of water. 'Charlie, I'm sorry,' she said. 'It was just stupid messages. They weren't meant for the whole street.' She looked at him with an expression that pleaded for camaraderie. For him to cringe at her humiliation rather than focus on the content of the WhatsApps.

But Charlie didn't smile. His face was blank.

A big hairy bluebottle zigzagged around the kitchen.

Julia didn't know what to say. She sipped her water.

Charlie was turning his phone over and over on its edges. Then he let it drop flat to the table. 'So you want to have sex with Hamish Warrington down the playground alley?'

Julia rolled her eyes. 'No I don't. It was a dream!'

The fridge hummed in the background. The bluebottle thwacked against the window, the claustrophobic heat pulsed through the room.

Charlie scoffed. Then he shook his head, brown hair flopping over his forehead. He exhaled, deflated. 'It's so humiliating. Jesus.'

Julia came round to stand on his side of the counter. 'I didn't mean it, Charlie. The dream was just a metaphor.'

'Oh right, yeah, for what?' he asked, tipping his chair back from the table, leaning against the cracked plasterwork. 'Your bored brain looking for excitement?' he quoted Meryl. 'Great metaphor, that makes it SO much better.'

Julia looked at the floor. At the dirt ingrained into the old linoleum.

Charlie scraped his hair back from his face, holding it there. They were both glistening with sweat. The bluebottle buzzed a circuit round the room.

Charlie flipped his chair upright so it landed on the floor with a whack. 'I don't know what to say. I'm working in a job I hate. I have no money. I knew the house stuff was stressful. But I at least thought *we* were OK.'

36

'We *are* OK,' Julia said but it came out like her mouth was stuck with treacle. It wasn't OK. She didn't know what she wanted, but she wanted different to this: the seed catalogue that Charlie had finally unearthed from the clutter and was now going through with annoyed flicks, the bleakness of their house, the spreadsheet. She hated herself for wanting an extension like everyone else's on the street, a jam-packed Instagram feed like Lexi's, a job offer in Hong Kong. Anything. A taste of something new. Anything that would counter her low-level dissatisfaction with the normality of life.

Standing in the sweltering kitchen, she found herself almost begging, 'Can you just put that seed catalogue away, Charlie, please!'

Charlie paused his flicking and frowned. He stared at her, incredulous that she had the audacity to be having a go at him right now. He slammed the catalogue shut and stood up. 'I'm so sorry I'm not good enough for you,' he said, pushing back his chair, then opening the back door added, 'I need some air,' and disappeared out into the garden where his tomatoes and man cave shed were waiting.

Julia stood where she was, feeling dreadful. She looked at her phone again, forced herself to face the WhatsApps. Across the street the party was still in full swing, music and BBQ smells infusing the hot air. How could Julia look anyone in the road in the eye ever again? Unsurprisingly the Cedar Lane group had no new messages. Disabling in its silence. There was nothing, not even a shocked face emoji from one of the other residents.

The fat bluebottle hit the bare overhead lightbulb and stunned itself, falling to the countertop.

Julia couldn't stay in the house, the walls closing in on her, the thump of the party music shaking the floor, Charlie outside in his man cave. Grabbing her phone, keys and bag she pulled her trainers back on and jogged outside, out the front door into the oppressive, sweltering heat.

CHAPTER FIVE

Amber Beddington had a love-hate relationship with the Cedar Lane WhatsApp group. The endless emojis grated and the 'Thanks hun' replies drove her barmy but it amused her to watch them all getting their knickers in a twist about the new Sainsbury's. Amber was quite looking forward to a Sainsbury's. She was particularly keen on their boil-in-the-bag mussels. Four minutes on the hob and you could just as well be in the South of France.

She was usually a silent observer of the thread but as she packed her suitcase in the unrelenting heat of her bedroom, her phone pinging with the screenshots charting Julia Fletcher's fantasies about that idiot Hamish Warrington posted by his more idiotic wife, Amber experienced a desperate itch to comment. To say something, anything that might bring Lexi down in return. Because Amber had a soft spot for Julia. She was clever. Amber always admired people who were cleverer than her. Or more talented – she had a huge girl crush on her Pilates teacher, Emma. She liked people who took the time to learn, took consideration with facts and figures, but also had time for others. Julia was like Amber's son, Billy. They had similar neat little brains that worried about interest rates, if there was milk in the fridge, if the car was taxed. Like a tidy patio garden with pots of begonias and an awning. Whereas Amber's was more like the ones they panned back from on *Homes Under the Hammer*, a confusing horror of brambles and bindweed.

Amber zipped up her suitcase and giving her bedroom one last glance – the tangle of sheets, she should really make the bed – to check she hadn't forgotten anything – ooh, underwear, she grabbed a handful from the antique dresser, and Nicorette patches, no she had them in her bag – she left the room, itching to go back for her emergency pack of fags but forcing herself to carry on out the door.

The afternoon sun was too hot. Amber squinted. The dreadful music from Lexi's party immediately got her back up, especially after the sticker she'd left on Amber's windscreen. She crossed the street to the VW camper van which she'd had to borrow from a friend because her van was currently having its third new clutch in Ray's Garage up the road. A kid in one of the windows stuck his tongue out at Amber as she walked past, she stuck her tongue out back, the little kid giggled. Behind him Peppa Pig was playing on a massive wall-mounted TV. All Amber saw down this road was Peppa Pig on giant TVs, or on a Saturday, the cricket. Every house on this side of the road was the same, all the Victorian terraces done up with plantation shutters and various shades of Farrow & Ball paint. On the walls were giant canvases of their children or themselves, making Amber wonder when art had become so narcissistic. Mind you, Picasso and Rembrandt were always painting themselves. Amber had never taken a selfie in her life; the idea was abhorrent. She didn't need a million likes to tell her she was beautiful. She caught sight of herself in the VW window and did a mock pout, grinning, she knew damn well how good-looking she was.

Throwing her bag in the back of the van she lamented the limited space. This was meant to be a buying trip and a camper van wasn't ideal for the job. Although it did have a kettle which was always a bonus.

Locking the van, Amber walked up to the high street to get some supplies for the journey, grimacing at the ridiculous oversized olive tree in Lexi's front garden that had been craned into position to much hoo-ha, and all the posers currently vaping around it.

What everyone in Cedar Lane referred to as a high street was actually a small strip of shops at the end of the road with a dry cleaners', chippy, double-glazing company and a Costcutter. Round the corner was a dreadful wedding dress shop and a veterinary practice. Amber pushed the door of the Costcutter and the little bell rang. Usually her son, Billy, was with her and this was his favourite part of the trip, chucking packets of mint Clubs and Mini Cheddars into the basket. Alone, she strolled round the fluorescent-lit aisles, not quite sure what to buy, grabbing a pint of full-fat milk and some slices of cheese.

Out the window she saw Julia Fletcher hurry past. Wearing the white dress she'd had on at the party, eyes downcast to the pavement.

For a second Amber wondered if she should go out and check whether she was OK, but then realised if she were in Julia's shoes she couldn't imagine anything worse than a busybody neighbour offering comfort.

She went back to perusing the aisles. Subconsciously

picking all of Billy's favourites – Pickled Onion Monster Munch, full-fat Coke, Mr Kipling French Fancies. But her mind kept drifting back to Julia, wondering if she was alright.

Amber had first met Julia when they had moved in at the end of last summer. Julia's dad had leant over the garden fence, and advised Amber, who had been reclining in her deckchair at the time, that the monkey puzzle in her garden needed chopping down because the roots would damage her foundations soon. Julia had been rolling her eyes, trying to shush him, to not get involved. Amber had got up, wandered over to the fence, bottle of beer in one hand, cigarette between her fingers. She'd turned her head so she could see what Julia's dad saw and replied with a blasé drawl, *'I'd rather the house fell down than the tree.'* Julia's dad had been momentarily flummoxed, like his brain was rearranging to account for such logic. Then he'd laughed, deep and loud, and stretched his hand over the fence to introduce himself. After the initial confrontation they'd got on strangely well. He couldn't fathom her, especially after she'd revealed good knowledge of share prices, which she suspected he quite enjoyed. Almost as an afterthought he had introduced Julia. And the moment had fast-forwarded Amber and Julia's friendship. Julia's clear embarrassment at her dad's involvement regards the monkey puzzle had made Amber laugh. Every time she saw her after that she made some comment about the tree. Then Julia had joined the Monday-night Pilates class at the Scout hut behind the high street where Amber was a regular and they often walked home together. On the walks Amber told her how her son Billy wanted to be a chef but Amber was a terrible cook and no help at all. It transpired that Julia had aced her way through Le Cordon Bleu cookery school – she'd been sent immediately to Paris one summer by her parents when she'd shown aptitude and delight in baking. So every Wednesday, Julia had gone round to teach Billy how to hold a knife properly, temper chocolate, spin sugar, truss a chicken, julienne, reduce and even, to Amber's arm-length fascination, how to kill a crab. And so, via the bonding power of their inability to do the double-leg stretch in Pilates and Amber's wine-sipping inquisitiveness in what Billy and Julia were concocting in her kitchen, they had formed the kind of acquaintanceship that came not so much from shared interest and opinion but from being comfortable in each other's presence.

Amber decided that once she'd paid she'd just go and see if she could see Julia and check if she was OK.

When she got to the checkout she said, 'Gary, don't let me buy any cigarettes.'

'Why? You given up?' asked the large white-haired man behind the counter.

'Yes. Well I'm trying. The reason's so pathetic though,' she laughed.

Gary started adding up her purchases. 'Oh yeah?' he asked, tapping numbers into his till.

'You remember my ex – Ned? Billy's dad? Yeah. Well he's got this annoying new girlfriend—'

'Marcia?' Gary said without looking up.

And Amber realised she must have slagged off Marcia in here before. She could imagine she had. Marcia was so annoying. Marcia worked at Google. 'Well between her and Billy they've got Ned from twenty-a-day to vaping. He's so smug. But I'm not a vaper. I'm iron will and about a million Nicorette patches. And maybe twenty Marlboro Reds, Gary, just in case.'

Gary shook his head and laughed. 'You said no, Amber.'

Amber made a face. 'Oh! That's so unfair.' She paid for her stuff, waved the offer of a carrier bag and piled everything up against her snakeskin print vest.

Outside the Costcutter, Amber was about to look for Julia when her phone rang.

'Hello,' she said, fumbling to answer the phone with all the food she was carrying, the shattered screen making it nigh-on impossible to ever see who was calling.

'Amber, it's Henri,' his voice boomed out.

Amber stood up a bit straighter. Henri Lupé owned the private members' club, Emerald House, which was the main source of Amber's income. An old, white-suit-wearing eccentric, they'd worked together for years, Amber supplying the vintage furniture for his hotel chain.

'Just checking you're all on target.'

'Oh yeah, absolutely, you know me, Henri.' She glanced at her watch, made awkward by all the junk food she was carrying, and then made a face to herself, aware she was now cutting things fine. Julia would have to look after herself, Amber figured, walking a bit quicker in the direction of the camper van. 'I'm actually on my way to France now. I'll get you all the best stuff,' she laughed, it sounded a little fake.

Henri paused for a second. 'I'm so sorry about what's happened, darling. You're not annoyed, are you? It's just Olga, darling, she likes to think she's in control now, but—'

'Well, with all due respect, Henri,' Amber said, trying not

to sound bitter, as she climbed into the van, 'she does seem to be in control now.'

Olga Lupé was Henri's niece and the new Emerald House Creative Director. Tipped to take over from Henri when he retired, tall, willowy and white-blonde, she had taken a dislike to Amber on sight. They were of different eras. Amber worked on instinct and Henri trusted her to deliver. She'd rock up with a van full of furnishings – some of which had been requested, some of which hadn't – and never failed to transform a room. She had won awards. Olga, on the other hand, liked planning, Pinterest and mood boards. She liked goals and teamwork and annoyingly wide-hemmed trousers that swooshed along the floor as she walked. She hated being caught off guard and, in Amber's opinion, had kiboshed two of the bedrooms Amber had worked on for the new flagship hotel in Russell Square purely to show Amber who was boss. It hadn't gone down well. Amber hated being told what to do.

Henri laughed, a rich, horsey guffaw. 'I knew you were annoyed.'

'Wouldn't you be? Henri, she literally banned two of my rooms and half of the furnishings for the bar.'

'Olga just has her own way of doing things, Amber, darling. She only wants the best.' Henri paused again. 'I don't want my two best girls arguing. You and Olga, you need to be friends.'

There was a fat chance of that happening, Amber thought. But she exhaled slowly through her nose and said, 'Yes, Henri.'

She could hear him do a little clap. 'Good girl.'

Amber bristled.

'Now, don't let me down, no?'

'No, Henri.'

Henri laughed, 'No Henri, Yes Henri. I love it. Have a divine time in France, Amber darling, we'll look forward to seeing the treasures you unearth next week, yes?'

'Yes.'

'*Au revoir, ma petite.*'

Amber ended the call. Quietly fuming inside.

She put the key in the ignition and as she looked up saw that the little witches' coven of Lexi Warrington, Alicia What-ever-her-surname-was, and the other blonde one, were stumbling down the street, arm-in-arm, in their white-hot garb.

Amber narrowed her eyes, watching them as they headed towards the high street, giggling. She turned the key in the VW and the engine rumbled to life. This van would not be a treat to drive.

Amber reversed and accidentally nudged Hamish Warrington's Porsche 911 Carrera Cabriolet. 'Oops,' she laughed to herself.

Then pulling out of the space, she drove up the road and saw the three blonde women totter out of the Costcutter unwrapping a packet of Marlboro Menthol, sneaking off round the corner to have a crafty mid-party fag. Amber was annoyingly jealous.

The van rolled on up the road, she watched them as they wobbled, drunkenly trying to light the cigarettes, all caramel-tanned and pinch-faced like the mean girls at school. Amber was half tempted to turn the wheel sharp and wipe them out in one go but they weren't worth going to prison for. It was an enjoyable fantasy though.

Speaking of fantasies. As Amber rounded the corner, there on a lone bench outside the dreadful wedding dress shop

– that was so incongruous on the high street, Amber was certain it was a money-laundering business – sat a rather forlorn, dazed-looking Julia Fletcher. Her hair fell limply half over her face, tangled with a ribbon that looked like it had once been part of a plait. Her eyes were red, her hands flopped in her lap, and her dress was still damp in patches on her boobs where the stripes of her bikini showed through. She looked a mess.

The three mean girls were just coming up to the bend.

'Oh shit,' Amber muttered to herself.

Lexi was opening a bag of strawberry laces. Amber saw the moment she clocked Julia. She saw her pause mid hair flick, her eyes narrow, a pause, a tug on Alicia's arm. Alicia's eyes zoned in in an instant, locking onto their target like a missile. Lexi tied up her hair and handed Alicia the packet of sweets, seemingly getting ready for a scene. Alicia took a long drag on her fag while the other blonde sucked on a strawberry lace. They stalked forward together, all pouty and catwalk curves. At that point, Julia glanced up and saw them, she looked momentarily startled, frozen to the spot, helpless.

Alicia flicked her cigarette just shy of the bench. 'Well, look who it is.'

Julia flinched. She brushed her hair out of her eyes, straightened her shoulders, tried but failed to get herself together in time for their attack.

'I'd like a word with you!' Lexi drunkenly sneered, getting closer to where Julia sat, such a vulnerable, easy target.

'Do something! Don't just sit there, Julia,' Amber muttered in the van.

47

A car behind flashed her for going so slowly. She waved him past.

'Living out your fantasy, Julia?' Alicia drawled, glancing towards the wedding dress shop.

Lexi did a mean little smirk, and in a tone of mock bemusement added, 'What I can't believe is why *she* would think *my* husband would ever want someone like *her*?' Asking as if Julia wasn't there.

The other blonde scoffed. 'Especially not in one of those dresses!' She waved her strawberry lace in the direction of the froufrou wedding shop.

Lexi grinned, hitting her stride, really starting to enjoy herself, she opened her mouth to say more.

'Oh for goodness sake,' Amber sighed, winding down the ancient window to shout, 'Julia, get in, for goodness' sake, just get in, now!'

And Julia, seeming to respond on instinct to the order, suddenly stood up and hurried head down as fast as she could into the van, slamming the door hard behind her. Amber roared the old VW up the road, loud and throaty, leaving a cloud of exhaust and Lexi, Alicia and the other one watching them go, stunned into bleary, drunken silence.

CHAPTER SIX

'Oh God!' Julia sat in the passenger seat of the old yellow van, hands covering her face, her skin sticking to the fake leather in the heat. 'That was awful. It was like being at school.'

Amber was driving. 'Yes,' she said, matter-of-fact.

Julia tipped her head back with a sigh. With the van's sub-standard aircon, there was no escaping the heat.

Amber indicated to pull out onto the main road. 'Do you want me to take you home?'

Julia thought of Charlie, angry in his man shed. 'No.'

Amber nodded, waiting for a gap in the traffic, 'So where do you want to go?'

'I don't know.' Julia shook her head. 'Did you read the WhatsApp?'

Amber glanced her way, pity in her kohl-rimmed eyes. 'Yes.'

Julia covered her face again, the endless replaying images of everyone at the party, Charlie at the kitchen table and now Lexi stalking towards her by the playground. She felt her life crumbling.

'You can come with me to France, if you want,' Amber said, reaching over to get a packet of French Fancies from the seat next to Julia. All blasé as if it were that easy. 'Traipse round an antique fair at five in the morning.' Amber seemed to brighten as she thought it through further. 'I could do with the company actually, I'm having a bloody nightmare with work.'

'But you work for Emerald House,' said Julia, unable to believe anything could be bad at Emerald House, where she'd heard everyone lounged at breakfast still in their dressing gowns and swam with famous people in the rooftop pool. Charlie would never be persuaded to eat breakfast in his dressing gown.

'Yes,' Amber agreed, musing over whether to eat a pink or yellow French Fancy, only half an eye on the traffic. 'And they've just axed six months of my work in one fell swoop and now I have less than a week to fix it.' She made her cake selection and turned to Julia, 'Come with me, it'll be fun. I'm only going overnight. The fair's in the morning. And I really hate driving on my own. Billy usually comes with me but he's in bloody Germany, isn't he? You'd be doing me a favour.' She was nodding, eyes wide. 'You should definitely come,' she said. The offer was so Amber, unthought-through, casual and off-the-cuff. She lived her life minute by minute as opposed to Julia who planned meticulously ahead. Amber went on, 'It'll get you away from that lot for a bit,' she gesticulated behind them to where Lexi and co. had been, 'And at the very least you can nose around a few French cake shops, you like that kind of thing, don't you?'

Julia watched Amber, all messy hair and dark snakeskin clothes, half a yellow French Fancy in her mouth, now gesticulating at the traffic jam in front of them and beeping her horn in annoyance. There was no way Julia was going to France with her. For one, seeing how she drove, she'd be dead before she got to Calais. And secondly, what would they talk about? While they were friends enough to stroll back from Monday Pilates and share a freshly baked raspberry mille-feuille, she definitely wasn't someone Julia would go on holiday with. She didn't know her that well. And Julia had a suspicion, admittedly stoked by her parents, that there was something slightly suspect going on with Amber's buying and selling because they didn't think anyone could make a proper living recycling old junk. To avoid answering, Julia changed the subject instead. 'How is Billy getting on?' Post A-levels, Billy had just left to go interrailing round Europe with his girlfriend Pandora.

'I have no idea. He sent me a message to say he'd arrived and then another of a really long German sausage,' said Amber, finishing off her cake.

Julia looked at the stack of playground food that was making her tired, emotionally overwrought body go slightly weak with craving. Stoking the desire to go with Amber to France if this was what they were going to be snacking on.

'So what do you think?' Amber asked, turning round to face Julia as the traffic inched forward. 'Do you want to come with me? You really would be doing me a favour. I get so bored driving on my own.' Then when she saw the expression on Julia's face she said, 'Nah, you're not keen? That's OK.'

Julia pretended to contemplate it further. Then said, 'I don't think I can, Amber. I'll just go to a Travelodge or something,' Julia said.

Amber shrugged, 'OK.'

Julia watched the shops on the high street disappear as

they pulled out onto the big McDonald's roundabout. Her office was just around the corner. She thought of the bags of clothes under her desk, the spare make-up bag she had in her drawer and the flip-flops she could put on instead of these bloody Supergas. 'Amber,' she asked. 'Any chance you could just pull in over there so I could get some stuff from my office? I'll only take a minute.'

Amber looked at her watch. Then she checked the traffic on Google Maps. 'Yeah OK, the traffic gets better after the roundabout, I've got five minutes.' She turned down the side road and parked in the loading bay outside Julia's office.

Just as Julia was hopping out of the van both their phones beeped in unison.

Amber's was in the cup-holder. Julia got hers out of her bag.

Cedar Road Group

Hamish Warrington: 'I would like to make it clear that I have never taken part in any extra-marital activities with Julia Fletcher. I love my wife very much and my family is the most important thing in my life. Hamish.'

Julia's eyes widened in horror as she read. 'Oh my God!'

Amber scoffed. 'He's a prat.'

Julia felt sick.

Amber grinned at her. 'See! Come with me. Fuck 'em.'

Julia shook her head, leaning against the open van door to calm her heart rate. 'I couldn't.'

'You'll regret it,' Amber said.

Julia looked at the WhatsApp again. She thought of Charlie reading it. Momentarily, she was tempted to say yes.

Amber could sense her wavering.

'I don't know.' Julia stood with her hand on her forehead. The temperature was soaring. Sweat was beading on her temple. 'What about Charlie?'

Amber shrugged. 'Maybe the break would do you good.'

'No. No, I couldn't go to France. I don't have the money.'

'It won't cost you anything apart from whatever food you eat,' Amber replied.

Julia paused then glanced up at her office. 'I have to be at work on Tuesday.'

'I'm only going for the weekend,' Amber said.

'No.' She shook her head. It was a crazy idea and she had to sort things out with her husband. Then she looked back at Amber, now cracking open a Coke wedged between her thighs, eyes sparkling like nothing was as hard as Julia made it out to be. 'Oh I don't know. I've never done anything like this. How would I come with you? Don't I need a ticket?'

'You just add your name to the booking, it's easy.' Amber rolled her eyes like all these technicalities were very boring. 'I even have a spare passport.'

Julia looked up, confused. 'Why do you have two passports?'

Amber shrugged and flicked open the glove compartment, 'One's a spare,' she said, reaching in to get the extra passport out and hand it to Julia.

Julia frowned. 'You can't have a spare passport.' She opened it up to the photo page and read the name on the duplicate. 'This says it's for Christine Miller. Who's Christine Miller, Amber?'

'No one,' Amber replied, all nonchalant. 'I think she's made up. I don't know. It's just for when I go to some countries, it's easier than going in under my own name. That's all. From stuff a long time ago. Nothing really bad per se, but you know, stuff you do when you're young.'

It was clear that Julia had no idea. That made Amber laugh. 'Seriously, don't look so worried. It's no big deal. My friend at the embassy got me that one. The woman apparently is infamous for looking like everyone. Like the Mona Lisa.'

'The Mona Lisa doesn't look like everyone,' said Julia, still concerned. 'She looks *at* everyone.'

Amber waved a hand. 'Oh well, you know what I mean,' she said, checking the traffic again on Google Maps.

Julia didn't know what she meant. Just touching the passport worried her – it would now have her fingerprints on it.

Amber looked across at her. 'Julia, it's fine. It's nothing. It's just a passport. I'm not a drug smuggler or anything.'

Julia couldn't hide her uncertainty. Amber really laughed. 'Oh my God, you think I'm a drug smuggler.'

'I don't!' Julia replied, trying to laugh the accusation off, but it sounded like a lie.

'Julia,' Amber said, trying to be serious, 'I am not a drug smuggler.' Then she grinned, unable to keep a straight face. 'Sorry, I'm not really laughing. I laugh when I'm put on the spot.' Amber was really chuckling. 'Now, please, put the passport away and go and get your stuff from your office. I'll add your name to the booking, just in case. You can decide on the way. I need to get moving.'

Julia was more than happy to put the passport back into the glove compartment and get out of the van. It was all too surreal. She walked in a bit of a daze up the path to the big glass doors of her office. Darren, the weekend security guard, was sitting at the front desk laughing at something on YouTube. He waved her through without looking up from the screen.

The office was eerily empty. Julia headed straight to her desk, conscious of holding Amber up. She grabbed the Primark bag of white-hot clothes meant for return and a pack of reduced men's vests that she'd bought for Charlie to wear in the winter because he got chilly at the office. She also stuffed in the flip-flops she wore if she ever had a shower at work after a lunchtime run and her spare make-up bag from her top drawer.

In the drawer was also her own passport, left there after a work trip to Munich last month. Her hand hovered over it as she thought about Amber and the trip to France.

There was no way she was going with her. Especially not after the fake passport revelation.

But then what would she do otherwise? Spend the night in a horrid hotel then go home and grovel to Charlie while hiding inside all weekend for fear of bumping into Lexi and Hamish? And she and Charlie would have to have a talk. Or maybe they wouldn't. Maybe they would just gloss over it. She would apologise again, tell him she'd lost her mind momentarily, make him his favourite curry for dinner and relent and let them paint the bedroom the colour Charlie preferred. And by the time it came to talking, a tentative version of normality would have resumed that neither would want to break.

Nothing would change.

Julia picked up the passport. Flicking through to her serial killer photograph. No. It was ridiculous, she wasn't going, she couldn't just up sticks and go to France with a possible drug smuggler. Saying the drug smuggler bit again in her head made it seem ridiculous. Even if Amber seemed like the type, Julia was pretty certain her son Billy wouldn't let her do it, and equally, she knew Amber wouldn't do anything that put Billy at risk. She knew from the time she'd spent teaching him to cook that Amber clearly adored him.

Outside was a loud beeping. Amber was impatient. Julia picked up her plastic bag, and put the passport back in the drawer. Then she spotted the leaving card that had been bought for Meryl to wish her well on her move to Hong Kong, signed by the whole office, that Julia had hidden in her drawer when Meryl came over for a chat by her desk. Julia was meant to have taken it to the drinks on Thursday. She picked it up, wincing at her mistake. The card had been bought by the CEO's PA, Tasmina, who loved nothing more than a motivational quote. On the front it read, 'We only regret the chances we didn't take!' And inside Tasmina had scrawled, 'Good luck on your adventure, Meryl! Whoop whoop!' in whiteboard marker alongside everyone else's well-wishes. Julia re-read the front cover quote, running her finger over the embossed letters. Then she propped the card up on her keyboard so she wouldn't forget to post it when she was back in the office on Tuesday. As she did, her eye caught a picture of her and Charlie on their wedding day, pinned up on the grey cubicle wall beside her computer. Not the best shot but the one where their smiles felt real rather than posed for the photographer. She hadn't looked at it properly for ages, it had just moved from desk to desk with her, becoming part of the furniture, unseen. She stared at it now but still couldn't really see it, the image of her in her strapless white dress and him in his grey suit so recognisable it was impossible to discern. The only thing she could make out was that she hadn't smiled like that in ages.

Amber beeped again.

Julia was about to step away when she turned back and got her passport out again, shoving it in her handbag just in case. Because maybe this was exactly the excitement she was craving.

Maybe she did need a break. Maybe it would be fun. Maybe she would regret it if she didn't go.

She left the office undecided, waving goodbye to Darren, the security guard, who looked up briefly from his phone to say, 'Enjoy your weekend'.

Julia nodded, wondering if that was possible. 'You too.'

She ran to the van when Amber honked her horn to hurry her up, and got in, breathless.

Amber rolled her eyes. 'You took ages!' she said, while doing a three-point turn at speed as Julia was still doing up her seat belt.

'Sorry!' Then, 'I got my passport.' She held it up so Amber could see.

'So you're coming with me?'

'Not sure,' said Julia, still undecided.

'Well add your details here anyway.' Amber handed her the phone to add an extra passenger to her Eurotunnel. 'The traffic's got worse on the M20, we have to get moving.' Julia did as she was told, keying in the passport details, buoyed by the possibility of excitement but secretly wondering who she was kidding. Then she put the phone away. Almost immediately it beeped with a text.

'Check that for me, would you?' said Amber. She reached into the cup-holder for Amber's phone. 'It's from Eurotunnel: We are experiencing a high volume of traffic. Please plan to check-in on time for your booked departure.'

Amber checked her watch. 'It's OK, we've got loads of time. I'm dropping you at a Travelodge, yes?'

The traffic had cleared. Amber drove like one of those people that zooms past on the motorway and everyone tuts at the speed.

'Can you just double-check the time of the train? That text has made me a bit nervous.'

Julia shook her head. 'I closed the page on your phone.'

Amber rolled her eyes. 'OK, it's printed out.'

Julia reached into the footwell for Amber's battered tan bag. She couldn't believe how much stuff was in there. It was chock-a-block with crap – there were lipsticks and empty fag packets, a bulging purse, sweet wrappers, receipts, scrunched up tissues, a book, a big bunch of keys and a million different coloured lighters. Julia's in comparison was small and neat with a pink furry pompom attached to the handle, which Lexi Warrington had given her as a birthday present when she'd been sent two accidentally.

'Found it?' Amber asked, speeding up to catch a green traffic light.

'No.' Julia shook her head. 'I can't find it. I'm not sure it's here,' she said, rummaging through various dog-eared papers.

'It's definitely there,' Amber said, swiping the bag onto her lap, half an eye on the road as she flicked through bits of paper.

'Watch out!' Julia heard herself squawk, as a car pulled out of a side road miles ahead of them.

Amber barely glanced up, Julia regretted sounding so panicky and uncool.

'Here!' Amber thrust a crumpled bit of paper into Julia's lap. 'Can you check the time?'

Julia cast her eye over the page. 'Your train departs at 17.36,' she read.

'No it doesn't.' Amber shook her head, indicating round a roundabout, the sun glaring as she turned.

Julia looked at the paper again. 'It does.'

Amber reached over and snatched it from her. Her eyes scoured for the departure time while also keeping an eye out for cars. 'Shit!' she said when she saw the time. 'How did I manage to mess that up?'

Julia didn't reply but feared her body language gave the impression that she thought it was quite obvious how Amber had messed up the booking.

'Shit.' Amber shook her head. 'Shit, shit, shit. Do you know how much time we have?' she said. 'We have minus time.'

Julia thought about travelling with Charlie, who always built in an extra hour for possible emergencies. 'What are you going to do?' she asked.

'We just have to go a bit faster. And hope there's no traffic. Don't look so worried,' Amber laughed. 'It's totally doable, even if the satnav doesn't think so. You just might have to get your Travelodge in Folkestone.' Amber grinned. 'It's a challenge. Fun. In a funny kind of way.' And she started to weave the van through the traffic like an ambulance, honking at anyone who got in her way. 'You could get a bus through there!' she shouted at the car in front that was edging through a gap in the traffic. Then they were out on the motorway and Amber's driving came into its own, zigzagging between lanes to maintain her speed. Julia found herself gripping onto the seat.

Amber said, 'Can I have another French Fancy? A pink one, I didn't really like the yellow.'

Julia was reluctant to take her eyes off the road. 'Isn't it illegal to undertake in England?' she asked, trying to sound nonchalant as she opened the packet of Mr Kipling cakes. She didn't even know they still made French Fancies.

'Yes.' Amber gave her a sidelong glance. 'Don't worry, I've been driving since I was fourteen, Julia.'

Julia nodded. She could just imagine it. She handed Amber a pink cake and took a yellow one for herself. Julia had failed her driving test first time round, causing quite a stain on her family's first-time pass rate. Her dad and brother never let her forget it. On family journeys she was never allowed to drive, as if one failure meant she'd never passed at all.

She looked out of the window, taking a bite of the little cake. They were cruising past patchwork fields and petrol stations. Amber was bombing along at a crazy speed. Julia thought how, since the house move and the spreadsheet, she and Charlie never drove above sixty-seven miles per hour. He set the cruise control after calculating the optimum speed for efficient petrol consumption to save money.

They sped past a Travelodge and then another. There would be no stopping, Julia realised, the synthetic sweetness of the French Fancy infusing her senses. And she was beginning to realise she was secretly quite pleased.

CHAPTER SEVEN

The sun was burning through the windscreen glass. They zoomed past fields of cows, the litter-strewn hard shoulder and giant adverts for a McDonald's and BP garage up ahead. Internally Amber was still sniggering re Julia's drug dealer fears and feeling a bit sick from too many French Fancies. She wanted a cigarette. The satnav was not hopeful about their chances of making the Eurotunnel, which would be a disaster.

Glancing across, she was quite pleased Julia was in the van with her. There was nothing worse than driving alone. And it made up for her son, Billy, not being there, sitting bare feet up on the dash, sometimes with his guitar that he strummed terribly but Amber didn't care because he let her sing terribly.

Julia was looking at the pile of food and drink on the passenger seat. 'Could I have some of your water, please?' she asked, tentatively polite.

'Of course,' Amber replied. 'You don't have to ask. Have anything you like.'

Julia picked up the bottle of Evian.

In the cup-holder, Amber's phone rang.

Traffic was pouring onto the motorway from a joining slip

road making her have to slalom through the available gaps in the traffic in order to maintain her current speed. Next to her, Julia was busy unscrewing the top off the bottle of water, so Amber reached forward and pressed answer, putting it on speakerphone.

'Hello,' she said, squinting against the sun streaming in overhead.

'Hi, Mum, it's Billy,' her son's soft deep voice filling the van.

'Hey, Billy, how are you? Is everything alright? How's Germany?' Amber asked, immediately alert as to the fact he was ringing. Billy never rang. He WhatsApped her messages or presumed she'd see his Instagram. He most likely wanted money.

'Yeah fine,' he said.

Amber glanced at Julia. 'Guess who's in—'

'Mum,' Billy cut her off. 'There's something I have to ask you,' he said, very seriously.

Amber frowned. Ideally she'd pull over at this point and take it off speakerphone but they had just under ten minutes to get to Folkestone. 'Can I call you back in about half an hour, Billy?'

'No,' he said. 'No, Mum, I just have to ask you a question.'

'What is it?' Amber asked.

'I want to know,' he said, quiet and serious, 'is my dad my dad?'

Amber realised suddenly that she had been en garde for this question his entire life. Except for right now. Because it took her so much by surprise she almost crashed into an overtaking Hovis van and beside her Julia had to brace herself against the glove compartment.

'Shit,' she said, braking hard and flashing the van to get out of the way.

'What?' Billy asked, concerned. 'What's happened?'

'Nothing,' Amber said, the Hovis driver swearing at her as he pulled back into his lane. 'I'm just driving.' She didn't know what to say to Billy. Her usually quite crafty, good-in-a-crisis mind was blank, frozen to just the sight of the cars up ahead, the central reservation and the endless motorway. She had a million answers prepared for if this subject ever arose but she couldn't think of one that would roll naturally off her tongue. And now she had been silent for too long.

'Well...' Billy asked, voice a bit tinny on speakerphone. 'Is he?'

Amber felt her cheeks get hot. She could feel Julia listening. If her son had been there, in front of her, she'd be able to handle it. She'd have a quick-fire reaction. She could touch him at least. But he wasn't in front of her. He was miles away in a different country. In the end she stammered out the first thing that came into her head, 'Why do you ask that? Of course he's your dad.' But the strange hitch in her voice was enough of a giveaway.

It was silent on the other end of the line.

Next to her, Julia shifted in her seat.

'I know you're lying,' said Billy, all sad, quiet voice.

Amber wiped the sweat off her forehead. She checked the speedometer. She checked the time. She glanced at Julia, who was head down, awkwardly toying with the pleats in her skirt. 'I'm not lying, Billy,' Amber said, feeling like she was sitting on an overstuffed suitcase, trying to close the clasps while everything inside made a bid for escape. This was completely the worst time for this to be happening.

'Mum,' Billy sighed, his disappointment in her evident, 'it was Dad who told me he's not my real dad.'

'Oh fucking Ned!'

'Mum!' Billy shouted over the speaker.

In the passenger seat, Julia looked like she was hoping the floor might open and suck her out onto the hot tarmac.

This was all going from bad to worse, spiralling out of her control. Amber gritted her teeth. She had a sudden memory flash of the farewell lunch they'd had for Billy at Ned and bloody stupid Marcia's. The world's best stepmother to her son, all calm and collected with her I-work-at-Google-so-I'm-really-rational take on everything. The moment Amber's ex-husband Ned married Marcia, Amber knew it was all going to take a turn for the worse.

For the whole time Amber had known Ned he had adored her. He was three years older than her and, growing up, had lived in Amber's block of flats on the floor above. He'd wait for her in the car park so they could walk to school together even when she'd tell him in no uncertain terms that she didn't want to walk to school with him. He'd give her his past Maths and English papers to copy and invite her to McDonald's for dinner but she'd always refuse. On Valentine's day, every year without fail, he bought her a Forever Friends teddy and a padded card. Amber had thought him a nice enough person but not someone she'd ever in a million years go on a date with. He had been her friendly nuisance – someone to talk to if there was no one else about, someone whose house she could eat Marmite on toast at and watch *Neighbours* if her parents weren't home. He was just average, nice but nothing special Ned from upstairs. But then suddenly he became her saviour when one day Amber appeared on his doorstep pregnant, alone and broke. By then Ned had a good job, his own flat and, still starry-eyed in love with her, he took Amber in, no questions asked, promising to raise her son as his own. For six years, Ned finally achieved the dream of catching Amber Beddington in his net. They split when Amber had become more financially solvent, Billy was happy in school, and their relationship had reached a level of platonicness that Amber felt it unfair to keep Ned tied to her, however much he was happy to be there.

And then for the following ten years, Ned had been happily single-ish in his ground-floor garden flat with a room for Billy, his neat stack of five work shirts washed and ironed by the dry cleaner up the road, his little white dog Alfonso, his PlayStation, his Mumford & Sons albums, and a constant supply of good Rioja that Amber would drink when she stayed for a drink after dropping Billy off.

Amber had Ned exactly where she wanted him. Life was good. Then suddenly, in waltzes bloody Marcia who had him dressing in Hugo Boss and eating coconut-infused lobster foam in Michelin starred restaurants. Marcia loved a man with long hair so suddenly Ned stopped getting haircuts and grew a man bun. 'Forty-year-olds can't have man buns,' Amber had scoffed.

Ned had done an infuriating smile and replied, 'Marcia says you purposely try to chip away at my self-confidence.'

Amber rolled her eyes. 'I do not,' she said, getting out her fags, offering one to Ned. 'I'm doing you a favour. People will be laughing at you.'

'See, there you go again.' Ned waved the cigarette away and got out his vape. 'I've given up. Marcia wants me around to see old age,' he'd said all sanctimonious.

And Amber had heard Marcia getting into Billy's head, too. Infecting him. 'You should study business and economics, Bill, and then after that maybe take a cookery course,' Marcia had said at Billy's *bon voyage* lunch.

Marcia had also taken the opportunity to drop the news that she and Ned were expecting a baby. A baby! Ned was too old to do all that again, surely? But Amber had smiled her disbelieving congratulations all the same. Marcia had carried on with her lecture to Billy. 'I just think these days, the best tools are those that will put you at the forefront in the larger corporate environment. You'll always be able to use a business degree, Bill. Don't you agree, Amber?'

'No,' Amber replied. 'He's good at cooking.' She had wanted to add: he's not going into the corporate environment, he wants to be a chef, you stupid woman, *and* don't call him Bill. But she hadn't, she'd sloped off for a cigarette in the garden to escape. Billy, who would usually have come out to chat with her, had got distracted by Marcia yapping on about Google's graduate programme while Amber stood outside and watched Ned come to stand behind her, his arms round her waist, hands protective of her tiny bump.

The scene had felt too good to be true.

When she'd gone back inside, aware of the pervading smell of cigarettes by the scrunched up look on Marcia's face, Billy was saying, 'Wow, could I come?'

Ned had shared a quick glance with Marcia and said, 'Of course.'

Marcia had tipped her head to the side and cooed, 'Oh Bill, that would be so fabulous.'

'Come where?' Amber said.

'Vancouver Island,' Billy replied.

Marcia stepped forward. 'It's where I'm from. We're moving back. It's a really nice place for the baby to grow up.'

'Nice.' Amber nodded, secretly thinking that when she got home she'd remind Billy that everyone knew Canada was the most boring place on earth. 'Don't forget, you're going to university in September, Billy,' she reminded him.

'Yeah, but I could go in the holidays or maybe I could defer?'

'Whoa,' Marcia laughed, 'I think let us have the baby first, Bill.'

Billy nodded, immediately reining himself in.

Amber shot her a look. 'Let the kid dream,' she said. 'He's just getting excited.'

'No it's fine,' said Billy, forcing a smile. 'Maybe next year or something.'

Marcia gave a simpering smile.

Amber fumed.

After lunch Billy took Ned's dog, Alfonso, for a walk so he could phone his girlfriend, Pandora, and talk about whatever they needed to talk about that wouldn't be covered in the next month on the train across Europe.

'What are you going to do about Alfonso when you go to Vancouver Island?' Amber asked, watching the little dog circling its lead round Billy's ankles out the window.

Marcia, who was arranging expensive-looking truffles on a plate, said, 'There's a couple across the way who said they'd take him, they love dogs.'

Amber almost spit out her coffee. 'Ned, you're giving away Alfonso! You can't – you've had him for years.'

Ned was about to say something when Marcia cut in, 'We love him, but I don't want a dog in the house when I have the baby.'

Amber made a face. 'What do you think's going to happen?' she asked, tone mocking.

Ned shot her a warning look.

Marcia ignored the question and settled herself down across the table from Amber, placing the plate of sugar-dusted truffles between them. Then she beckoned for Ned to sit next to her.

Amber hated truffles.

Once Ned was seated, Marcia gave him a nudge on the elbow. 'OK,' he said in a slightly harassed whisper.

Amber put her cup of coffee down. 'What's going on?'

Ned cleared his throat. He looked mildly terrified. 'Marcia would like—'

Marcia nudged him again on the elbow.

Ned corrected himself. 'We would like,' he paused, cleared his throat again, 'to tell Billy the truth.'

'About what?' said Amber, wondering if she still hated truffles as much as she thought she did because she was still really hungry, Marcia's lunch portions were decidedly small.

'About his parentage,' said Marcia.

Amber's head shot up. 'Excuse me?'

Marcia raised her brows. 'I think you know.' Then in quite a slow hushed voice said, 'About Ned not being his *real* father.'

Amber stared wide-eyed at Ned. 'I can't believe you told her.'

Marcia slipped her hand over Ned's. 'We don't have any secrets.'

Ned was staring intently at the truffles.

'Why would you tell Billy? It's been eighteen years. He's your son. You *are* his real father. I can't believe this.' Amber stood up, fast, spilling her coffee.

Marcia immediately mopped it up with a napkin.

'Jesus Christ!' Amber swiped her fringe out of her eyes, holding it back with her hand on her head. 'Why would you do this to him? Just to stop him popping over to Canada every now and then for a holiday? He's not the bloody dog, Ned! You can't just give him away just because Marcia doesn't want him upsetting the baby.'

'OK. Time out.' Marcia stood up doing an intensely annoying T shape with her hands. 'Let's all take a minute.'

'Fuck off.'

Marcia gasped.

'Amber!' Ned stepped in front of Marcia like she needed a shield. It was all very un-Google.

They stood in a silent stand-off.

Marcia held up her hand and said, 'You need to go someplace and cool down, Amber.'

'I do not need to cool down, thank you very much. Come back to me in eighteen years when some jumped-up pain-in-the-arse tries to screw your kid over.'

'I'm not trying to screw him over, Amber,' said Ned, the tips of his ears going red like they did when he was stressed. 'Marcia – I mean – we just thought that maybe the truth would be better, but I— I don't want to upset Billy,' he stammered.

Amber glared at him, incredulous. 'What did you think it was going to do?'

'I don't know,' Ned looked at his hands for a second, then at Marcia who was clearly unhappy at this capitulation but was saying nothing. 'The last thing I want to do is hurt Billy,' he said, looking at Marcia, imploring.

Marcia folded her arms over her chest. She did a little shake of her neatly bobbed hair. 'No,' she said, looking only at Ned, refusing eye contact with Amber. 'No, we don't want to hurt Billy.'

Well, thought Amber, as she hurtled along the M20, a silent Billy on the other end of the phone, they had clearly changed their minds.

Why had she not suspected? Because she had presumed she'd silenced Ned – that he would do as he was told, as he always did. And she had stupidly thought that if she could just get Billy to eighteen it would all be OK, it would never come out. How wrong she'd been.

'Billy,' said Amber, the satnav was showing a line of red, gridlocked traffic up ahead, 'let's not talk about this now. Don't ruin your holiday.'

'It's already ruined,' he said.

Amber bit her lip. 'Don't be daft. Listen. I can't talk to you properly now.' The traffic was slowing to a standstill. Amber could see her turning up ahead. She glanced at the clock, trying to work out what to do – how to catch the train and placate Billy just for long enough to formulate a plan. In the end she decided to appeal to his neat little brain's constant concern about her ability to pay the mortgage and said, 'Billy, I've got to get this train otherwise there's a possibility I'm going to lose my job.'

'What?' Billy said, suddenly all worry. 'Why?'

'It's OK,' said Amber, feeling suddenly bad for worrying him, while also deciding that the only thing to do was to bomb it up the hard shoulder, bypassing three lanes of gridlock. 'There's just been a couple of problems with some of my Emerald House rooms. So, Billy, I need to get this train and then I'll call you and we can talk properly. OK?' The van hit a branch of a low hanging apple tree. 'Shit!' Amber gripped the steering wheel as it smashed against the windscreen.

Julia screamed, clearly thinking they'd hit something much worse.

'Mum, what's going on?' said Billy, concerned.

'Nothing, darling. Nothing.'

'Don't drive like a maniac,' he warned.

'I'm not.'

Julia made a sound of disbelief next to her. Clearly regretting coming on this trip. No amount of French Fancies would make up for the current debacle.

'OK listen, darling,' said Amber, 'I'll call you when I get off the train. Yes? Are you OK?'

'Yes fine,' said Billy, his mind now distracted by the practical concern of Amber not killing herself. 'Please drive safely.'

'I will,' Amber replied, speeding along the slip road past lanes of hot, sweating holidaymakers inching forward at a snail's pace, furious with Ned, worried about Billy, trying desperately to work out how best to handle the situation so it didn't escalate, while also wondering if a VW camper van counted as freight because, if so, she could bypass the car check-in traffic and hurtle up the lorry lane.

Billy hung up.

CHAPTER EIGHT

'Are you OK?' Julia asked hesitantly as the phone call ended.

'Yes,' Amber replied, curtly concentrating on the network of Channel Tunnel roads.

Julia nodded, then twisted in her seat to have a look at the signs they were passing. 'Hang on, isn't this the lorry lane? Amber, you're in the lorry lane.'

'I know,' said Amber, zooming along the empty freight lane, bypassing the stream of holidaymakers.

'But they won't let you check-in, you're not a lorry.'

'Yes they will.'

'They won't! They'll send you back.'

'Christ, you're as bad as Billy,' Amber snapped and right at the last moment, with less than a minute left on the clock, she swerved right and cut back across the dividing bollards into the car traffic.

'Oh my God!' Julia gripped the seat as the van made a crunching noise like the bottom was being ripped off. 'Amber, what are you doing? You can't drive over them. You'll be arrested.'

'I'm not going to be arrested,' she scoffed, nipping in front of a hot, idling people-carrier to push to the front of the automatic check-in.

Julia slithered down in her seat so no one would see her as all the cars around them honked their horns in disapproval and there was at least one annoyed wave of a hand out a window. 'What do you think they're going to do?' Amber asked, her attention honed on the Eurotunnel screen as she keyed in her booking details, waiting to learn their fate.

PLEASE HEAD STRAIGHT TO BOARDING AT GATE E.

'Yes!' Amber thumped the steering wheel.

She cruised through the barrier, head tipped back in relief.

They wove their way through the terminal, a snaking line of cars following the signs to France, and joined one of the waiting-area queues where a man in a fluorescent flak jacket ushered them onto a loaded train. Once inside, a woman with a clipboard beckoned the van forward to within touching distance of the bumper in front. 'Windows open, handbrake on, leave the vehicle in first gear,' she said, moving on to issue the same instructions to the car behind.

Amber unclicked her seat belt. 'I have to call Ned,' she said to Julia, who nodded.

The tannoy gave safety instructions in English and French, and then the train pulled out of the station.

Julia sat back with her head against the headrest.

Suddenly Amber's face appeared at the van window. 'I completely forgot, you were meant to get out at a Travelodge!'

Julia shrugged like she'd forgotten too. But she hadn't forgotten. She'd kept her head down and allowed the situation to run away with itself, hoping she wouldn't have to make a decision. Wanting, but not allowing herself to admit to wanting, to run away from her life for the weekend.

'Well, you're here now,' Amber said, vaguely amused by

the fact anyone could forget to get out of the van, and went back to call her ex, Ned.

The train chugged on. Slowly the wires and telegraph poles out the window retreated, then faster and faster became a blur behind them.

Julia thought about Charlie, what he would be doing without her.

In the corridor, leaning against the yellow handrail between a window and a what-to-do-in-an-emergency poster, she could see Amber on the phone, hear the tirade she was giving Ned.

'I can't believe you told Billy??... Oh who cares if Marcia wants to start your life with total honesty. Do you know how pathetic that sounds?... You may have looked after him for eighteen years, but you're still a spineless insensitive jerk.'

Julia looked away, out the window at the blurry country-side, the lines of colour, the fields and trees zooming past.

She felt bad for Billy.

Amber shouted, 'You promised, Ned. You were in this for life!!!'

Julia glanced back at the sound of Amber's raised voice. She looked stressed and tired. She felt sorry for her, too.

'Yeah, well, sorry's not good enough,' Amber snapped and hung up. She smacked the handrail in frustration, then turned so she was leaning against the wall, head tipped back, staring up at the fluorescent light.

Julia wondered what was happening back at home. She wondered if the party was still going on. Of course it would be. She clicked on her phone and saw a snap of Lexi, Alicia and

Nicky, on Instagram, all in the hot tub, holding up glasses of champagne #bffgoals #blondesjustwannahavefun. A rising sickness rose up in her throat as she thought about what they'd said about her. She imagined Charlie at home alone. She wondered how he was feeling. If he was worried about her.

She sent him a message: I know it's a bit weird, Charlie, but I've gone to France for the weekend with Amber from next door. x

Immediately her phone rang.

'What are you talking about?' It was Charlie. 'What do you mean you're in France?' There was a pause. 'Julia, are you having a breakdown? Should I be calling an ambulance or something? Or the – what are the police called in France?'

'No, I'm not having a breakdown. I just...' she paused. 'I just thought we could do with some space.'

Charlie huffed a laugh. 'No kidding.'

Julia sunk a little lower in the faux-leather seat. Neither of them said anything for a while.

Then Charlie asked, 'So where are you?'

'In the Channel Tunnel. I don't think I'll have reception for much longer.'

'Right. That's lucky,' he said, as if she'd planned it that way.

'Don't be like that.'

'Like what?'

'It was just stupid dreams,' she said.

'Yeah right, so you said,' Charlie replied. 'And all that at the hot tub? You've made me feel like a fool, Julia. Like I'm not good enough. I can see Hamish bloody Warrington through the window right now so pissed he's trying to climb his bloody olive tree, and I think, Christ, if that's who Julia wants, how can she possibly love me?'

Julia swallowed, she looked down at her feet, tried to picture Charlie's face and home but it was all a bit blurry. 'I do love you.'

Charlie scoffed. 'Sounds like it.'

Neither of them said anything again. The silence stretched like chewing gum till finally it snapped and Charlie said, 'Look you're going to run out of reception soon, I'd better go.'

'OK,' Julia replied.

'And you're sure I don't need to call whatever the French police are called?'

Amber's voice cut in at that point, saying, 'The gendarmerie.'

Julia glanced over to where Amber was leaning against the railing. She cringed that she'd clearly heard the whole thing, as she had heard Amber's argument with Ned. 'The gendarmerie,' Julia repeated to Charlie.

'Yeah that's it,' he said, momentarily off-brand with pleasure that they had stumbled upon the answer. 'So I don't need to call them?'

'No.' Julia shook her head.

Then the train went through the tunnel and she lost all reception cutting Charlie off. She put her phone away and sat for a moment, feeling unexpectedly empty. Then she got out of the van. Walking tentatively towards Amber. Leaning against the yellow railing next to her.

'Are you OK?' Amber asked.

Julia nodded. 'You?'

Amber pulled her hair back off her face. 'No.'

Julia smiled. 'Me neither.'

Amber laughed.

Julia laughed.

'Why is this funny?' Julia asked.

'I don't know,' Amber replied. Then she closed her eyes. 'Shit.'

Julia ran her hand back and forth over the yellow railing, not sure what to say.

They both stood for a bit. In the car in front of their van, an old couple were having a little picnic. They watched the old man reach over to get a thermos from the back seat.

Amber went to the van and got a Nicorette patch.

Julia replayed the conversation with Charlie in her head.

Then suddenly Amber shot back, flattening herself against the wall, eyes a bit wild.

'What?' Julia asked, looking around for a problem. 'What's happened?'

But Amber just pinned her back too with her outstretched arm. 'Just stay here.'

'Why?'

'Because,' said Amber, ripping the back off the Nicorette like her life depended on it, 'there are two possible candidates for who is Billy's real dad, and one of them is in the white van in the compartment in front of us. Damn,' she huffed, slapping the patch on her arm underneath the one that was already there. 'I didn't think he was coming to this fair. Damn, damn, damn.'

Julia tried to lean forward again to have a look. 'That's really bad luck,' she said.

'Don't look!' Amber ordered. Julia flattened herself against the wall again. Then Amber sighed, her energy deflating. 'I won't be able to avoid him at the fair. He's probably staying in our hotel. Bollocks. I'm going to have to talk to him as if nothing's happened.' She retied her hair, bracelets on her arm clattering. 'God it's such a mess.'

Neither of them said anything. Amber was staring up at the ceiling, eyes closed. The overhead tannoy said something in French. The toilet door had been left open and banged repeatedly as the train sped through the tunnel. The old couple having the car picnic had put some Billie Holiday on the CD player.

Julia said, 'I went on a crisis-management away-day at work once.'

'I bet that was fun,' Amber replied, dryly.

Julia grimaced, 'We each had to say three interesting things about ourselves at the start. It was awful.'

Amber smiled.

'Anyway,' Julia said, picking a bit of dust off her skirt, 'they said you need to try to change a negative to a positive.'

'Yeah, I don't see how that is going to happen here,' Amber replied, fingers tapping on the railing. 'There is no positive.'

'OK well,' Julia persevered. 'The other main thing was to manage key stakeholder expectations.'

Amber snorted. 'What the hell's a stakeholder?'

'The people involved,' said Julia.

'Why don't they just say that? Why say stakeholder?' Amber shook her head in despair. 'I'm so pleased I don't work in an office.'

Julia shrugged. 'I just think, maybe it's worth thinking about now. For you and Billy. I mean,' she hesitated before pushing on, 'especially if, you know, his real dad—' she pointed towards the other train compartment where this guy's van was parked. 'You just need to manage expectations.'

'Julia, this is not a work crisis,' Amber replied, brow raised with disdain.

Julia felt her cheeks go pink and looked down at the dirty concrete floor.

Amber said, 'Sorry. I know you're trying. It's just really stressful.'

Julia nodded.

Amber gave her a sidelong look. 'So how are you going to manage your key stakeholders?'

Julia huffed. 'Same as you,' she said with a laugh. 'By hiding out on this train.'

Amber gave her a wry smile. 'See, that's the best plan I've heard.'

After a second or two of doing nothing, Amber pushed off the handrail and crept covertly back to the van to grab two bags of Monster Munch and the newspaper she'd bought. Then darting back, she handed Julia a packet of crisps and they stood side by side, leaning against the railing eating Monster Munch and Amber reading out the questions of the *Times 2* crossword to take their minds off it all.

When the train finally came to a stop, they climbed into the van, Amber with her head down out of possible view. The concertina dividers between the compartments opened and cars ahead started their engines. Amber waited so long to move, clearly putting as much distance as she could between her and the van of Billy's possible father, that the cars behind started beeping. In the end, she exited the train way too fast, swearing at the honking cars behind, sun blinding, staff in orange flak jackets ushering them to slow. Her focus was on finding her sunglasses, locating them finally on her head.

Julia gave the staff a cheery wave to make up for their speed and Amber's disinterest.

Out on the road, the view from the van was an endless piercing blue sky. It was hotter here, which seemed inconceivable. The motorway shrubs and grass had yellowed in the heat. The odd patch of cloud did nothing to shade against the burning orb of early evening sun bellowing through the windscreen.

Their phones started pinging as they found reception. Amber's was in the cup-holder and came up with a missed call from Billy. And a text from Ned: I really am sorry, Amber.

Julia read her own messages. One from O2 Roaming saying Welcome to France!

'Anything from your husband?' Amber asked.

Julia glanced across, more disappointed than she'd imagined. 'No, nothing.'

CHAPTER NINE

Outside the window were perfect lines of forest trees, the light flickering through the tall trunks. They cruised the wide motorway. Signs pointing to Paris and Boulogne. The petrol gauge on the van beeping.

'We need fuel,' Amber said. She hated stopping. She just wanted to get places, get journeys done. She especially hated service stations. A hang-up from her youth when her mother decided they were one of the many places to find a replacement husband after Amber's dad died: *'You meet all sorts at a Little Chef, Amber, everyone has to stop for a pee and an empty tummy however posh they are.'* Amber shuddered at the memory of having to hang around places like this, sitting sullenly teenage, with her mum all dolled up, furtively rubbing lipstick off her teeth, while practising all her tricks to get attention from men at other tables. *'I'm going to face this way, Amber, you tell me when he gets up to go to the loo. I don't want to look too obvious.'* She remembered her mother once accusing her of deliberately acting sexy when a guy came to join them at their Burger King table. As if Amber were the competition rather than her daughter. It was all in vain anyway, because in the end, her mum had found her new man down the King's Head pub, but she could just have easily have scraped him off the bottom of her shoe.

Right now though, Amber didn't just need petrol, she needed a cigarette, some proper food and she wanted to call Billy.

They pulled into the next service station. The concrete miraging in the heat as sparrows fluttered in dust puddles.

Julia queued for food while Amber bought fags, and a toothbrush at Julia's request, she was desperate to unwrap the pack but forced herself to wait till she'd made the call to Billy. The whole experience of giving up smoking was a battle with herself. Creating self-imposed hurdles to try and put off the inevitable.

She joined Julia in the cafeteria just as she was paying, all her purchases stacked neatly on a little tray. There were two espressos, two cheese baguettes, water and two apples.

Amber was not impressed with the apple and rejoined the queue to get a massive bag of crisps and a bar of Milka chocolate because it was Billy's favourite.

Walking outside, they stood by a tall table in the shade of the main building to eat their sandwiches. It was an ugly, concrete place, all pitted walls and sharp angled glass, brutalist and efficient, Amber's dream. Beside them was a lake with white ducks then nothing but fields.

Mayflies danced on the water and the sun shimmered through a wooden slated awning overhead.

Amber ripped off a bit of her baguette for the ducks.

'You shouldn't feed them bread,' Julia said, covering her mouth with her hand as she ate and spoke. Then swallowing added, 'It bloats them.'

'I know the feeling,' Amber said. 'That's why I'm giving it to the ducks.'

'They like rice and peas.'

'Bullshit do ducks like rice and peas. I have never in my life seen a duck eat rice and peas.'

'Oh yes, in the pond at the village it's all birdseed and rice and peas,' Julia nodded.

Amber shook her head, despairing.

Julia suddenly laughed. It clearly took her by surprise because she nearly choked on her baguette. 'Sorry,' she said, coughing. 'Sorry. It does suddenly seem really ridiculous – the rice and peas.'

Amber half-smiled.

Julia searched through her handbag for a tissue. Amber noticed the pink furry pompom, just like the one on Lexi Warrington's handbag, and everyone else who trotted past her house like little matching sardines, and wondered how often Julia allowed herself to have her own thoughts. To question. No doubt ducks did like rice and peas, but seriously, Amber liked caviar and Richard Gere in his *Pretty Woman* days, didn't mean she was going to get them.

Amber screwed up her baguette wrapper, drank the espresso and was about to dial Billy's number when a booming voice said, 'Well if it isn't Amber Beddington?'

Amber froze. She felt all the hairs on her body stand on end and the blood rush to her skin. She could feel her cheeks get hot as she looked up to see two men walking towards them. The first was a tall solid figure, dark hair greying slightly at the temples, his face grooved with laughter lines, hooded eyes glinting. He wore a dark grey shirt open at the neck and black jeans. His sleeves were rolled up to reveal a tattoo of an arrow from his wrist to the crook of his elbow.

When he got to Amber he leant in and give her two big kisses on the cheeks, all wolfish grin and arrogant swagger. Amber could feel her tenseness locking her rigid, making her movements unnatural and her voice sound strange as she said, 'Hi, Lovejoy.' All her senses were on high alert, this was who – in light of Billy's phone call – she was planning to avoid. This was real-dad candidate number one. She could feel her pulse thumping.

Lovejoy stood back, arms wide, oblivious as to any weirdness on Amber's part. 'Aren't you going to say anything?' he said, gesturing to himself. 'Look, the beard's gone.'

Amber nodded in acknowledgement, taking in his smooth, tanned jaw, but she felt like her movements were false, she was too self-conscious. 'It does look better,' she said, begrudgingly admitting to herself that he did look good.

The other guy who was with him was Martin, Lovejoy's sidekick. He was younger, muscly but petite, with glossy blond hair down to his shoulder blades that hung in a centre parting. Always guaranteed to have a good outfit on, today he was dressed in a leopard print T-shirt, tartan kilt, chunky white socks and tan Timberland boots. He stalked forward and air-kissing Amber said, 'I gave him a makeover.'

'It's not just better, Amber,' said Lovejoy, admiring himself in the pane of window glass. 'I look bloody fantastic.'

Amber would usually have rolled her eyes at this point, made some wise-crack, that was how their relationship rolled. But instead she found herself standing like a lemon, doing a slight huff of a laugh.

But it was OK because Lovejoy's attention was elsewhere, he had clocked Julia in the reflection. 'And who's this?' he asked, turning round to give Julia his well-practised winning smile, wolfish eyes glinting.

'This is my neighbour, Julia. She's *married*,' Amber said, stressing the word for Lovejoy's attention. She could feel her seriousness and hated herself for it, *just be cool, Amber* she chastised, *it's all fine*.

'Well, everyone has to have at least one fault, don't they?' he grinned, sauntering over to shake hands with Julia. Amber thought he'd lost weight, he'd clearly been going to the gym because he was definitely flexing his arm muscles as he took Julia's hand in his, lifting it to kiss the back. 'Pleased to meet you, I'm Lovejoy and this is my nephew, Martin.'

Julia was blushing blotchy up her neck, clearly embarrassed by the attention. 'Lovejoy?' she asked. 'Isn't that the guy off the TV?' she had a vague memory of having to watch BBC reruns of the roguish, swindling antiques dealer on Sunday nights with her parents.

'It's a self-appointed nickname,' Amber called over, deliberately trying to undermine him, confused by her warring emotions – her sudden fear and nervousness coupled with a defensive desire to put him down in order to make the situation less serious in her head. *He's just your friend*, she told herself, *that's it, that's all this needs to be, nothing's changed*. 'His name's Dave.'

'Everyone calls me Lovejoy,' he said, acting as if Amber hadn't spoken, the lines on his face creasing as he smiled down at Julia, all cocky and self-assured.

'He's a crook,' Amber added, unable to help herself, almost

needing to reiterate to herself his faults. To remind herself why the situation was as it was. 'You'd be advised to steer well clear.'

The blond, Martin, who was snapping a selfie on his phone, laughed.

'Erm excuse me, don't *you* laugh,' said Lovejoy to Martin. 'You're meant to be on my side.'

Martin tied his hair up and took another selfie, while musing, 'Not for much longer.'

'Why where are you going?' Amber asked.

'I've fired him,' Lovejoy said with a laugh.

'You haven't?' Amber was shocked.

'Course I bloody haven't.' Lovejoy stole a handful of Amber's crisps, giving her a look like he was surprised she'd believed him. 'He's got another job. Leaving me, high and dry.'

Martin shook his head, incredulous, grabbing a crisp for himself. 'Only because you refused to offer me more than just ad hoc work, Lovejoy. Anyway it's not confirmed, I'm in the running for a styling job on a makeover show on Channel 5.'

'You'd be mad to take it,' Lovejoy cut in, leaning against the table, eating the crisps. 'No one watches Channel 5.'

As they were bickering, Amber could sense Julia trying to catch her eye. She was so unsubtle that in the end Amber had to look her way in case Lovejoy or Martin noticed. Once she had Amber's attention, Julia did equally unsubtle wide-eyes in Lovejoy's direction. And Amber was so concerned that Julia was going to mouth something like 'Is he Billy's dad?' that she cut her off with a quick, concise nod.

Julia's eyes widened even further as she took in the tattoo, the square jaw, the Lothario eyes, and she too seemed to suddenly lose her ability to be natural, sitting up a bit straighter, fixing a smile on her face. Amber hoped she didn't look as false.

Beside them Martin was still talking and fighting with Lovejoy for crisps, 'He's basically a nightmare to work for. No security, no respect. No nothing—'

'That's bullshit,' said Lovejoy and with a roll of his eyes wandered off towards the lake to inspect the ducks while calling back over his shoulder, 'He's just saying that now because he feels guilty about abandoning me.'

Martin looked at Amber, exasperated, like he'd been through this a thousand times.

Behind them Lovejoy got out his phone. He came back to the table and already onto the next subject said, 'I've joined Tinder. Are you on it?' he asked Amber, then without waiting for a reply said, 'Get on it. It's unbelievable. I'm literally flooded with offers from gorgeous women with a burning passion for antiques dying to go on a date with me. I'm thinking at the very least I can get a new assistant out of it. Bit easier on the eye than this one,' he nodded his head in Martin's direction. 'Kill two birds with one stone.' He laughed, then his attention was caught by a prospective date on his phone and he was suddenly grinning and firmly swiping right.

'You're unbelievable!' said Amber, feeling herself snap. He was exactly the same. For eighteen years she had haughtily disparaged Lovejoy's morally dubious love life but suddenly it seemed too much. Like he was letting her down again. She could feel a buzzing in her ears that she wanted shot of. She would not allow him to be Billy's father. She would not allow him into their lives.

She could feel Julia watching her.

Lovejoy looked up all confused, raking his hand through thick, wavy hair. 'What? Why?'

Amber shook her head, what was she doing? This was not playing it cool. 'Nothing,' she said, 'Nothing, forget it.'

But Lovejoy's attention was piqued. 'What's wrong with you?' he asked, putting his phone away, coming to stand at the table, rifling through the packaging remnants to see if there was anything else he could eat. 'Why are you so moody?'

'I'm not moody,' said Amber, looking away at the white ducks. The sun was reflecting on the water in bursts of blinding light. In the distance the fields were crisp and arid yellow from the heat. Even the shade under the awning felt like it was hotting up. Amber could feel the sweat begin to trickle between her shoulder blades, she wanted to get going. Get away from here.

Lovejoy was inspecting his fingernails, running them through his teeth to get rid of the dirt.

Then, to her surprise, he said, 'It's not because I'm doing this Emerald House thing, is it?'

Amber straightened up, forgot about the ducks and looked back at Lovejoy. 'What Emerald House thing?' she asked slowly.

Lovejoy swallowed, clearly regretting the fact he'd volunteered the information. 'You know?'

Amber raised a brow. 'Clearly I don't.'

Lovejoy suddenly refused to meet her eye, went back to sifting through the food detritus on the table. 'They asked me to look out for some stuff they might like. That hits their vibe.'

'Ri-ight,' Amber said, unable to believe what she was hearing. 'Who did?'

'Olga, is that her name?' Lovejoy said, crossing his arms over his chest, now looking Amber straight in the eye, almost as if in challenge. 'She offered me one of the rooms to dress in the flagship.'

Amber frowned.

Lovejoy went on, pulling at his T-shirt like he was too hot, clearly a bit uncomfortable. 'I said to her, I thought Amber did your rooms and she said you did but she just wanted to explore all her options.'

Amber narrowed her eyes. 'And you agreed?'

Lovejoy tipped his head to one side and made a face, dark hair flopping over his eyes. 'Of course I agreed. It's work. You'd have agreed.'

Amber's eyes widened. 'So you're taking one of my rooms?'

'I'm not taking one of your rooms per se. I'm taking what was offered to me by the lovely Olga.' Lovejoy grinned.

Amber glared.

'Oh come on, Amber,' he said, pushing a hand through his hair. She focused on his arrow tattoo as he spoke. 'Don't look at me like that. You'd have done the same. We've fought for jobs before. It's fair game.' He shook his head. 'Anyway, I don't see why you care. You always go on about how much better you are than me, so what are you worried about?'

Amber scoffed, trying to tramp down any emotion. 'Don't flatter yourself, Lovejoy, I'm not worried.'

'Well what's your problem then?' he snapped, clearly confused because this wasn't the way their relationship usually worked. It was normally just banter.

Amber couldn't answer. She was upset that Emerald House were looking elsewhere but more so that they had chosen him and he had agreed. At every turn he seemed to live up to expectation, but she realised, that was what people did.

There was silence.

The heat rose from the concrete pavement, the metal table glimmered. A wasp landed on a discarded crisp.

Lovejoy stood, hands in his pockets, face taut.

Both Julia and Martin seemed to be trying to make themselves as small and inconspicuous as possible.

Amber took a breath in through her nose and told herself off for getting annoyed but she couldn't shake the feeling, like a shallow hurt had flooded her body and refused to let her perk up. 'There's no problem,' she said, voice annoyingly flat.

A young, sullen waitress came to clear away all the dirty wrappers on the table.

Lovejoy bit the inside of his lip as they waited for the waitress to finish. Julia helped scrunch up the rubbish.

When the waitress had gone, Lovejoy said sulkily, 'So is that it now, you're pissed off?'

'Yeah, maybe I *am* pissed off.' Amber turned to face him. 'And we'd better stop talking because we're basically in competition now. So bye bye.' She waved her hand to shoo them away.

Lovejoy huffed, 'I don't need this. Come on, Martin, let's go.'

Amber narrowed her eyes and watched as Lovejoy stalked away. Martin following with a sheepish little wave to Julia. 'Nice to meet you,' he whispered.

Julia smiled quietly in return.

Lovejoy raised a hand without turning round. 'See you at the start line, Amber.'

'Yeah,' Amber called after him. 'You can pick up the scraps we leave you, Lovejoy.'

He laughed, loud and booming. 'In your dreams,' he said, having seemingly recovered his laissez-faire composure and turning to walk backwards a couple of paces added, 'We're going to wipe the floor with you! And *you*,' he said, pointing to Julia, 'I'll see in the bar.' Then he turned again, grin as wide as his face, and swaggered away.

Julia was blushing wildly for having been singled out for Lovejoy's attention.

Amber watched as they got into their van. Martin was in the driver's seat, hair pulled up into a bun on the top of his head. Lovejoy was lounging, knee crossed over ankle, attention back on his phone, one arm extended out the window. Immediately relaxed and OK with the world while Amber seethed. As they pulled out of their space, Lovejoy glanced up and deigned a casual wave in their direction.

The van sped off into the burning heat of the motorway.

Amber immediately unwrapped the cellophane on the cigarettes. She pulled out the tab and got a fag out, holding it between her fingers as she dialled Billy's number. Thrumming her fingers on the hot metal table top.

Julia said, 'Are you calling Billy? What are you going to say?'

Amber ignored her. Billy answered.

'Hey, Billy, we made it.' She smiled into the phone as she talked, trying to sound upbeat. 'By the skin of our teeth.'

Next to her, Julia was listening, her hands clasped neatly in her lap.

Amber walked a couple of paces away towards the river.

'Listen, I'm sorry I couldn't talk properly before. I know this must be such a shock and I'm sorry you had to find out from your dad.'

'Except he's not my dad,' said Billy down the phone. She imagined his face, all cross and frowning. He'd push his glasses up his nose.

'Well he is, Billy,' said Amber, watching the ducks dipping up in the water, their white bums waggling in the air. 'He's the best dad you've got. And you've had a great life with him. He's given you a great life and been a great father. Still is a great father.'

'I know that,' said Billy.

Amber sucked her bottom lip in. Julia watched her like a wary conscience. She had always intended to lie and say she didn't know who the real father was, tell Billy she'd had a one-night stand with a stranger. If only she'd realised that Ned would waver, then she could have told him herself before he went travelling. She could have managed the message as Julia said. All Amber could see now was Lovejoy's grinning face as he'd walked back towards his van. She couldn't let this escalate. For the good of all of them.

She took another step away from Julia's earshot.

'Well the thing is, Billy, I don't actually know who your real father is.'

There was silence on the other end of the line. Amber looked down at her boots. It was too hot here. She hated the heat.

Billy said, 'I don't believe you.'

Amber bristled. 'Well, there's nothing I can say to that, is there?'

It was silent again. The ducks quacked and splashed. A pigeon ate a stray bit of Amber's baguette.

All she could think about was how Billy's skin smelt when she kissed him goodnight as he slept. When she stood over him watching when he didn't know, when he couldn't shove her away with a grin as she dragged him into a hug, when he didn't politely have to tell her that he didn't need help with his homework because she knew that he knew that she didn't know the answers. How she would stroke his hair across his forehead so she could see his face, usually hidden by his glasses and his long black fringe. How desperately she didn't want to lose that.

'You really don't know?' Billy asked.

'No, I really don't know,' said Amber.

There was another pause.

'Fine,' said Billy, curtly.

'OK,' Amber replied, trying not to show her relief, glancing down at the cigarette in her hand and scrunching it into a ball. 'We can talk about it more when you get home.'

'OK,' he said. 'Bye.'

'Bye, darling.' She looked at the phone for a second, then out at the water, taking a deep breath of the tangy river-scented air.

Then as if nothing had happened, she went back to the table and scooped up her bag and the bottle of water, leaving the packet of fags for whoever ate there next. Without quite meeting Julia's eye, she said, 'Let's go. It's still a long drive.'

Julia gathered her stuff and hurried alongside.

The van handles were hot to touch, the metal of the door scorching.

'You're not going to tell Lovejoy?' Julia asked as they climbed into their seats, the pervading smell of melted chocolate and hot leather.

Amber started the engine. 'He's an arsehole, Julia. He's always been an arsehole.' She reversed out of the space. A car beeped its horn because Amber had cut in front of them. The sun was beating down hard through the windscreen, prisms of light scalding their skin. 'He left me just after my dad died, did you know that? If that's not arsehole enough then I don't know what is. I can't tell him about Billy,' she said, heading out on the motorway, vehemently shaking her head. 'He doesn't deserve to know.' She glanced at Julia. 'I can't tell him.'

Julia was nodding. 'OK,' she said. 'OK, I understand. I agree, that sounds fair enough.'

Amber nodded. She reached forward and turned on the radio. Good, she thought. Good. She was right. Julia had agreed. She tried to ignore the mocking identikit pompom, currently dancing in her eye view as Julia dug around for something in her handbag. And the fact that when Julia had been round at theirs teaching Billy how to kill the crab, she'd alluded to the fact her workplace personality test had categorised her under the heading 'People Pleaser' making her wholly unsuitable for the job of sticking a screwdriver into a fridge-numbed crustacean.

No, she had definitely agreed with Amber because Amber was right, not because Julia agreed with people to please them. Amber was right. That was it. Done. Amber could box it up and move on.

CHAPTER TEN

They drove on steadily for another two hours. The van rumbling along in the relatively traffic-free fast lane. Julia had her legs tucked up underneath her. Amber would reach an arm up to the van ceiling every now and then to stretch. They ate Tunnock's Caramel Wafer bars and Aero Bubbles. They started googling answers to the crossword to help them along. They listened to the radio and various podcasts of Amber's about antique dealing, interior design and forgery-spotting techniques. Julia dropped off occasionally. There was only so much lulling drone she could take on the difference between Bakelite and Celluloid.

The only thing not discussed was anything of a personal nature. As if they'd signed some silent treaty, both aware that any question asked would have to be reciprocated. Alternatively, it was that Julia was too afraid to ask Amber anything and Amber was too wrapped up in her own predicament to question Julia.

Whatever the case, Julia spent a lot of time staring out the window at the French countryside. Noticing the differences. The flatness, the vastness, the yellow of the fields and the hazy brightness of the evening sky.

It made her remember a holiday she hadn't thought of in years, of coming to France with Charlie the summer after they had left university. They had taken a tent and their sleeping bags and jumped on a Ryanair flight at the most unsociable time for less than fifty quid. Charlie had wanted to hitchhike but Julia had thought it was too dangerous. Instead they had bought a couple of rusty bikes from a junk shop and cycled and got the bus around the Dordogne. When it rained and soaked their belongings they had moved from camping to stay in little hotels. She remembered sitting in a French café, and musing, 'The light really is different here,' and Charlie rolling his eyes, and saying, 'I just don't get that. How can light be different? Light is light.' He'd gestured to the horizon adding, 'It's exactly the same!'

In the van, Julia laughed unexpectedly at the memory.

Next to her Amber said, 'What's so funny?'

'Nothing.' Julia shook her head and turned her attention to the podcast and the crossword clue they were stuck on.

Every now and then, when Julia dropped off, her head would fall forward and then jerk back up again. Each time it happened, Amber snorted a laugh, so Julia promised herself it wouldn't happen again and then suddenly her head was jerking again and she was saying, 'Oh sorry, I fell asleep,' and Amber shrugged and said, 'You can do whatever you like.'

Julia woke up with her head against the window, a crick in her neck and an embarrassing film of drool around her mouth. The sun was no longer overhead but hovering on Amber's side and they were out of the countryside, driving along roads lined with petrol stations, swimming pool shops and Mr Bricolage DIY stores.

Julia rubbed her eyes. She felt dreadful. She checked her phone.

Lexi had Instagrammed a Boomerang video of Hamish lifting her above his head and twirling her round on the makeshift dance floor. The scene played over and over, backwards and forwards, backwards and forwards. Giggle, grin, giggle, grin. Her white skirt pooling over him, his arm muscles bulging. Alicia was laughing in the background. *'So much love xxx'*

In contrast, Charlie had uploaded a picture of a particularly odd-shaped tomato.

Amber's voice cut in, 'Put your phone away, Julia, you're missing out on what's going on…'

And Julia glanced up to see they had driven into a town decked out like a carnival. Every street preparing for tomorrow's antiques fair. There was bunting strung from lampposts and tissue paper flowers tied to railings. The cobbled streets with wonky mediaeval timber-framed buildings were blockaded, chalk pitch numbers scrawled on the narrow pavements. Bars were being built, scaffolding banged into place and beer barrels hauled out of lorries and onto trollies. Police were everywhere directing the traffic. Along the main road yellow cones stopped parking and hundreds of metal market stalls were under construction.

Julia wound the window right down, breathing in the scent of the setting sun and car fumes and café extractor fans. It smelt foreign and exciting and other. She stuck her head right out the window. She gazed at cafés with their red and white latticed chairs around little tables on the pavements, full to the brim of people. A kids' merry-go-round played fairground music as one kid sat crying on a giant plastic elephant. The heat seemed to echo off the walls, the atmosphere loud and enticing.

All she could think was that Charlie would love it here. He would love the sights and the smells and the colour.

Next to her Amber swore about roads that were closed and where she was going to park. 'That wasn't closed last year. What are they doing? Where am I meant to go?'

A man in a bright orange official's waistcoat waved his hands frantically at her when Amber turned the corner and started shouting.

'I don't know what he's saying,' Amber said.

Julia listened, 'He says it's a one-way street.'

'Oh for God's sake,' Amber reversed. 'Do you speak French?' she asked Julia.

'Not really, well not very well, I'm OK,' Julia said. 'My brother can speak Mandarin.'

Amber paused, checking the traffic as she backed up the road. 'Fat lot of good that would be right now.' Then she winced as she hit a bollard on the corner as she turned.

As Julia looked worriedly out the window to inspect the damage done to the bollard, which now tipped at a precarious angle, a voice shouted from outside one of the cafés, 'You made it!'

Julia looked up to see Lovejoy sitting with a glass of pastis, Ray-Bans on, thoroughly enjoying Amber's driving debacle. 'You're going the wrong way, Amber!' he laughed, feet up on the chair in front, chucking an olive into his mouth.

Amber gave him the finger as she drove away.

Lovejoy smiled.

Tense now, and riled by Lovejoy, the heat exacerbating

the stress, Amber stopped the van in the middle of the road, holding up the traffic behind and said, 'I'm sure the hotel's up by that café. It's always up there.' She chucked Julia her phone, 'Can you google Hotel Croissant?'

Julia, who was uncomfortably conscious of the fact a lane of traffic was at a standstill because of them, said, 'Oh I saw that back there. Down the road opposite Lovejoy's café. I remember the name.'

'Oh he could have told us,' Amber muttered. 'See, he's an arsehole.'

Julia was itching to make her drive on. Horns were honking. Completely oblivious, Amber did a three-point turn and drove back towards Lovejoy's café.

He started slow clapping when he saw them. Amber glared as she turned right and, about fifty yards up the side road, pulled into an underground car park next to a narrow hotel building with a giant gold croissant hanging above the door.

Amber was clearly bad-tempered and tired as she found a space. Getting out of the van she slammed the door so hard it echoed round the dull fluorescent dimness of the car park.

Julia cleared up the rubbish on the front seat and shoved it all into a plastic bag. Amber got her case out of the boot.

As Julia stood with her plastic bags, shaking the crumbs from her new dress, worries that had been percolating in the background suddenly sprang to the top of the list. Were there going to be twin beds in the room? And what about the bathroom? She made Charlie leave the room when she had to go to the toilet. If Amber was there she was bound to get stage fright. God, what was she doing here? She suddenly wished Charlie was with her.

Her phone beeped with a message from her friend Meryl: How's it going?

Amber was checking stuff with the van, so Julia wrote back: All your and my texts got sent to entire road's WhatsApp group inc Charlie. Shit hit fan. Am in France with a neighbour. Charlie and me not really speaking.

Four rapid-fire messages came back from Meryl.

Wow

Sorry.

That sucks.

You got your adventure!!!

Julia rolled her eyes. She looked around the grey, echoey car park, Amber swearing as she tried to get the boot on the VW van to lock, the sound of the fair setting up outside. Yes, she supposed she had got her adventure. She had wanted excitement and now she had it. She should embrace it, regardless of the bed and bathroom situation. If only the guilt re Charlie didn't loom so large over proceedings.

Amber finally got the van locked. 'Come on!' she ordered briskly, picking up her case and dragging it across the car park. Julia followed, keeping all her questions to herself, because she knew instinctively that they were not things Amber would worry about – especially not with everything else she had going on. Amber pushed open the heavy metal fire door and they stood quietly side by side in the rickety lift. Rather than thinking too much about the room and how many beds there would be, Julia focused on the idea of heading to a café for a glass of wine and some dinner.

The lift doors opened onto the hotel lobby, a shabby beige area with brown tiles the texture of orange pith and smoked glass windows. There was a rack of leaflets about things to do in the area and an old telephone booth. On the floor was a brass jug filled with dusty dried flowers. A wispily bald man sitting behind a cracked glass hatch stood up and greeted Amber like an old friend, coming out through his little door to clasp her hand with his fat one and kiss her on both cheeks. Amber cracked her first smile in a while. '*Bonsoir,* Erik.'

'Amber, *ma chèrie*. Lovejoy, he is already here.'

'Yes I've seen him,' said Amber, glossing over the news. 'How are you, Erik?'

Erik made a so-so gesture with his hand then mused, 'I am old, I am tired.'

'Aren't we all?' Amber joked.

As they talked, Julia surveyed the hotel lobby. It reminded her of one of the places her and Charlie had stayed on that post-university trip. Stony broke, they had lived off cheese and one euro bottles of red wine for the week. Charlie had insisted they didn't book anywhere before they left to make it more of an adventure. The first afternoon had been spent traipsing round the boiling streets, trying to find a campsite that wasn't where it said it was on the map. Then when they moved from their soaked tent to a hotel, the exact same thing happened, a morning searching for a hotel that wasn't *complet.* They had finally stumbled on a place very similar to this. Down to the bowls of potpourri and the residual scent of vacuum cleaner. Like Hotel Croissant, it was the kind of place her parents would have immediately phoned the travel agent to complain about, and then high-tailed to the nearest functional business hotel until the mistake could be rectified and compensation arranged.

Instead, Charlie had forced her to enjoy the basicness of it. To see charm in the original brown tiles and the grumpy man behind the counter, to enjoy the scent of warm wool as the sun streamed through the old blanket curtains.

At the Hotel Croissant, Amber was still talking with Erik the owner, who handed her a key and said, 'I save your favourite room.'

'*Merci*, Erik.'

Julia followed behind Amber as they climbed the stairs, observing the wonky black-and-white pictures hanging on walls – papered with a similar patterned Anaglypta to the one in her own house – the mismatched door numbers, the carpet frayed under their feet, the bannister dark from greasy hands.

She couldn't get that holiday out of her head. The rose-tint of memory made them honey-tanned and always smiling. Although Julia was almost certain she'd had a strop about wasting time searching for a hotel and used the patchy Wi-Fi to book the remaining three nights someplace different, much to Charlie's dismay, but then he was happy because the next place was of an equal-level of shabbiness.

She would never think to have that kind of holiday now, ten years later, adults with proper jobs. She expected more luxury even though they were broke. She'd rather go nowhere. Save instead for something better. Her holiday bookmarks on her computer were of three resorts Lexi and Hamish had been to this year alone. Julia had noted down the names from their Instagram location pins.

Her and Amber's room was on the very top floor, up in the eaves. Amber bashed the door with her shoulder to get it to open. 'Here we are,' she said, walking through into the bedroom, chucking her case onto one of the two twin beds.

Julia internally sighed with relief that they wouldn't be sharing a bed.

'Bathroom's on the landing,' Amber said. 'You can do your business in private,' she added with a laugh, as if she could tell just by looking that Julia was the type of person who would worry about things like that.

Julia put her plastic bags down on the other bed. The covers and pillows, curtains and carpet all the same shade of blue. There was an old veneer wardrobe and matching dressing table, a sink and a basket lampshade. It smelt of cleaning product and warm dust. The last of the sun was streaming in the paint-flaking sash windows and outside the evening sky was a rainbow of pink, red and orange.

Amber stretched herself out on the bed. 'I'm exhausted,' she sighed.

Julia looked out the window, it was half open, the room flooded with the sound of traffic noise, chatter from the cafés, the bashing and clashing of the antique fair stalls being built and from over in the park on a giant bandstand, came the music from a sound-test.

Julia could see Lovejoy and some antique-hunting friends at the café, Martin was at the bank next door getting money out. She could see the bunting and flags swishing between lampposts, the sparrows bobbing about in the road and the last arc of the setting sun silhouetting the starlings lined up along rooftops.

Julia wanted to tell Charlie that the light *was* different in France. The sky felt bigger and brighter. The sunset more majestic.

She was about to take a photo when she realised her battery was low. 'Oh God, I don't have a phone charger.'

Amber opened one eye. 'You can use mine.'

Julia shook her head. 'No, yours is an iPhone, mine's a Samsung.'

Amber shut her eye again.

'Oh no.' Julia slumped down on the bed.

'Don't worry about it,' said Amber.

But she did worry about it. How would she keep in touch with Charlie? How would she get the addictive, self-flagellating hit of Lexi's Instagram and see what was happening at the party? How would she know if the Cedar Lane WhatsApp group said anything more about the humiliating screenshots? She turned back to where Lovejoy was sitting to see that more people had joined the table, Martin had stood up to air kiss someone, the group kept expanding. A waiter was frantically taking orders, a guy in a leather jacket said something to make Lovejoy laugh, Julia could see the deep grooves in his face, felt like she could hear his laughter. Strings of lights twinkled along the awning, a tabac sign shone red.

She suddenly wanted to be out there, to be talking, laughing. She wanted to be ordering an Aperol Spritz while Lovejoy – who of course was *persona non grata* but clearly held good hierarchy – suavely introduced her to everyone, not up here panicking about losing contact with everyone back home.

But when Julia turned around, to her dismay, Amber was wriggling underneath the covers of her bed, setting her alarm on her phone.

'Are you going to bed?' Julia frowned, taken aback.

'I'm shattered,' Amber yawned. 'And it's a really early start in the morning.'

Julia swallowed. 'But you haven't had dinner.'

'We had those baguettes and I've eaten so much crap today I couldn't eat any more,' Amber said. 'You go out if you want, the key's on the table. I have to be up at five a.m. but you can stay in bed if you want.' Pulling her red satin eye mask down she rolled over and seemed to fall immediately to sleep.

Julia stared in horror at the turn of events. Amber with her earplugs in snuggled down into her pillow. She looked back to the window, brows drawn, breath shallow. Where was her vin rouge as the sun set #livingmybestlife? She felt suddenly claustrophobic in the tiny rooftop room with all that light and space and company down below. Yes, she could don her white dress and head out on her own but what would she do? She couldn't fraternise with Lovejoy, the enemy. She'd have to eat on her own – dwelling on how shit she felt about Charlie and working out how she'd face Lexi – before sloping quietly back to the hotel.

She flopped down on the bed and looked around the bare blue room, Amber snoring next to her. The feeling of foolishness washed over her again. Home seemed ever such a long way away. She missed Charlie. Not the reality of him, their argument and their falling-down house, but the idea of him: his smell, his warmth, the comfort of the crook of his arm. Everything amplified by the loneliness.

On the bed next to her, Amber rolled onto her back, mouth open, eye mask skewwhiff. She snored a couple of big snores, then turned again so she was curled up facing Julia. She slept as she lived, uncaring and sprawled. Julia anticipated herself lying straight and rigid drifting off lightly as she waited for the ungodly alarm.

There was a half-eaten bag of crisps on the dressing table. Julia reached over and hooking the bag with her finger started to shovel them into her mouth. Her phone bleeped a low-battery warning.

She took the risk that there was enough juice to call Charlie.

'Hi,' he said, voice bland.

'Hi,' she replied, suddenly feeling nervous that they were chatting. 'I just rang because we're at the hotel.'

'That's nice,' he said, but didn't sound like he meant it. He actually sounded like he was doing something else.

'What are you doing?' Julia asked.

'Staking my tomatoes.'

'Oh.' Julia looked out the window, saw Lovejoy signal to the waiter for more drinks, unperturbed about a lack of sleep. The noise and chatter drifted up to the room. She knew Charlie was being defensive, had a shield up to protect himself, that was what he did when he was hurt, but rarely did he use it against her and she didn't like it at all. 'I am sorry, Charlie.'

He sighed like he was over it all. 'Listen, Julia, it's fine. Just go and do your thing. I'm really tired. Give your bored brain some excitement, I'll be here, doing my stuff. Oh and sorting out the damp patch that's appeared on the ceiling.'

'What damp patch?' Julia frowned.

'It's fine. I've turned the water off,' he said. 'And called the plumber.'

She knew it wasn't fine. 'Sorry I left you with that to deal with.'

But he said, 'Easier probably, on my own.' And that felt like a blow. She could feel him closing in on himself.

Her phone bleeped critical again. 'I'm going to have to go. I don't have any battery and I don't have a charger. I'll try and buy one in the morning.'

'OK.' He sounded nonplussed. Distracted again by his vegetables. 'Well, you'd better go, save your battery.'

'Yeah.'

'Bye,' he said.

'Bye.'

Julia sat on the bed, phone in hand, uncomfortably hollow inside. She didn't know what she wanted from Charlie but nonchalant disinterest certainly wasn't it. Her dad would raise bushy eyebrows and say, 'Be careful what you wish for, Julia.'

Then a Cedar Lane group WhatsApp pinged through. Julia's finger hovered over the screen before she could bring herself to read it. It was the first message since the Hamish fantasy screenshots. She felt sick as she clicked to read. It was from Linda at number eighty-seven who was a nurse and hadn't gone to the party because it clashed with a work shift, Guys, just FYI, 40% off at Boden till midnight! Quick, grab a bargain!

Julia exhaled. God, even the Cedar Lane WhatsApp had moved on.

She finished the crisps, licking out the remaining salt crumbs from the ripped open bag. She scrolled through Instagram despite the fact her battery was dying.

Nothing new there – pictures of her brother posing by his new Audi, her work-colleague's new puppy, her parents holding up a trophy having won the tennis club league again, then another from Lexi of her, Nicky and Alicia, their blonde heads together posing in the hot tub with #pornstarmartinis. Julia stared at the picture, feeling so foolish for how much she had tried to impress them.

It felt imperative suddenly that she had to make things right with Charlie. She wrote a last quick message, her phone on two per cent battery. I really am sorry, Charlie, I'm about to go to bed but I just want to check you're OK? X One kiss. Normally she put two or a heart-blowing emoji. But even one felt like she was putting herself out on a limb.

Outside, the waiter was carrying a tray high above his head crammed full of teetering beer glasses. The cigarette smoke wove in wispy tendrils, there were laughing faces, the sky was a wash of vermillion lines.

Beside her, Amber snored.

Charlie messaged back: Yeah, seriously, I'm fine. Hurt, embarrassed, but I'm fine. To be honest, Julia, I just want you to work out how to be happy so everything can get back to normal.

Normal. Julia flagged at the word. OK, she replied just before her phone died.

No kisses from either of them.

CHAPTER ELEVEN

The alarm went off at five a.m. Julia was wide awake, having woken practically every half hour and checked her watch to ensure she hadn't overslept. The attic room had heated up and up during the night so she'd got up to open the window. She'd finally dropped off, only to be woken by the loud noises of the market starting.

Amber was grappling with her eye mask and so tied up in her sheet that she almost fell out of bed, having to grab the side table and knocking over the light as she tried to silence her phone alarm.

'Jesus. Where am I? What is this? Holy shit, you're here,' were Amber's first and only words for a while. Amber was clearly not a morning person. She stalked around the room semi-naked, yawning and rummaging through her case. She showered and dressed in black jeans, a black lace-trimmed vest, zebra-skin bumbag and huge black sunglasses in about two minutes flat and looked sensational.

In contrast Julia had a white shimmery polyester Primark skirt and an oversized white vest from the pack she'd bought Charlie, the outfit felt painfully prim and clean-cut when compared to Amber. Her and Lovejoy were all rugged and grooved, wiry and hard-edged, there was something primal about them, like they'd been dug out of the earth together. But the skirt and vest were all Julia had. Then she realised she didn't have any clean pants. 'Oh no.'

'What's wrong?' Amber was tying her hair up and slicking on some red lipstick.

'I don't have any pants,' said Julia. 'Just my bikini bottoms.'

Amber laughed. 'Wear them inside out. You can buy some at the market.'

'Urgh.'

'Or don't wear any,' Amber offered, brow raised in challenge as if she knew on instinct Julia was not the type of person to go knicker-free.

The suggestion did indeed spur Julia into wearing yesterday's bikini bottoms inside out. Then she hastily got ready and packed up because Amber was waiting at the door, clicking her fingers, antsy to get going.

Outside it was already light. Stallholders were adding the finishing touches to their sprawled tables. White vans blocked every roadside, horns honked, furniture was being dragged on dollies up the centre of roads while police were trying to unmuddle knots of traffic.

They crossed the road past a council truck washing the hot concrete kerb-side. Other buyers traipsed out of the hotel yawning. Amber clearly had her routine down pat. Marching down the centre of the road, her battered bumbag bouncing as she went straight into the café where Lovejoy had been the previous evening. '*Deux* espresso,' she said, then to Julia, 'Wait here,' and disappeared out the door.

All Julia could think about was breakfast. Her stomach was gnawing.

The waiter slammed down the two little cups just as Amber came back with two piping hot *pains au chocolat* from the boulangerie next door and two bottles of water. She paid the waiter, downed her espresso and with a huge bite of gooey chocolate croissant in her mouth said, 'Come on, Julia, let's go.'

Julia felt like she was on fast forward. Downing her own coffee and ravenously tearing at her *pain au chocolat*, wondering if she had time to buy another.

Everything shimmered in the early morning sun. They walked fast up a cobbled side street, past stalls piled high with silverware, 'This isn't for us,' Amber said when Julia slowed to look.

There was so much to see. Julia was dying to get her phone out, to snap a picture of the bright red sunrise behind the cathedral spire. Maybe get a great shot of her own face reflected back in a heap of silver teapots. But her phone was dead. It was just her, the croissant and a shit loads of antiques.

A woman selling jewellery saw them and called, '*Bonjour*, Amber!'

Amber offered a brief wave but didn't pause. Another guy, pulling a chest of drawers on a trolley up the road greeted her like an old friend. Amber turned and walked backwards, greeting him with pidgin French before turning and marching on.

'Keep up, Julia,' she called, tearing off some *pain au chocolat*. 'We've got bargains to find.'

Julia hurried to keep up.

Another stallholder waved. Even the wrinkled old man in a colourful hat with only one good eye, selling novelty whistling birds, said, '*Bonjour*, Amber.'

'Do you know everyone here?' Julia asked.

Amber laughed. 'Pretty much. I've been coming here for years. And they all knew my dad. Everyone knew my dad,' she smiled proudly at Julia. 'He was larger than life – you couldn't not know him.'

Julia thought about her own father. Was he larger than life? Only when it came to holding court about share prices over the dinner table.

Amber pointed towards the cathedral. 'The best stalls for me are here.'

In the shade of the giant church, it was cool enough for Julia to shiver and wish she had a cardigan. Amber had no regard for the weather and was already a stall ahead of her haggling over some plaster-cast hands and feet.

To Julia it all just looked like a sea of objects. Most of them awful. There were jugs shaped like ducks, horrible dirty plastic lights, mangy teddy bears and wood-worm riddled boxes. It resembled the crap they'd found in their house when they'd moved in and boxed up in the attic. She didn't desperately want to touch anything let alone ask how much it was.

She tried to envisage Emerald House and what might suit. What might appeal to someone like Lexi. It was Lexi and Hamish's living, breathing dream to be members of Emerald House. One of their friends had nominated them but the waiting list was impenetrable. Charlie would hate it, he hated anything that was members only. Only by pleading did she get him in a jacket and tie for Sunday lunch at her parents' tennis club. In the past, Julia had always listened wistfully to Lexi talking about the time she'd been a guest of her friend at the Barcelona Emerald House, they'd had evening massages by the subterranean plunge pool and sipped espresso martinis for breakfast dressed in white fluffy gowns in the morning room.

Amber could most likely wrangle Julia membership now, but who would it impress?

On the next table Julia saw a turquoise glass vase almost identical to one Lexi had on her coffee table, one Julia had always coveted. 'How about this, Amber?' she asked, holding it up.

Amber turned back and said disparagingly, 'Too trite.'

Julia was about to defend the vase but stopped herself when she realised it was strangely liberating to hear someone not immediately like something of Lexi's. Instead she put the vase back with a '*Pardon*,' to the stallholder in apology for Amber's dismissal but he couldn't have cared less.

She caught up with Amber who had paused to ask the price of a whole box of old gilt picture frames.

'Oh, they're nice,' said Julia, knowing Amber would be the type of person who could artfully arrange a wall of natty mismatched frames like the ones she saw on Instagram.

The stallholder, a guy with a roll-up hanging from his lips was giving Amber a price.

'That's cheap,' Julia said, holding up a small gold frame.

Amber shot her a look.

Julia immediately shut up.

Amber waved her hand at the guy's price and started to walk away. Julia put the frame back in the box and went after her.

The guy shouted another price after them.

Amber paused. Turned back. Quoted lower. The guy shook his head. 'Not even for you, Amber.'

Amber shrugged. Then finally, when they were almost out of earshot, he relented and Amber strolled back and paid him for the whole box. Writing down what she'd bought in a little notebook and making a note of the stall number so she could pick it up later. 'And please, Julia,' she said, without looking up from her pad, 'please don't comment when I'm haggling. It really doesn't help.'

They continued in a similar vein. Julia seeing just a table full of tat, Amber plucking out some amazing gem that out of context Julia could see would sit perfectly in Emerald House. A bronze palm tree lamp that Julia hadn't even noticed in a box beside a big van. A life-size porcelain sausage dog. All haggled with military efficiency. Amber tried to buy a big round mirror with a gilt trim but the stallholder wouldn't budge on price, no matter how hard she turned on the charm.

The cobbled street opened out onto a riverside promenade. Water glistening in ripples, an ancient arched bridge in the distance, rowers pulling into a boat club on the far side.

As they walked along the wider, less crowded promenade, Julia noticed that Amber's strides were much longer than hers, the pavement like her catwalk, her step a strut. It made Julia work a bit harder to be by her side, to improve on her normal hurried, head-down walk. To almost strut herself. To put her shoulders back and hold herself a bit higher. It was enjoyable to be by Amber's side, to be in the glow of her notoriety.

Julia found herself wanting to impress her.

She pointed things out, but Amber just shook her head. A glassy heat rose from the river. Julia wiped the sweat off her brow. Out of the corner of her eye she saw a mirror almost exactly the same as the one Amber hadn't been able to afford earlier.

'Amber! Look! How about this?' she called.

Amber paused where she was studying an etched carafe on the next table. She put it back and walked across the cobbled street to look where Julia was standing. She pulled her sunglasses down to inspect the mirror. 'No.'

'But it's the same—' Julia started.

'It's not the same, Julia. Look,' Amber picked up the mirror. 'It's new. Look at these fastenings. And this trim, it's painted gold.'

Julia peered. 'Oh,' she said.

Amber gave her a pitying look. 'You've got to go with what *you* like, Julia. Not with what you think I might like. You've got to get a feeling for something, a connection. You have to feel it here,' she said, pointing to her heart.

Julia wasn't sure she'd ever be able to feel anything in her heart for the stuff on these stalls. She was annoyed because usually with enough study she could ace things pretty fast. 'OK,' she said, but didn't point anything out after that.

They walked on and on. Up and down snaking back streets in the now blistering sun. Past so many Instagram opportunities. Julia was tired, hot and hungry. Her white vest was getting dusty and black from handling the antiques. She wondered what Charlie was doing. Lounging on the sofa enjoying the peace and quiet? Painting the living room maybe? Or chatting with Frank the plumber who was giant and loud but really sensitive and actually quite good fun to have in the house. She remembered when he'd plumbed the upstairs bathroom, Charlie had been his sidekick while Julia had stripped the wallpaper in the bedroom. They'd all sat on the dust-sheet-covered bed eating cheese and pickle sandwiches for lunch, lamenting the amount of plaster that had crumbled off the bedroom wall as the wallpaper was stripped and discussing Frank's penchant for Japanese anime movies on Netflix.

Walking the hot cobbled street, Julia chastised herself for being so nostalgically homesick when she was mid-adventure. In reality, she and Charlie would probably be having a row about something DIY-related, or just the fact they should be doing DIY, while Frank sucked in his breath over the price of the ceiling leak. The house was like an endless task on the horizon. She couldn't actually remember the last time she and Charlie had done something nice together. Even trips to the pub were frustrating conversations trying to explain how the other envisioned the bedroom, indecipherable diagrams drawn on napkins, until one or the other retreated into their phone.

As Amber and Julia turned the next corner they passed Lovejoy and Martin next to a giant lorry, its tarpaulin side completely concertinaed back to reveal sofas and tables for sale on platforms. They were examining a glossy wooden bedstead. The type that might have once been in a hotel like The Savoy. There were mini crystal chandelier sconces attached above the polished walnut shelves and a built-in radio. It looked expensive, decadent and perfect for an Emerald House bedroom.

When Lovejoy clocked them, he stopped what he was doing, draped his arm protectively over the beautiful swirling wood of his purchase and said, 'Jealous, Amber?'

Amber inspected the bedstead over the top of her sunglasses.

Even Julia could tell it was gorgeous and exactly the type of thing Amber would buy. Inlaid around the edge of the wood were strips of gold, the drawer handles were shiny gold half-moons and the spindle legs ended in an elegant gold-tipped point.

'Not in the slightest,' Amber replied.

Lovejoy grinned.

Amber beckoned for Julia to walk away. Muttering under her breath when they were out of earshot, 'Shit! That was a really nice piece.' From then she stalked from stall to stall even quicker, more focused.

The air was getting hotter. Julia's feet hurt, her shoulders were burning.

Amber's phone rang. She looked at the name flashing on the screen. 'Oh God, what now,' she said, voice worried, before answering with a cheery, 'Hi, Billy.' She walked as she was talking, casting her eyes vaguely over the stalls.

Julia listened.

'Lovejoy?' Amber said with an incredulous laugh. 'Course it's bloody not. Whatever gave you that idea?' Amber stopped, pushing her sunglasses up on top of her head, she covered her eyes with her hand. 'Ned said it? Well Ned doesn't know what he's talking about.'

Julia turned, she could see Lovejoy and Martin walking in their direction. She leant forward and tapped Amber on the arm, gesturing with a nod of her head at Lovejoy's proximity.

Amber swore under her breath. 'Billy, it's preposterous. Don't be silly. Listen, my phone's about to die. I forgot my charger.' Amber looked away from Julia as she lied. 'I'll call you when I get home, yes. I'll be home tomorrow and we can discuss properly. I have to go. Literally, darling, it's bleeping that it has no battery.' Then she hung up. 'Shit!' she said.

Julia looked at the pavement. It felt like the web was tangling. That Billy wouldn't be so easily deterred. 'Amber, are you sure you're doing the right thing?'

Amber waved her concern away. 'Yes. It's fine. All I need to do is hold it off till I get home. I just need to get this sorted and then I can come up with a proper plan. It's fine.'

Just then, Lovejoy strode past with Martin. 'Having a nice little chat?' he asked, eyes sparkling. 'You snooze, you lose, ladies. You snooze, you lose!'

Amber ignored him. Putting her phone away as if nothing had happened she walked off in the opposite direction.

But the air around her was charged. Like she too knew she was on borrowed time. Billy was tenacious, Julia knew that just from teaching him to cook. She wanted to tell Amber that, as an observer, she really should be telling him the truth, but then who was Julia to talk? Why hadn't she spoken to Charlie sooner? Because like Amber she was trapped. Not by lies but by expectation. A too big mortgage, no money, bad DIY, and all the aspirations of tradition on the horizon: a baby or two, a bigger car, exotic holidays, good schools, extensions, bi-folds, loft conversions…

Julia needed a break. She needed some sanity. She wasn't comfortable with the way Amber was lying to Billy. She liked Billy and it felt weird being party to his deception. She looked around at the miles of antique stalls still to cover. Then noticed that down a side road to her right the stalls looked a bit different. More of a market selling new things. Somewhere where she might pick up a charger and some pants.

'Amber, I'm just going to get some stuff down there,' Julia said, pointing in the direction the stalls.

Amber's attention had been caught by a taxidermy fox, she was turning it this way and that in the light, completely absorbed. 'OK, I'm going up round the park, it's a big circle so you'll find me.'

Julia nodded. 'OK, see you in a bit.'

Down the street, the stalls were more commercial. There were knock-off phones for sale, new clothes, toys, and fruit and veg polished till they glimmered in the sunshine.

Julia queued at a cashpoint to get some money out, wincing at their overdraft. Trying to blot the debt out of her mind, she went in search of a very cheap phone charger. A very vociferous salesman on the knock-off phone stall tried to flog her a battery pack to use straight away as well as a charger, sweetening the deal with a hefty discount. Julia's desire to connect with the outside world won and she bought the bundle. Then she turned her attention to the underwear stand. Everything appeared to be pastel shades of ginormous. The biggest pants she'd ever seen hung stretched on a hoop at the back. Rummaging through all the crates filled with underwear, the only knickers she could find in her size were baby blue and had waistbands that went over the belly button of the woman in the picture. Reluctantly she handed over five euros.

Pausing to look around, Julia realised she wasn't in any hurry to rejoin Amber. She liked this bit of the fair, it was fun. A break from all the mountains of old tat. A mime artist followed her for a bit which was so uncomfortable in the end it made her laugh. There was a huge stand selling wine in small plastic tumblers for a euro and griddled merguez sausages in buns.

There was a cake stand just at the point the stalls started to curve round the iron railings of the park. Julia stopped to have a look. There were giant chocolate éclairs, fresh strawberry tarts, tiny mille-feuille, cream oozing Paris-Brest. Julia knew how to make them all. She had agonised late into the night on her Cordon Bleu cookery course to perfect the glossy tempered chocolate sheen of a Sachertorte just like the ones in front of her.

She wasn't actually a massive fan of fancy desserts. She liked a Victoria sponge with cream and raspberry jam best, but the idea of doing something for something's sake growing up was an alien concept. Julia had displayed an aptitude for baking so that skill had been honed by her parents to within an inch of its life. Till she had sweated over trays of delicate rose and pistachio financiers and delivered top-of-the-class choux buns. One of her dad's all-time favourite phrases was: 'Good enough isn't.' Closely followed by 'Show me a good loser and I'll show you a loser!' which he had on occasion taunted Charlie with over a game of Scrabble at Christmas. Thinking of it now made Julia feel awful. Especially as she also remembered her parents' wedding anniversary, when she had made a croquembouche profiterole tower and two hundred macarons – the croquembouche alone had taken seven and a half hours – leaving her so exhausted, she had missed most of the party, falling asleep on a leather sofa in the tennis club lounge while everyone danced, everyone except Charlie who came and sat next to her, drinking whisky and reading Twitter till she woke up.

Charlie's favourite cake Julia made was a basic all-in-one chocolate cake. It reminded him of the ones out of a packet his mum used to make. Every time it was his birthday, Julia would whip it up for him and Charlie would stand in front of the oven salivating as it baked. She would ice it with chocolate butter icing and sandwich it together with strawberry jam. It occurred to her she hadn't made it this year, they had been too busy moving house and the oven had blown up the first time she'd turned it on – another expense she'd forgotten. She had bought him a chocolate cake from Costcutter instead that tasted of air and cardboard and they had thrown it in the bin after eating a slice each.

'The lady wants cake,' she heard Lovejoy's voice and turned to see him and Martin sidling up beside her.

Lovejoy was dressed all in various shades of grey with a black bandana round his neck, tanned, earthy and piratically good-looking, while Martin wore cut-off denim shorts, a vibrant Hawaiian shirt, white socks and white Reeboks. His blond hair was tied in a bun high on top of his head.

'Oh no I don't, I was just looking,' Julia said, embarrassed that they had caught her eyeing up patisserie.

'Rubbish, you're salivating,' Lovejoy laughed all deep and rumbling, as he casually reached to get his wallet out. 'What do you want?'

'Really I'm fine,' she said, conscious that she was chatting with the enemy, taking a step away from the stall.

But the woman behind the counter was poised ready with her tongs, indicating to the creamy éclairs or strawberry tarts.

'Have a cake,' Lovejoy pressed, eyes sparkling as he encouraged her.

'I'll have one,' said Martin, lifting his bright mirrored sunglasses up so he could get a better look as he pored over the display.

Lovejoy held his hands wide, euros poking out the top of his battered wallet. 'That was not the point, Martin.'

Martin ignored him, then said, 'What are you having, Lovejoy?'

'I don't really like cakes,' he said, turning his nose up at the offering. 'I'm more of a savoury person.'

Martin inspected one thing then another, umming and ahhing before deciding. 'I'll have one of those,' he said, pointing to a coffee-éclair which he took from the shopkeeper's outstretched tongs and polished off in two bites. '*J'adore le France*,' he sighed.

Julia decided it was probably easier to just accept, rather than making more of a fuss, and chose a madeleine. Another of her favourites. Practised to perfection at the Cordon Bleu. Simple lemony sponge. No icing. No cream, no fuss. She could eat them by the bucket-load.

The lady behind the stall handed it to her. Lovejoy paid. Julia determined to keep the whole transaction from Amber. It was making her feel very uncomfortable.

But then she took a bite of the little golden cake. The sponge was zesty and soft. The crusty shell firm between her teeth. The taste immediately conjured a certain confidence. A happiness. The feeling she got when alone in the kitchen whisking eggs and sugar, watching the mixture puff in the oven, slipping the little golden shells from their moulds. Sampling the first one when it was still warm, savouring the flavour before it was marred by anyone else's opinions.

She wondered if she had closed her eyes as she chewed. The flavour filling her senses and reminding her of her own baking skill. When it was finished, she realised that the eating of the madeleine seemed to make her look at things differently. To remind her that she had a couple of days out of her life and urge her to enjoy them. Make the most of them. What was the point otherwise? She had wanted freedom and escape, a pause from reality, and here it was. Yes, she almost nodded to herself. It made her see things on the stalls in a different light too as the three of them walked on. Enjoy the hunt rather than be blinded by panic. She worried less that she was accompanied by the enemy and looked instead at the towering trees and the lush green grass of the park. She smiled as the band on the bandstand started to warm up. It felt suddenly more like a holiday, the taste of the madeleine still on her tongue.

'Amber ahead of us, is she?' Lovejoy asked.

Julia nodded.

'Damn it.'

At one stall they came to, Lovejoy picked up a small stuffed owl that had seen better days. It was the same stall where Amber had been inspecting the taxidermy fox. Julia noticed it was at the back with a sold sticker on it. The mangy thing would be in the van home.

'I bet Amber bought the fox,' Lovejoy said as he handed over the money for the owl. 'It's got her name all over it. Did she buy it? I'd have bought it.'

Julia shook her head. 'I don't know.'

Lovejoy grinned. 'Yes you do. You've gone all red. Brilliant.' He clapped his hands. 'You've got the worst poker face.'

Despite her redness, Julia still found herself trying not to laugh as Lovejoy bashed her on the shoulder. She felt like a traitor but she quite enjoyed the attention. 'I should go,' she said.

'Nah,' said Lovejoy, all blasé like she'd be a fool to hurry off. 'Don't worry about it. Just walk and look and you'll catch her up.'

Martin sauntered over to the stalls on the other side of the street, kneeling down to rummage through a box of paintings. Lovejoy lagged behind to study a desk light.

Julia was on her own again. Her shoulders had relaxed. She found she was enjoying picking things up and putting them down. She even gave an old book a little sniff.

She saw a wooden ruler with the kings and queens of France on it. Charlie had a ruler just like it left over from his school days. He had a photographic knowledge of the English monarchy, and close enough with the French. He loved history. Julia struggled to know the difference between Mary Queen of Scots and Mary the First. Geography was her thing and politics – put through her paces in her father's weekly pop quizzes. Together they made a formidable pub quiz duo because Charlie also had an encyclopaedic knowledge of sports trivia and a weakness for reality TV. They used to win the pub quiz every Thursday. Julia had stopped going when Lexi started up a book club.

She shook her head, trying to make herself live in the moment, to stop thinking about home.

The sun was blistering as it moved into mid-morning, there were tourists buying now not just antique dealers so she had to push to get to the front of some of the stalls. A wrinkled old woman in a shawl tried to hand Julia a posy of flowers but she waved her away. A little terrier yapped at her feet. In the distance the band started up and the air filled with lively music. A man behind one of the stalls started to dance with his wife and another clapped his hands in time with the beat.

Julia perused stall after stall, she even rummaged in a couple of boxes, picking up an old doll that reminded her of one she used to have as a child and a Wedgewood plate that matched the set her parents had got for their wedding and kept for best. She imagined their displeasure at seeing it here for sale for, she turned it over to look at the sticker, three euros. They had visions of them passing down through the generations, it was in the will that her brother would have them, but he wouldn't be caught dead with them. He was all swanky black square plates for his daily Deliveroo. She looked at the plate, remembering a heated discussion with her mum and dad before her own wedding about gifts. Her parents were aghast that they were asking for money for a honeymoon instead of requesting fine china and towels from John Lewis. They thought it was very bad form and something she would regret. To Charlie's dismay, Julia had succumbed to the pressure and now they had a cupboard full of fine china they never used. And more debt from a honeymoon-esque holiday on the Amalfi coast. Julia winced at the memory. It reminded her of Lexi's WhatsApps, of how much Julia tried to live up to a standard. *Stop thinking about home!*

She put the plate back down on the stand and strolled on,

rolling her shoulders, telling herself to relax, arms behind her back, sun warm on her shoulders, casting a glance from one stall to another. And then she saw it.

Right at the back of the stand, almost completely obscured by an Impressionist imitation of the *Mona Lisa*, was a gold and glass drinks trolley.

It had Emerald House written all over it. It was definitely original, as far as Julia could tell, the metal was tarnished, the etching on the glass was delicate and hand cut. It looked Art Deco, like something out of the *Poirot* films her and Charlie used to watch on Sunday afternoons. It was beautiful. She immediately understood what Amber meant by a connection, a feeling. Julia had to have this trolley. If Amber didn't want it, she'd keep it herself.

'*C'est combien?*' she asked the stallholder, a short round man with a panama hat and a shirt unbuttoned one too many.

He named an extortionate price, far more than Julia even had on her.

She didn't know what to do, she thought about going to get Amber but she didn't know how long it would take her to find her and someone else might buy it in the meantime. She knew the trolley was good, she could feel it in the tingling of her fingertips.

She bit her lip and looked back at the stallholder.

Then Lovejoy's voice behind her said, 'Halve it.'

She turned. He looked at her with lazy confidence, his voice quiet as he said, 'Go back to him with half what he just said.'

'No I can't, he won't accept it.'

'Trust me.'

Julia looked from Lovejoy's urging half-smile back to the stallholder. She offered half.

The stallholder laughed. He told his mate who also laughed. As she suspected would happen, she'd made a fool of herself. She turned to go.

'Stick with it,' Lovejoy urged. She could feel him right close to her, bodies almost touching. She could smell him, all aftershave and earth. His breath was warm on her neck.

She shook her head, uncertain.

'Do it, just stand there and stare at him.' Lovejoy was suppressing a grin. 'I promise, it'll work.'

She sighed, took a breath and turned back, held her ground, urged on by the physical presence of Lovejoy behind her, shoring her up, she didn't want to fail.

The stallholder was still chuckling.

Julia forced her expression to look serious. She stayed, rooted to the ground like the tree in the yoga videos Lexi invited her to do with her in her lounge but then spent most of the time asking Julia to take photos of her for Instagram.

Julia realised she hadn't thought about Instagram since she'd bought the battery pack and charger.

After a little while the stallholder stopped laughing, he took in Julia's expression, he went over to look at the trolley, lifting the dreadful fake *Mona Lisa* out of the way to examine it properly, weighing up its worth. His mate came over and had a look, they oohed and aahed a bit, they held their hands wide, his mate turned away, lighting a giant cigar and shaking his head, the stallholder turned and quoted a price just shy of the original.

Behind her, Lovejoy whispered, 'No.'

Julia glanced over her shoulder.

Lovejoy put his hand softly on the middle of her back

to make her stay looking forward. 'Stand your ground,' he murmured. 'Now, make an offer that splits the difference.'

Julia could feel where his hand had touched. Something about the complete otherness of the situation gave her the desire to succeed. The desire to be and do something different to the person who caved to the pressure of fine china wedding gifts and suffered public shaming on WhatsApp. She took another deep breath and quoted her new offer.

'Good girl,' said Lovejoy, low and husky.

The stallholder made a big show of exhaling. Julia winced, tried to turn to look at Lovejoy but he pressed her back again. 'Hold on,' he whispered. 'Just hold on.'

The stallholder glanced at his mate who puffed out a plume of cigar smoke and shrugged. He turned back to Julia. 'OK.'

Julia's eyes widened. 'OK?'

She heard Lovejoy hiss a 'Yes!' and give her shoulder a squeeze. The whole transaction smelt of him, merged with the touch of him in her euphoria. She felt momentarily like she could turn around and hug him tight.

'OK,' the stallholder said, hand outstretched to shake.

Julia shook it. Lovejoy gave her a wink and a lazy grin.

She felt the rush of success. She thought how impressed Amber would be. She thought how she might replay the entire haggle – with or without mentioning Lovejoy, she'd judge Amber's mood. Even Charlie might be impressed if she told him – definitely without the mention of Lovejoy.

It was all so exciting. She rummaged through her bag for the money to pay the man.

Just then her phone started ringing. Newly charged, it trilled loudly in her bag. '*Un moment,*' she said to the stallholder.

It was her mother.

'Why do you have an international dial tone? Are you abroad, Julia?'

'I'm in France. Just for the weekend,' Julia said. 'I can't talk, Mum, I—'

Her mother carried on regardless. 'I'm surprised you and Charlie have got the money. I saw his picture on Instagram of a leak in your ceiling. It looks dreadful. What happened? Do you need the number of our plumber?'

'No, we have a plumber.' Someone else was asking the stallholder a question. Julia gestured that she'd just be a sec. Scuffing the floor with her foot, she said to her mum who was asking more and more questions re the leak diagnosis, 'I'm not actually sure what the plumber said. Charlie dealt with him. He's still at home.'

'Why is Charlie still at home?' Her mum paused. 'Have you had a row?'

'No,' Julia said too quick.

Her mum had a talent for letting a silence hang suspended till the other person caved. It was why she was such a good lawyer.

'Sort of,' Julia admitted.

'What do you mean, sort of?'

Julia stared up at the sky. 'We just needed a little break. You know what it's like?'

There was a short silence on the other end of the phone, then her mum said, 'Did I tell you that when Suzy Maynard's son's marriage was in trouble he whisked his wife off to the Canaries for a second honeymoon. Worked a treat apparently.'

Julia rolled her eyes. 'No, you didn't tell me that, Mum.'

'Well I'm just saying. Nothing smacks more of divorce than heading off on separate holidays. You remember Suzy Maynard's son, don't you? Works for...' she paused, 'Terence, who does Suzy Maynard's son work for?'

Her dad shouted the answer in the background.

'Oh yes. Van Cleef and Arpels. You know the diamond people. If you'd married him you'd have got a bloody good engagement ring.'

All her life, Julia's mum had been desperate for Julia to get together with Suzy Maynard's son. She'd had them practically betrothed as children.

'Mum!' Julia halted her, unable to quite believe she was already trying to move her on to a more suitable match. 'I'm not getting a divorce.'

'Sorry, sorry, I know you're not getting a divorce. What's the row about?'

'Just stuff,' Julia said, not wanting to go into any more detail, hoping the call would end soon.

'Hang on, your father's asking something. What, Terence?' Another pause as her dad shouted something else in the background.

'Mum, I have to go.'

'Yes, quite right,' her mum said, clearly having a separate conversation with her dad. Then to Julia she recounted, 'He's saying that if you'd bought the shares in that Fever-Tree tonic when your brother suggested, you'd have enough now to go to the Canaries and do up the rest of your house.' Then she mused, 'I don't really know what all the fuss is about gin nowadays. What happened to good old Schweppes? Oh, I've just remembered why I was ringing. What's happened with that promotion at your office? Have you updated your CV yet? You said you'd send it over for me to have a look.'

Julia squeezed her eyes shut. Sweat trickling down her back from the heat. So much for her break with reality. 'I'm doing it,' she said, when really she hadn't done anything because she wasn't completely sure she wanted the new job. It was more hours and a bigger team and not really in her preferred field of expertise and enjoyment. But they needed the money.

In the background her father shouted, 'The secret of getting ahead Julia, is getting started!' Then he added, 'If you're getting euros use your Santander 1,2,3 card, there's no fee for foreign currency.'

'I don't have a 1,2,3 card,' said Julia.

'She doesn't have a 1,2,3 card,' her mum called to her dad. Then she came back on the phone, 'Why not? He says he told you to get one.'

'I don't know, I didn't have time. Look, Mum, I really have to go, OK. I'll get one when I get home.'

'I hope you didn't use a cashpoint because it's daylight robbery. Oh there's someone at the door. I don't know who that is. Terence, can you get the door? I've got to go. Bye, Julia.'

'Bye, Mum.'

Julia hung up, feeling as she always felt when she spoke to her mother – small and a little disappointing. She took a deep breath. Then turned round to buy her trolley.

The stallholder and his mate were sitting smoking cigars.

Julia got the money out of her bag then looked around to see where they'd put it.

The stallholder hoiced his trousers up, puffed out a breath and said, 'It's OK, the man paid for it.'

'Which man?' Julia asked, puzzled.

'The man. Your man. The tall one.'

Julia shook her head. 'He's not my man. He's not with me.' She felt her stomach sink. 'It wasn't his trolley, it was mine.' She looked around trying to catch sight of Lovejoy. To rectify the situation. But he was nowhere to be found. 'I bought it. It was mine,' she repeated to the stallholder. Her previous high like sand slipping through her fingers.

The stallholder shrugged like it wasn't his problem and sat down again with his mate.

Julia couldn't believe it. 'This can't happen. It was sold to me.' But the man was completely indifferent to her protestations.

Julia walked a few paces away from the stall and stood still. She could just imagine what Amber would say – 'Well you've learnt what a dick Lovejoy is' or 'You must always do your own deals!'

She couldn't believe it. The disappointment was exponential. Not only was it the first thing she'd ever successfully haggled for, it was the first antique she'd had a feeling for. It was going to impress Amber. More than that, it felt like a symbol of her skill and independence.

Julia went over to a doorway and slumped down on the concrete step. There were some people playing boules in a café garden to her left. She got out her phone. Whether out of habit or desire, she wasn't sure, she found her fingers hovering over the keys to call Charlie.

She dialled his number.

'Hello?' he said, voice sharp and unwavering.

As soon as he answered, Julia knew it was a mistake. They

were still at loggerheads and any explanation about the trolley would sound stupid and pathetic. 'Hi,' she said.

On the other end of the phone, Charlie waited. 'Julia, is everything OK, because Frank's here.'

'Oh right, no it's nothing,' she said, pushing her hair from her face, fanning herself with her hand. Feeling silly for ringing. 'It was just that Lovejoy stole my trolley, but it doesn't matter.'

'I have no idea what that means,' Charlie replied. 'Hang on, Julia. Yeah, mate, great, that's great thanks,' he said to Frank the plumber. 'Yeah, enjoy your weekend. No, hopefully I won't see you soon,' he added, all jolly and laughing. 'OK, he's gone,' Charlie said back to Julia, voice immediately curt and clipped.

Julia heard him walk down the corridor into the kitchen. It was weird to envisage Charlie's every move but not be there to see it.

There was a silence.

Julia picked at the pebble-dash of the step she was sitting on. 'So do you miss me?' she asked.

Charlie sighed. 'I'm having quite a nice time, actually. It's quite peaceful.'

'Oh right,' Julia said, unable to mask her disappointment. She looked up, shaking her head. Saw the boules players all laughing at something. In the distance a jazz band was playing on the stage, there were little kids dancing and the smell of buttery crepes being cooked on hotplates filled the air.

'Oh come on,' he countered. 'You're living it up in France.'

'I'm not living it up in France, Charlie. I'm only here because things aren't right at home.'

'Things are fine,' he sighed.

Julia put her head in her hand, staring at the blackness of her palm. 'They aren't. You can blame this all on me, Charlie, but it's not all me. You can't just get married, you know, and then stop trying.'

Charlie laughed in disbelief. 'I haven't stopped trying. I'm knackered. I've had a stressful week at work, I spent most of yesterday evening peeling wallpaper off the living room ceiling and this morning making small talk with Frank. Do you know how much it costs to get a plumber out on bank holiday weekend?' he added, his tone not expecting a reply. 'Now I want to relax. Is that allowed? Or would you prefer if I was cycling with Hamish Warrington? What do you want from me?'

'I don't know,' said Julia, standing up, pacing up and down in the space between the stalls and the doorway. 'Something. Anything.' She knew it was selfish and awful but she just wanted him to fight for her. 'Something to show that you care that I'm not there.'

'Like what? You want me on a plane? Coming to get you? I'm really not Hamish Warrington, Julia!'

'I don't want you to be Hamish Warrington.' Although at that moment she could completely imagine, if she *was* married to Hamish Warrington, him suddenly tapping her on the shoulder having flown to France because he couldn't live without her. 'There's a middle-ground, Charlie.' Julia sighed. 'I don't know. I don't know what to say. It feels like this has got too big. You know I've just had my mum on the phone telling me Suzy Maynard's diamond-dealing son flew his wife to the Canaries after a row.'

There was a pause on the other end of the phone.

Julia suddenly realised that probably wasn't the best thing to have said. Charlie knew her mother had harboured a secret desire for Julia and Suzy Maynard's son to marry.

'And what did you say?' Charlie asked slowly.

'Nothing,' said Julia. 'I didn't say anything.'

'You didn't say, "Charlie's not going to do that because it was me writing messages about having sex with the guy over the road that started all this"?'

Julia cringed. 'No, because I'm not talking about sex with my mother. I just told her we weren't getting a divorce.'

'Divorce?' Charlie repeated. 'Who said we were getting a divorce?'

'No one! Nothing.' Julia was in way over her head. This had gone too far. She felt even worse. All she'd wanted was for Charlie to talk her down about her parents. And now, as he was pushing back, she realised suddenly how much she relied on him to calm her down about things that wound her up. How often he made her laugh about things that seemed disastrous. What was happening right now was not the order of things. She back-pedalled furiously. 'It was stupid, Charlie, I shouldn't have said anything.'

'Yes you should' said Charlie, clearly steaming. 'You should have stuck up for me. Christ, you'd probably quite like a diamond dealer. Go and compare rings with Lexi.' He snorted with rage. 'I'm going now, Julia. That's enough for me.'

Charlie hung up.

Julia stood with her phone. God. She tipped her head back against the wall, eyes closed. The sunlight flickered in colourful patterns on her eyelids.

From beside her, she heard Amber's voice say, 'That didn't sound like it went very well.'

Julia jumped upright 'I didn't know you were there.'

Amber shrugged. 'I came to look for you. Thought you might have got lost. I wasn't listening, but it did get quite loud at one point.'

Julia stepped away from the wall. 'I don't think Charlie and I bring out the best in each other at the moment,' she said, resigned. 'I don't even know if we like each other anymore.'

Amber looked sadly at her.

Julia changed the subject – not wanting to think of the phone call and her goading about Suzy Maynard's son – she recounted what had happened with the silver drinks trolley. 'I was really stupid and got duped by Lovejoy,' she said with a shrug, blowing wisps of hair that had escaped her messy ponytail out of her eyes. She felt tired and bedraggled.

Amber listened, then said simply, 'That's Lovejoy for you.'

'I can't believe he took it,' Julia said, unable to let it go. 'It was really good, Amber, I promise, you would have been really impressed.'

Amber nodded, attention already caught by a stall selling old postcards ahead of them.

Julia bit her lip, looked down at her sandals and kicked a bit of loose shingle. 'I really wanted you to be impressed.'

Amber paused on her way to the postcard stall and turned to look at Julia. Then she reached forward and momentarily touched Julia's arm. It felt like a gesture she didn't do very often. Awkward and quick. Amber didn't seem like a toucher. Her skin was cool. It made the moment Lovejoy touched Julia's back seem purposefully manipulative and practised.

Then with a hint of amusement in her big brown eyes, she said, 'I'm very rarely impressed, Julia.'

And for a second Julia forgot her despondency and laughed. Amber too.

'Come on,' Amber said in a voice that seemed as if it were usually reserved for Billy, 'it's getting late, we've still got work to do.'

CHAPTER TWELVE

For the next few hours they walked together side by side at every stall. Julia pointing out things that Amber deigned to give a cursory glance. When Julia picked up an old school test-tube clamp purely for the nostalgia of science lessons, Amber bought it as a possible bedside lamp stand. They stood together staring at an old green factory pendant light – would it work draped over a club chair in the corner of the bedroom? Amber got her notepad out, flicking through to one of the pages dedicated to the room redesign and showed Julia where she could replace the standard lamp in the corner with the pendant, amending the little sketch.

Julia looked at the drawing. 'You're really good at drawing.'

'I know,' Amber replied.

Julia stared at her in surprise.

'What?' Amber stopped what she was doing, confused by her expression.

'Just...' Julia shrugged. 'Not many people just agree to a compliment.'

'What would you prefer me to do?' Amber looked at her puzzled. 'Go all coy and dopey?' She put her notebook back in her bumbag.

'No, no,' Julia waved a hand to show she wasn't disagreeing, 'no, I *want* you to say yes. It's just most people deny it, don't they, if someone says they're good?'

Amber narrowed thick lashes. 'Well most people care too much what other people think.'

Julia paused for a second. 'Yes, I suppose they do,' she mused as she followed behind Amber, snaking through the mass of people, her contemplation of the fact making Amber smile under her breath. Maybe she'd have Julia ditching the Lexi-esque pompom on her bag before the end of the holiday.

They finished off the south section of the fair by zigzagging up a network of side streets where Amber bought a handful of Emerald House pieces. It was just before lunch by the time they'd done the main bulk of the fair. There were only the stalls on the north of the river still to do but Amber explained that was all the smaller stuff – jewellery and more antique pieces that they would have a cursory look at but it wasn't that relevant to her.

So they retraced their steps, picking up everything Amber had purchased and lugging it back to the van. They had to do four trips, borrowing a trolley to wheel a little chest of drawers Amber had bought along with three big mirrors. Julia carried a bag filled with lamps and candlesticks that cut deep into her skin. Amber hoisted the taxidermy fox under one arm and the cardboard box of picture frames under the other. They were hot, dirty and sweaty by the time it was all collected, and only then did Amber sanction a quick stop for lunch at her favourite crepe van. It was where her dad always took her when they were here. As a kid, he'd lift her onto his big broad shoulders so she could watch as the woman in the van scattered the pancakes with grated cheese that bubbled and melted as soon as it hit then she'd crack an egg and when done, she'd fold the finished crepes into perfect quarters with a palette knife and slide them into their little cardboard envelopes, handing them over with a flourish. Always with a big grin and a sneaky double helping of cheese for Amber's dad. It was one of Amber's favourite memories – everything about it was good. Behind the counter it was still the same woman making the crepes, back hunched and wrinkled skin, but the same beaming smile.

Julia and Amber stood under the shade of a plane tree and drank Perrier from bottles, runny yolk dripping on their chins, silently surveying all they still had left to cover. The vans glistening like flames in the incessant heat. A mirage of winding lanes ahead of them.

Lovejoy and Martin strolled past. Lovejoy spotted them and with a tip of his head said, 'Ladies.'

Julia glared at him sullenly.

Amber shouted, 'That was a dirty trick you pulled on Julia, Lovejoy.'

He held his arms wide with a smile. 'What are you talking about? I had to buy it, someone else came along and offered him more.'

Amber groaned, 'Oh please, that's such a lie.'

Lovejoy crossed his heart, 'God's honest truth.' Then he grinned at Julia, 'Aww, don't look at me like that. I promise, I had to buy it!'

Amber replied with a dismissive wave, sending him on his way.

Lovejoy held up his hands, still protesting his innocence. 'It's the truth.'

Amber tossed the cardboard wrapping of her crepe in the bin, then got her compact out and redid her lipstick.

Julia said, 'I don't think that's true.'

Amber smacked her red lips together. 'Course it's not.' She chucked the compact into her bumbag.

Lovejoy had paused by an adjacent plane tree to answer his phone. Amber's attention was immediately caught when she heard him say, 'Billy?' Her gaze shot to Lovejoy, his smiling, quizzical face as he spoke into the handset. 'What are you calling me for? I'm standing right by your mum.'

Amber felt her heart start to hammer. 'I'll talk to him,' she said, striding over towards Lovejoy. 'He's just calling you because my phone's died.'

But Lovejoy held up a hand to fend her off. The light through the branches of the tree played on his face. 'Sorry, mate, I didn't quite catch that. Your dad? What do you mean, your dad?'

Amber watched with horror as Lovejoy started to frown, listening to whatever Billy was telling him on the other end of the line.

'Christ, Billy,' Lovejoy blew out a breath, leant one hand against the peeling trunk of the tree. 'No it's not me. Definitely not.' He laughed. 'Bloody hell.' Then he paused again, nodded. 'No, there's no way your mum wouldn't have told me—' He looked up, caught Amber's eye as if to convey the fact this was big news being discussed, almost sorry for Amber that her and her son were going through this.

Amber stopped a metre or so away from him. She

swallowed. Waiting. Waiting for the hesitant moment of doubt to cross his face.

But she needn't have worried. Lovejoy wasn't going to give it any credence. She should have known. Should have guessed. He would never want to even consider the possibility.

He shook his head, looked at Amber, all regretful. 'Nah, mate, you've got the wrong guy. Sorry, kiddo.'

And his expression took her back to exactly the moment when he had looked at her exactly the same way. Used exactly the same tone. Finished the sentence with that slightly off-hand laughter that always served to make the other person feel just a tiny bit silly for asking.

It was the same afternoon her mother had left with Keith, one of the many boyfriends she'd handed herself over to after Amber's dad died, but this one stuck. It was a Tuesday, she remembered because the dustbin men were collecting the rubbish and she remembered the sweet, rotten smell as she stood in the wind-tunnel corridor of their flat block with her rucksack. A couple of cleaners hired by the landlord were already working on the flat she'd lived in with her mother, getting it ready for his next cash in hand tenants. She saw them shoving stuff into bin bags – Amber's eighteenth birthday cards still on the windowsill, a vase of dying tulips, some old shells they'd picked up on the beach, a stack of condolence cards for her dad that Amber's mother had shoved in the drawer as soon as one of her new boyfriends came on the scene – all grabbed and discarded by the rubber-gloved hands of a stranger. She remembered having no idea what to do, shocked that even though she knew what her mother was like, she had never expected her to leave. Amber had been so lulled by her mother's desperate dependency on her that she had never prepared for the eventuality of being left.

When she'd had enough of watching the stuff she couldn't carry being unceremoniously junked, Amber had turned and walked three doors down to Lovejoy's. He'd been her best friend since she was ten years old.

His mum, Carole, was the complete opposite of her own mother. The type of woman who glowed with open friendliness. She made vats of jam – with quinces and apples from her allotment. She had symbolic tattoos up her arms, smelt of washing powder and was always lamenting the fact she wasn't lying on a Lanzarote beach. She was an antiques dealer too, she'd been a great friend of Amber's dad's, and her mother loathed her. Jealous of their shared laughter. Carole laughed a lot. She hugged a lot. And when she looked at you she could see right into you.

She'd opened the door with a beaming smile, an offer of a cup of tea and an apology about the state of Lovejoy's bedroom as Amber disappeared down the corridor in that direction.

Amber's friendship with Lovejoy had recently developed from its teenage bantering one-upmanship into a tentative relationship. She'd tried to resist – she'd seen enough of his girlfriends leave the pub in tears or watch as he got bored and dumped them with a text. She had been the friend he whined about them all with and she'd vowed to never step into their shoes. But then one night, their flirty peacocking had slipped into an illicit, never-mentioned kiss round the back of the King's Head and she hadn't been able to forget it. She had woken up at night thinking about him. Lovejoy had been trying to get her into bed since they were sixteen, it had been part of their banter, so when she finally caved in he was delighted. Then it was covert nights spent over, and finally to what it was at that point – coy hand-holding when they walked down the street and an understanding that they'd go home together after a night out. Their friendship, initially unchanged, had just started to tip, to veer into territory where not everything could be said out loud, where vulnerability and pride were suddenly at stake. And neither was willing to be the first to dip their toe into the water first.

When Amber had walked into his room, he'd grinned like a Cheshire cat at the sight of her. And she had grinned back. She climbed over the discarded clothes on the floor and onto the bed where he'd been lying listening to music, where he'd opened his arms wide to envelope her, where he'd smelt of warmth and sleep, Lynx and sweat.

Where she'd found herself shy suddenly. And for the first time in need. Where she had allowed herself, as she slept on his grey patterned sheets, as she'd heard his mum watching TV in the living room, as she'd fought the drag of the blank hoarse loss of her dad dying and the bewilderment of her mum leaving, the momentary luxury of safety.

She had woken up in the morning to find Lovejoy sitting up, T-shirt thrown on, fidgety like he'd been waiting for her eyes to open. When he'd smiled, this time his face was too vibrant. His eyes too wide. He started talking about a plan he'd had. He wasn't hanging around here, he said. His mum had come into a bit of cash selling some old photographs of vegetables she'd found in an attic clearance. She was lending him some. He was going to go to the States. Did she know there were warehouses in Brooklyn packed with the antique equivalent of solid gold? Buy it cheap, ship it over. No messing. His hands moved fast as he talked. Then he might go east, he thought. There was so much to see. He wasn't staying around here, no way. Amber had barely wiped the sleep from her eyes. All she noticed was that he kept looking furtively at her rucksack in the corner, panic on his face. Like it was going to rise up and tie him down where he was on the bed, forever. Not once did he mention the possibility of her going to America too, of them buying stuff cheap and shipping it back together.

Amber didn't need to be told twice.

They got up and had breakfast with his mum. She remembered Carole asking, 'How's your mum, Amber?' And Amber had said, 'Oh she's fine. She's just gone on holiday actually. Back in a fortnight.'

Carole looked uncertain.

Amber's expression was too neutral to challenge. But she knew Carole knew that she was lying.

'That's nice,' Carole said in the end. 'Very lucky.' She glanced at her son. Amber had seen her mouth, 'Have you told her?' And Lovejoy nod as unsubtle as ever. Carole had turned back to Amber and said, 'I know Lovejoy's going away, but there's a home for you here, always, you know that?'

'Alright, Mum, I'm not going till next week, you can't rent my out room yet.'

And Amber had smiled almost quizzically, as if even the mere mention of her needing a place to stay was completely unnecessary – she had a home, a mother, a place to sleep.

As soon as she could leave, without seeming too hurried,

Amber had picked up her massive rucksack, as if it were no big deal, and with a casual 'See you at the pub later' to Lovejoy, she strode off down the biting, wind-tunnel corridor. Then she had got into her dad's battered old van and driven off to nowhere. That night she slept in the back. Shivering in a car park.

And here Lovejoy was, at an antiques fair in France, with that same off-hand, bright-eyed emotionless expression on his face. It made Amber feel sick. It made her take those few final strides towards him, snatch the phone and say, 'It's not Lovejoy who's your father, Billy. I told you that. If you must know, it was a guy called Richard. He was in a band called something like Open Water or Something Ice, I can't remember. I don't know where he is. He's probably dead from all the drugs he was taking. Alright? There you go. That's all I can tell you.'

On the other end of the phone, Billy was silent for a second, then he said, 'Richard. Something Ice or Water... ' slowly as if he was writing it down.

Amber exhaled. 'Billy, you don't need to do anything about it now. OK. We can talk about it properly when I get home.'

'Yes,' he said, completely unconvincing. 'Bye, Mum.'

'Bye, darling,' she said, but he'd hung up.

Lovejoy looked vastly relieved. Like the status quo had resumed.

When Amber handed him back the phone he said, 'Well that was interesting. I never knew Ned wasn't his real—'

But Amber wasn't listening. Every part of her body was telling her she had to leave. She had to get as far away from him as possible. She couldn't cope with any questions. She couldn't look at the expressions on his face. She couldn't cope with the tendrils of him curling into her world. 'Come on, Julia. We have things to do.'

Julia hurried to catch up as Amber started to stride away from the shade of the trees.

'Amber?' Lovejoy called after her.

But she ignored him.

CHAPTER THIRTEEN

'Where are we going?' said Julia, having to trot to keep up as Amber pushed blindly through tourists and traders.

'To the van,' Amber said without turning round.

'The van?' Julia said, surprised, but didn't argue. Amber was almost radiating fury.

When they broke out of the main crowd and hit the road leading up to the hotel, Julia finally caught up with her side by side. 'Was it true?' Julia asked. 'What you said about that guy Richard in the band. Is that true?'

'Course it's true,' snapped Amber.

But there was no 'of course' about it in Julia's mind. It seemed it was impossible to trust Amber from one thing to the next.

They got to the garage of the Hotel Croissant. Inside it was freezing. Dark and gloomy. One of the fluorescent lights flickered. Amber opened the back doors of the van and checked everything was packed properly. The taxidermy fox stared out at them, beady yellow eyes making Julia jump.

'Are we leaving?' Julia asked, confused as Amber slammed the doors.

'Yes.'

'But we still have the north side of the fair to do.'

'Just get in the van, Julia,' said Amber, who marched to the driver's side, yanking the door open.

Julia hauled open her door as Amber was starting the engine, her wild eyes making Julia panic. She didn't want to drive off into nowhere with Amber. If she was honest, she quite wanted to go home even if her husband wasn't talking to her and everyone on the street knew her humiliating business. This fiasco wasn't much better. 'Where are we going?'

'Away from here.'

'But where?' asked Julia, looking around unsure. They couldn't just leave the fair.

'I'm thinking,' said Amber, sighing, trying to concentrate while also crunching her gears to find reverse while reaching across to get her bag from the footwell.

'What do you need?' Julia asked, taking it from her.

'About a hundred Nicorette patches.'

Julia handed her the box. 'Amber, why don't you just wait a second,' she urged, hoping she might pause and calm down rather than just peel multiple patches off and thwack them onto her arm. 'Why don't we get a cup of coffee or something and then you can talk to Lovejoy.'

Amber finally slammed the van into reverse. 'Why?' she said, off-hand, checking her mirrors as she pulled out of the space at speed.

'Well because...' Julia started as if it were obvious, then paused because Amber didn't look as if it were obvious. Julia was suddenly torn. She wanted to say nothing but Amber was glaring at her in challenge.

'Why?' Amber said again. Outside the garage, the roads

were still blocked by market traders. Amber had to weave the van through the traffic diversion of narrow back streets.

'Nothing,' said Julia.

'No, go on,' pushed Amber. 'You want me to talk to Lovejoy because…?'

When Amber frowned she looked like Billy. When he was all earnest with Julia, diligently following her cooking instructions. Pushing his thick-rimmed glasses up his nose. His studious, geeky seriousness.

But it wasn't just Billy that Julia was thinking about. Part of her was let down because she thought Amber was so strong and so together and now they were running away. From Lovejoy of all people. It was that which made her say quietly, 'Because you're lying to them,' as the van was heading up towards the main road. And then to quickly make amends, to make it seem said more out of concern for Amber, added, 'It's only going to make things worse, I think, lying. Maybe you should just be honest with them? I don't know.' She shrugged. Wishing she'd never said anything. Beside her Amber's face was setting, hard and sharp.

'No you don't know!' Amber snapped, like a whip. 'And who are you to talk, anyway?' she said, almost visibly puffing up, like a cat backed into a corner, instantly ready on the attack. 'Be honest – that's a laugh! You can't even be honest with yourself.'

Julia gripped her seat belt, wide-eyed with surprise.

'Don't look so shocked,' Amber scoffed, pulling out at a roundabout even though it wasn't her right of way, sneering at the angry on-coming driver. 'You have this nice husband. Well he seems nice enough, bit scrawny but nice enough.

A nice house. You're clever. You don't have one problem in the bloody world. But there you are decked out like Lexi bloody Warrington and her minions. Constantly mooning over her Instagram.'

'I am not,' said Julia, defensive.

But Amber wasn't listening. 'Fantasising about her idiot of a husband. Moaning at your husband that he's not making grand enough gestures to keep you. I mean, what the hell? Just open your eyes and admit you've fallen into the trap,' she went on. 'Take some bloody responsibility.'

Julia swallowed. She felt like she had scratches on her arms.

Amber was flooring it up the street out of the town. She shook her head, despairing. 'You're so busy blaming your husband, you're incapable of taking any blame yourself. Maybe *you're* driving *him* bananas! Always bowing to other people, pleasing them. I mean, who the hell agrees a deal on the most *amazing* trolley ever and then takes a phone call from their mother rather than paying? You want to know about lying. Look in the bloody mirror, *Julia*.'

Julia was clutching tight to the seat belt now. 'Why are you being so mean?'

Amber huffed. 'Because you're so frustrating!'

'Well so are you!' Julia found herself snapping back, hurt. Almost shocking herself. She immediately wanted to suck the words back in, feeling not quite up to the challenge of taking on Amber. Like a duckling waddling into a boxing ring.

'Oh really?' Amber drawled.

'Yes,' Julia replied, a touch less confident.

'Why?'

They pulled onto the motorway, the sun ahead of them

pooling out over the rolling hills, horses in fields and giant white windmills looming still and silent in the thick muggy heat.

'Where are we going?' Julia asked as the van powered along in the fast lane.

'Don't change the subject,' Amber snapped. 'Tell me why I'm frustrating.'

'No,' said Julia shaking her head.

'Go on,' Amber baited, clearly gunning for a fight.

'I don't want to,' said Julia fiddling with her skirt pleats.

'Go on, tell me why. I've told you. You can't, can you?' She laughed. Julia flinched. 'Come on,' Amber went on. 'Stand up to me, Julia, I can take it. Tell me what's so frustrating.'

'OK, fine,' Julia snapped. Feeling the tension of the day wound up inside her, the humiliation of Amber's words. 'You blame everyone but yourself, too. You act like you're so right but you're not. You should have told Lovejoy and you know it. However bad he was. It's people's lives. Not just yours. I agreed before but I actually think you're wrong. He has a right to know. Billy has a right to know. You're just afraid of getting into trouble.'

'It's not school, Julia!'

'I know it's not school. You know what I— I mean.' Julia was stuttering now. She'd lost her train of thought. She was panicking. 'I just think you're afraid of them getting angry, maybe. Because—'

'Because what? What?' Amber snarled, blowing her hair out of her eyes. Driving faster now. 'Because you think it's all my fault? That I denied him the right to a child when he wouldn't have stuck around for a child in a million years. It's me that's angry.'

Julia hesitated. 'Yes, fine. Maybe you all have a right to be angry! It's just I would be afraid of them getting angry and not speaking to me, because I had lied,' she started to lose her fight, she was worried about how fast Amber was driving, 'I think it's going to get worse if this carries on. That they're more likely to not speak to you. And you and Billy have such a lovely relationship. Oh I don't know, I don't know.' She held her hands up like she was done. 'I just— I think you should slow down.'

Amber snorted with disgust at the idea, eyes fixed on the road, undertaking, overtaking.

Up ahead, the sky was almost white, the heat engulfing.

A beep from Amber's phone cut into the tense silence between them. It was in the cup-holder and Julia could see it was a WhatsApp message from Billy.

Amber reached forward and clicked on it.

The message read:

Was it this guy?

And there was a photo, a screenshot from an old newspaper. Clearly the result of Billy's obsessive googling.

'*Richard Shepherd, of band Thin Air, and girlfriend, Amber Beddington, brave the Glastonbury mud,*' the caption read.

Julia craned across to see the photo better. The guy in it wore a black pork pie hat, a loose white T-shirt with a black eagle on the front, a rosary round his neck and skinny black jeans that were caked in mud up to the knee. A cigarette hung from his plump lips and there was another one behind his ear. His arm was draped casually over a very skinny, very young-looking Amber. Moody and beautiful in a sludge green mini-dress, low boho belt and mud-encrusted wellington boots. Her long platinum-blonde hair hung in a centre parting half over sullen, dark-rimmed eyes. She had the look of a child playing at being a grown-up.

Amber smacked the steering wheel. 'Shit,' she muttered darkly. 'Shit, shit, shit.'

Julia winced as the van accelerated. 'Amber,' she said, tone warning, trying to get her to pause, to calm down.

But Amber was going faster now. Faster and faster in her stony silence.

Then the sound of a siren pierced the air behind them.

Julia had never been pulled over by the police before. She presumed for Amber it was a more regular occurrence because she sighed with annoyance rather than shook with nerves as she pulled the van over to the hard shoulder, the interior of the van lighting up with flashing blue.

Julia was terrified.

Other cars went past slowly rubbernecking.

The tarmac sizzled with heat. The grassy verge was an arid mix of rubbish and mangy gorse bushes. A tall white windmill towered ominously over them. Up ahead was a wide expanse of patchwork field.

'Don't look at me like that,' Amber said, turning to Julia.

'We were going too fast,' Julia said quietly. Then she added, 'Do you have all that stuff you need to drive in France? All the yellow jackets and triangles?'

'Yes,' said Amber, all stubborn. Then she said, 'No.'

Julia exhaled.

'Don't sigh, it's not helping. I don't need your dad in the

car with me.' Amber was tapping her fingers on the steering wheel watching the police officer approaching.

Julia was silent. She did feel like her father.

Just as the police officer appeared at the window, Amber said, 'Now play it cool.'

Julia nodded.

Amber beamed as the stern-looking policeman approached. '*Bonjour,* Officer.'

He narrowed his eyes.

Julia waved her hand. '*Bonjour.*'

The officer was chewing gum, he had his arms crossed over his dark blue jacket. His gun in its holster. 'English?'

Amber nodded.

'Madame, you know the speed limit?'

'*Oui,*' Amber replied, trying to look nonplussed. 'I was going at the speed limit, wasn't I – 140 kilometres an hour? Yes?'

'*Non,*' he shook his head, chewed his gum some more. Then he looked across at Julia, 'You think she was driving at the speed limit?'

Julia swallowed. She didn't know what to say. 'Maybe she was possibly a little above the limit, I'm not sure.'

Amber rolled her eyes.

The police officer raised a brow. He wrote something in his pad and walked back to his car.

'What did you say that for?' Amber snapped.

'What? He knows you were speeding,' Julia hissed back.

'You just admitted guilt.'

'Technology tells him you're guilty, Amber. Lying isn't going to help.'

Amber scoffed, 'You know the first rule of driving, Julia, is not ever admitting guilt.'

Julia pursed her lips. 'I don't think that's the first rule of driving, Amber.'

'Just keep your mouth shut from now on, Julia.'

Julia turned away and looked out the window, at the big white blades of the windmill static in the breezeless heat.

The officer returned. He lifted up the speed gun he had bought back from the car with him. 'The vehicle was travelling at 191 kilometres an hour.'

Amber pursed her lips.

'This is an automatic fine of seven hundred and fifty euro.'

'What?' Amber shrieked. 'No way. It's never been a fine like that before.'

The officer shrugged.

'I'm not paying that much.' Amber reached over for her bag in the footwell. 'Come on,' she said, 'What'll it take? A hundred euro?' she asked, opening her purse and folding up two fifties ready to slip them to the officer.

'Madame, are you trying to bride me?'

Amber laughed. 'No.' But still she held out the fifties.

'Put the money away,' the man said, humourless.

Julia hissed, 'Put the money away, Amber.'

Amber put the fifties back in her purse. 'Well what can I do?' she said to the officer. 'I'm not paying seven hundred and fifty euros, this is a joke.'

The officer ignored her. 'For refusing to pay the fine, we are going to take the van, madame, and you are forbidden from driving it in this country.'

'No,' gasped Amber.

'Madame, you need to get out of the van.'

'Absolutely not.' Amber shook her head. 'It's my van.'

'You are beginning to annoy me,' he said, looking angry.

Amber just crossed her arms and sat staunchly where she was.

The policeman glared at her. Then he paused, considered the options and with a sly smile said, 'You have something to hide in the van?' Then he peered in through the window at the grey blankets covering Amber's stock.

'Of course I don't,' Amber said, sitting up to look where he was looking.

Julia suddenly thought of Amber's fake passport. For the woman called Christine Miller who looked like the *Mona Lisa*.

'Maybe you do,' said the police officer. Then he radioed something too fast for Julia to understand.

'What's he saying?' Amber asked Julia, voice hushed.

'I don't know.' Julia felt a slight dread creep up her spine. 'But I don't think it's going to be good.'

The officer was laughing at something that was being said on the radio. Then he turned back to Amber all serious and said, 'Madame, I am impounding your vehicle on the suspicion that you carrying stolen goods.'

'No, you're kidding, you can't!' Amber shook her head. 'Come on, I was only speeding. I'll pay you the fine, but you're not having the van.' To Julia's surprise, Amber added, almost to herself, 'I've got to find my son.'

'Out!' The officer opened the door.

'No!' said Amber, steadfast.

Just then another police car pulled up, sirens blaring, and the officer said, 'Madame, I am arresting you—'

Julia put her hands up to her face and gasped.

'OK! OK!' Amber huffed. 'OK I'm getting out.' She made a big show of undoing her seat belt and taking the key out of the ignition. Then as she leant over and grabbed her bag she whispered to Julia, 'Get the passport.'

'How?' Julia whispered back but Amber was climbing out of the van. As she did she dropped her keys, clearly trying to distract the officer so that Julia could open the glove compartment and try her best to slip the spare passport into her bag. But it was all so hasty and unplanned, that when Julia did try to get the passport out unnoticed she did it very badly and very obviously, fumbling it with nervous butterfingers.

The officer looked up. 'What are you doing?' he asked Julia.

Julia went bright red. 'Just getting my passport,' she said. Amber closed her eyes.

The other police officers were getting out of their car, chatting as they came over to stand with the arresting officer.

The policeman clicked his fingers for Julia to hand over the passport.

Julia could see her hand trembling. If she really was her father, right now she'd turn Amber in without a second's hesitation. She could feel her heart thundering in her chest. She didn't know how long a French prison sentence for passport fraud was but it would be more than speeding that was for sure. She couldn't meet Amber's eye. She could feel the colour begin to rise up her neck as she opened the passport on the photograph of Christine Miller, taking her time pedantically flattening it out, trying to disguise the tremble in her hand.

The officer clicked his fingers again, impatient. When she

gave it to him, he studied it for a second then stared at Julia. Narrowing his eyes.

Julia swallowed. Barely able to move.

The officer showed it to his pal. Who also looked at Julia.

'Name?' the man said.

'Christine Miller,' Julia replied, unable to quite believe that this was happening, that he believed the picture was of her, trying to keep her voice even.

'Date of birth?'

Julia closed her eyes. She felt sick. She was lying to a police officer.

Julia reached up and scratched her blotchy neck, she pictured the page she had just spent precious seconds flattening. 'Fourteenth of February,' she said, 'nineteen eighty-two.'

There was a pause. She could feel Amber looking straight at her. Then the officer nodded, closed the passport and handed it back to Julia. 'Ms Miller, you need to get out of the van,' he said. 'My colleague will give you a lift to the station.'

'Fine, yes,' said Julia nodding, stumbling in her movements, overwhelmed with relief and fear and something else, a tiny flicker of excitement. Maybe even pride. Her hands shook as she tucked the passport deep into her bag.

Amber clearly couldn't believe it. She was staring at Julia with a new-found respect.

'And you,' the officer said, tugging on Amber's arm. 'You are coming with me.'

CHAPTER FOURTEEN

The police station dominated one edge of a town square boxed in by giant plane trees. Across the road was a mini-Carrefour and a signpost up the hill for a boulangerie, a gymnasium and what looked like a picture of a viaduct. Baskets of pink geraniums hung from lampposts and there were tables on both sides of the square from two cafés. Under normal circumstances, Julia thought, it might be a nice place for a mini-break.

She sat on a bench under the dappled shade of the plane trees still coming down off the nail-biting horror of being questioned about the passport. The aftermath of fear had turned into a shivering surge of adrenaline. She wished she had her cardigan or something to wrap round her shoulders but all the clothes she owned were in a plastic bag which was in the van that was currently impounded just visible through a window in the police station, jacked up with no tyres, all their antiques scattered over the floor and the door-panels ripped off. She wondered what the friend Amber had borrowed the van off would make of the destruction. But, she supposed, that was the least of Amber's problems, currently incarcerated behind the big white swing doors in the police station that Julia wasn't allowed through. A long and frustrating discussion in broken English and AS-Level French with the beautiful flame-haired desk sergeant told Julia nothing about Amber's case or how long she would be locked up. The redhead had nodded to the hard green plastic seats and said, 'You will have to wait.'

But Julia hadn't been able to sit still. The fake passport burning a hole in her handbag. So she had gone outside into the square. Where she now sat, on a bench, waiting.

She got her phone out and went on Instagram.

There was a story posted by Lexi. It was a video documenting the carnage of the party. Then Hamish walking in from the gym, all sweaty, and ignoring the fact she was recording him with her phone, giving her a long, wet hello kiss. Lexi pushed him away with a grin and said, 'I'm mid-Insta-story, babe.'

Julia watched as Hamish nodded, opened the fridge and said, 'I got two hundred views for my bench-press routine this morning. Guys, check it out!' he added, drinking Tropicana straight from the carton. 'Babe, a glass...' said Lexi from behind the camera. Then it cut to Lexi at the hairdressers post-blow-dry, dressed in monochrome athleisurewear. A glass of Prosecco and a magazine next to a pair of GHDs. Her stylist behind her grinning. Julia read the caption: *Sun-kissed!* #newhair #lexistyle

Julia held it on pause to stare at Lexi's hair. It looked perfect. All artful waves and glossy blonde streaks. She thought of her own hair in comparison, wishing it too was sun-kissed.

The wind blew gently and rustled the plane tree leaves like maracas. The sun flickered on her screen. On her hand, the skin on her arm, the pavement. Probably if she could see a mirror, on her hair.

She *had* sun-kissed hair, she realised. Actual sun-kissed hair.

Julia thought suddenly of what Amber had said, about her mooning over Lexi's Instagram. She felt immediately ashamed. Stupid.

She was about to click it off but her finger hovered over the button for her own Instagram page. She clicked onto her timeline. The last photo was of her in the Whistles rip-off white dress holding the cakes #partytime. The dress wasn't as flattering as she'd hoped. Her hair was as flat as she'd feared. She scrolled down some more to older photos. A picture of all the swatches of paint she'd done in the living room #whichone? She remembered writing it, she had actually wanted one of her sixty-three followers to choose for her. A selfie with a paint roller that she remembered using to daub her face with a splodge of paint before taking it so it looked funnier, more authentic. She scrolled some more, further and further down, past the photos of the #newhouse and her and Charlie holding up a bottle of champagne her parents had brought them to celebrate, posing in front of the dreadful ear-of-corn kitchen tiles #excitingtimes.

She went back further still, past her wedding. Past the too-expensive honeymoon in Amalfi and a video of her unwrapping all the fragile bone chinaware they'd never used. Further and further until she got to pictures of her and Charlie lounging in their tiny studio flat in the eaves of a red-brick house in Acton, the first place they'd rented together. Eating popcorn, drinking tea, feet up on the coffee table. Then further back still. To the holiday in France when she was new to Instagram and treated it like her photo stream, nothing curated, just a day by day account of the cheese they ate, the gorges they canoed, the camera faces they pulled, the old bikes they cycled. All filtered to the max. There were no hashtags. There was just her life. Her plain and simple life with Charlie.

In one photo they were eating hot dogs from a little shack by the canoe-rental place, sitting under an orange umbrella, squinting from the sun. Julia had been a reluctant canoer. She had never done it before and didn't want to look like an idiot but told Charlie it was because she didn't want to fall in. But he wouldn't take no for an answer and it had been one of the best mornings of her life. The water calm, the sides of the gorge high. It had been Charlie who had fallen in, much to her hilarity and his droll ambivalence. In the post-canoeing hot dog picture, she zoomed right in on their faces, on their skin, on their eyes. He looked so young. She looked so happy.

The T-shirt he was wearing was the same one he'd wanted to wear to the party before she'd made him change into the white polo shirt. Now holey and threadbare. She hadn't recognised it. And strangely she suddenly remembered it as the same T-shirt he'd worn when she'd met him. Bright green, like he worked in a garden centre.

Julia stood up from the bench. She needed to move – delving so far back into her life made her feel a little uneasy. At how fast time passed. At how easily smiles faded. So she did a lap of the square, past the tweed suits in the window of the boutique and the waitress laying out napkins and cutlery at the café. At the far end of the square was a small fountain of cherubs and then a couple of old tables with rickety chairs where old men were playing chess, while some onlookers drank glasses of pastis. She went and watched for a while, listening to the trickle of the fountain and the angry challenges to the chess moves.

She thought of Charlie and his bright green T-shirt. The first time she'd seen it she'd been at university, late for her business studies lecture and in her mild panic she had spotted the bright green of Charlie's T-shirt like a beacon next to an empty chair that she could slip into without drawing any more attention to herself. The door had already slammed causing the lecturer to sigh. The only interaction she and Charlie had was for him to move his jacket slightly so she wasn't sitting on the edge of it. But about half an hour in, the lecturer said something that prompted one of a group of jocks lounging at the back to shout out in response some really clichéd TV catchphrase as a joke. The whole room sniggered at the heckle, except Julia, who frowned because she always felt sorry for the person being interrupted, she didn't like seeing anyone made a fool of. Next to her Charlie leant over and said dryly, 'Not funny.' Which did make Julia laugh, more unexpectedly than anything. Especially as in her world – the jocks, being much like her brother, and her father for that matter – the norm was to automatically be impressed by these guys and their crowd-pleasing humour.

She sat next to Charlie a couple of times again after that, not every time. Their relationship was slow to progress. Once she asked him why he was studying business, whispered it while the lecturer was setting up a PowerPoint. Charlie said, 'I don't know really. I want to live off-grid.'

Julia had laughed. 'Yeah but you have to do something.'

He'd shrugged.

'Well what do you like?' she'd asked. 'Do you want to live off-grid because you want to be alone or because of climate change?'

Charlie frowned. 'Not sure, maybe both.'

'And you can't just live off-grid. You have to get a job.'

'Yeah,' he'd shrugged.

'So maybe you could work in something like renewable energy?'

He'd pondered the idea. 'Maybe I could.'

She'd been incredulous at his lack of a plan

'How about you?' he'd asked. 'What do you want to do?'

'Something in the city,' Julia replied, a whisper now because the slides had started.

'What in the city?' Charlie sounded confused.

Julia shrugged. 'I've got an internship at a management consultancy in the summer,' she said the name of the company, Charlie hadn't heard of it, 'And hopefully they'll take me on again over Christmas,' she said, hushed, trying to look like she was paying attention. 'Eventually I want to work with food – you know, be a chef or a baker or something. Maybe own a restaurant.'

'But?' he'd asked, completely uninterested in the lecture.

Julia said, 'My parents think I should get a proper job first, you know, earn some money, get a good pension and then go and do that later.'

'Screw your parents,' Charlie said, making a face.

Julia giggled. 'You know I'm the only person in my family in six generations who didn't get into Oxford?'

'Congratulations,' Charlie replied, dryly.

A couple of weeks later, Julia had sat down next to Charlie and one of the jocks, a guy called Ed Grainger, had walked past her on his way to the seats at the back and said, 'Julia, still on for tonight?'

Julia had blushed, 'Yes.'

Charlie had made a show of looking confused, then when she'd admitted she had a date with Ed, openly mocked her for her lame choice. But Julia hadn't been able to resist Ed's offer, he was six foot four, dark-haired, captain of the rugby team, and she was still trying to chase the dream of fitting in.

But the date had been as bad and as dull as Charlie had told her it would be. And in the morning, all Ed's rugby housemates had jeered when she'd walked through the kitchen to the front door. She'd only learnt about their points-based score sheet when she'd sat red-faced in the lecture as one of Ed's mates had shouted, 'Grainger's number five at three o'clock, people.'

Charlie had raised a condescending brow. 'Should have stuck with me,' he'd said. And somehow the words transformed and hung between them taking on more meaning than suddenly poor blushing Charlie had intended but pushed through the layers of perfectionism and FOMO around Julia's heart to the sweet bit that liked baking vanilla sponge cakes and wasting time with him after lectures drinking horrible coffee. They had gone to see a movie together that night.

And they had been together since that first accidental invitation for a date. Charlie gave her a quiet liberation from the overachieving ambitions instilled in her. While she encouraged in him a sense of direction and self-belief to counter his laid-back disregard. But more than that they laughed. And they believed in each other.

Charlie got a job in a tiny wind farm company that didn't believe in hierarchy or office wear and suited him down to the ground. Julia got a job in the marketing department of a London restaurant group that paid badly but gave her loads of responsibility and a lot of free dinners for two where she tested the restaurants incognito. They had shit salaries and lived in their top-floor flat that was a hovel inside but out the window they were level with the trees so it felt like they lived in a forest. For a few years they brought out the best in each other. Then came the wedding and the expectation. Charlie's inheritance, the mortgage and the house.

In the town square, one of the chess games ended and the old men packed up the board. Julia stood up from where she'd been perched against the brick wall and wandered back to her bench, the sun casting dancing shadows on the wood through the plane tree leaves. She sat down, one eye on the jail just in case Amber might appear. Then she glanced at her phone again, scrolled back through her Instagram till she got to the shots of her and Charlie moving into the house. The champagne and the dreadful tiles. They had been like kids in a sweet shop. Their eyes bigger than their pockets. Julia's parents had pushed for her to aspire to more – her brother had recently renovated a Kensington loft apartment big enough to host the whole family. Julia got sucked in by Rightmove and estate agent spiel and Charlie went wide-eyed at renovation possibilities. And they got the house on Cedar Lane that they could just about afford the mortgage each month as long as *nothing* in their lives changed.

A month later Charlie's company was bought out by a Japanese company who, while dedicated to wind power, were more dedicated to profit and they liked to see their staff in a suit.

Charlie would put on his tie like a garrotte. Julia remembered a conversation she'd had with her family one day after Charlie had come home with the news that one of his colleagues had the backing to set up a vegetable delivery start-up. He had offered Charlie a job and a seat on the board. Julia's mother had frowned, 'Do start-ups need a board?' Her brother had said, 'Every company needs a board, Mum.' Her father had said, 'But at this stage he'd be on the board of nothing. Could be a Monopoly board for all the money he'd make. Remind me how much your mortgage is again, Julia?'

Around the same time Julia had taken a job at the corporate giant TPX Consumer Healthcare that had a great salary, pension and excellent maternity package. Her dad had been one of the management consultants who had, a few years previously, raised profits by 40 per cent and was very friendly with the board of directors. It had felt like the secure, grown-up thing to do, especially with Charlie wavering, and she was good at it. The salary was such that it might give Charlie a bit of slack, perhaps be able to drop down marginally if he did want to change profession. Then the boiler blew up and the builder muttered about asbestos and the guttering collapsed. The unexpected bills mounted.

Charlie had stuck at his job because they simply couldn't afford for him to leave. But he retreated into renovations, ripping up half the carpets but with no money he ran out of energy to do more, and then in the spring he went out into the garden to his precious tomatoes like he could escape his work by feigning retirement.

When Julia had mentioned the possibility of her applying for the promotion at work, the extra money that might buy them some slack, he'd paused his digging of the vegetable patch to say wearily, 'We can't both hate our jobs, Julia.'

Julia stared at the Instagram picture of the champagne she'd hashtagged #excitingtimes. She realised it was one of the last she'd posted of the two of them together. It had been the start of their divergence. That afternoon their new neighbour, Lexi Warrington – all tanned and gorgeous fresh from a week in the Maldives – knocked on the door to deliver a vegan cheesecake and slip into casual conversation that she was an Instagram influencer, while beckoning them into a photo. The dormant FOMO had sparked again in Julia's eyes and she'd been consumed.

Julia stared at the champagne photo. Then she turned off Instagram. She was tempted to delete the app but couldn't quite bring herself to. The only thing she really wanted to do was talk to Charlie.

CHAPTER FIFTEEN

Amber sat on the hard blue prison bench. Inside the small cell it was hot and stuffy and smelt of public toilets. The walls were bare concrete bricks, their surface rough to the touch. The ceiling was dappled with black spots of mould and the old linoleum floor was speckled with various coloured stains. The harsh electric lighting flickered like a twitch. Opposite Amber, leaning against the chipped white bars, was a skinny girl with bad skin who sat scratching furiously at her arm. In the far corner was an angry old purple-haired woman who reeked of booze and was clearly sleeping off a heavy night, the police officers seemed to know her well. Every now and then she opened one eye and shouted to the skinny girl to stop scratching, more out of annoyance than care.

Amber tried to sit as still and silent as possible. She needed the loo but there was no way she was using the stainless steel toilet in the corner. Instead she focused on trying to control her cortisol levels that if left to spin into overdrive would have her screaming at the bars in frustration to be let out.

How dare Julia have said all that stuff about her. She didn't owe Lovejoy anything. He was untrustworthy and selfish and always had been.

Amber glared angrily at nothing.

But then Julia had helped her with the passport. She could easily have handed it over as a fake. It had surprised her, the fact she hadn't. It had probably surprised Julia, too, she thought.

The purple-haired woman in the corner smelt like Amber's mother. The pervading sweet stench of rotten red wine.

Amber didn't want to think of her mother.

She could suddenly imagine her peering through the bars, feet crammed into gold stilettos, old raggedy fur coat pulled tight up round her neck. 'Oh Amber, how have you ended up like this? No I can't help you, honey. Keith's in the car waiting. You'll work out what to do, you always do. So resourceful. Not like your mother.' Amber could hear her self-deprecating titter. See the lipstick on her teeth. She doubted she was still with Keith, but there would be some bloke in the car waiting with bad teeth and shiny skin.

Amber couldn't sit any longer. She stood up and went to lean against the bars. To try and breathe in some fresh air.

The old purple-haired woman watched her.

Touching the bars of the cell was like the cool hardness of her mother's hand as she thrust her a wodge of cash, and with a quick hug, said, 'You're on your own now, honey. I'm sorry, it's Keith, he doesn't want children. Don't look at me like that. You know I'm hopeless on my own. It's not my fault, honey, blame your father. Why he gets to be the saint just cos he's dead? Blame him for his cholesterol. No one says that do they? No one says the stupid fool thought more about a bacon sandwich than he did about us.'

And suddenly there was her father, collapsed behind his

stall at Newark Antique Fair while she was queuing to get them both their usual sneaky bacon sandwich – banned from his diet a couple of months before by the doctor. She heard the holler of teenage Lovejoy, who was manning the stall next door, shouting her name. She remembered leaving the sandwiches unpaid for at the burger van. She remembered mundane snapshots, of bumping into an old man with a stick as she ran, a snatch of a song on the radio. And then her dad, the huge bulk of him lying prostrate on the floor. Comical, almost embarrassing. Too big to be vulnerable. She remembered the strange feel like squeezing a rubber ball of pressing down on his chest.

She leant her head now against the cool metal of the prison bars.

She could still remember the taste of his breath as she pressed her mouth to his. The overwhelming helplessness. People told her a nurse who'd been browsing antiques had taken over from her within minutes but to Amber it had felt like hours.

She wondered what he'd say now if he saw her like this. His large hands on the cell bars. His smile and his crooked teeth. His belly wobbling as he chuckled. *'Fine mess you're in, kiddo,'* he'd say, as if the whole world were just a joke.

Amber turned her back on the bars and the harsh electric light, trying to keep her face impassive. The stagnant heat pressing down and engulfing her senses.

She used to wonder all the time what life would have been like if he hadn't died. Had she not had to pause her own existence to support her grieving wreck of a mother who cracked the moment she heard the news. She wondered

172

what it would have been like to finish school rather than pick up her dad's business, unloading the stall in the ice-cold darkness, fingertips blue. Getting completely shafted by wily dealers taking advantage of her age. Hauling great pieces of furniture on her own. Getting muscles where once had been puppy fat. Panicking about whether between her and her mother, they'd scraped enough together to pay the month's rent. Living for those moments when occasionally her mum was some semblance of the woman she was before her dad died, and they had some semblance of family. But it never lasted long.

In the cell, the woman with the purple hair caught her eye, head tipped, intrigued. She grimaced, her teeth the same wine-stain of Amber's mother's.

Amber closed her eyes to make it go away. But it wouldn't. She remembered the boyfriends. The one who'd chased Amber round the living room swearing that he'd break every bone in her body because she'd found him smashing her mother's head into a door, and then, when she'd grabbed one of her father's antique samurai swords mounted on the wall and pressed the tip to his throat he'd called her an effing psycho and sloped off back to the pub. She remembered the one who climbed into Amber's bed, unaware that she slept with that same samurai sword. And then the ones who broke her mother's heart, making her curl up, cool and bony beside Amber, smelling of Nivea cold cream and stale wine, while Amber stroked her brittle hair. Then her mother had met Keith, another of the identikit idiots, and once again she handed herself over to him and this time he stuck.

The prison cell was getting hotter, stuffier. The sun glaring

173

in through the dirty windows along the corridor. Amber pressed herself back against the bars. She stared at the old purple-haired woman crumpled in the corner in matted fake fur and laddered flesh-coloured tights.

For the first time in Amber's life she wondered suddenly if she was like her mother. When she'd asked Ned for help, had she too picked a man to save her and never looked back. Had she made herself a victim. A user.

She put her hand to her chest. Her heart was beating faster. The purple-haired woman grinned, it felt like a victory for her mother, whispering at the bars, '*Oh Amber, we're the same you and me, you've always known that.*'

'No!' said Amber out loud. Making the young, scratching girl jump and the purple-haired woman scoff.

Amber turned round to grip the bars and shout for the police officer, 'Hey! What's going on? How long am I in here?'

The response was a hard bang on the wall.

CHAPTER SIXTEEN

Julia took a deep breath and rang Charlie's number. The sunlight flickered on the screen. Her palm was sweating. She sat back while it rang and stared up at the big green leaves dancing above her.

'Hello,' he said, his tone clearly showing that he was still unimpressed with her.

'Hi, Charlie,' she said. 'I know you're annoyed.'

'I *am* annoyed,' he replied.

'I'm sorry about what I said about my mother and Suzy Maynard's son. I should have stuck up for you, I don't know why I didn't,' she said, squeezing her eyes shut, hoping, praying that he was in the mood for listening. She went on, 'And I'm sorry I hurt your feelings. And made you feel like a fool about Hamish. It was just stupid texts, Charlie, I promise. Not reality.'

He didn't say anything.

Julia sat biting her lip, waiting. 'Are you going to reply?' she asked.

'I shrugged,' he said.

Julia nodded.

'Are *you* going to reply?' he asked.

'I nodded,' she said.

He half-laughed.

She could hear birds singing and knew he was in the garden.

'So what's going on there?' he asked.

Julia watched the sparrows pecking the dust around her bench. She told him everything about Amber's arrest, tone hushed in case somehow they might hear at the police station, and finished with, 'And now I'm supposed to be bloody thirty-eight-year-old Christine Miller.'

Charlie blew out a breath. She heard the noise of the garden bench creaking as he sat down. 'You don't look thirty-eight,' he said.

She laughed. 'Thanks.'

'What are you going to do now?' he asked.

There was a wariness between them. Both sticking to their corners. Charlie especially.

Julia scuffed the sandy floor with her foot. 'Don't know. Hope they don't keep Amber in overnight. Where would I stay?' She looked around the square, there was no visible sign of a hotel.

Charlie said, 'Tell me the name of the town and I'll google somewhere for you.' She heard him go in the back door, probably to get his laptop.

'Thanks,' she said, feeling a sense of relief at the kind normality of the offer.

'Blimey,' Charlie said, voice distracted from whatever was on his screen, 'there's not much. A couple of Airbnb rooms and that's it. You'd better hope she gets out.'

Although Julia knew he was probably sitting at the kitchen table, surrounded by all the mess, it was nice to hear his voice detached from the image of the falling-down house and the mountains of debt. She felt for the first time in ages that she was talking to just him rather than the angry, tired, stressed face he had become. To pass so easily as thirty-eight-year-old Christine Miller she figured her face must look the same.

'It all sounds quite exciting though,' he said.

Julia rolled her eyes. 'Like I'm in *The Wire*.'

He snorted. 'More like *The Bill*.'

'I could have been arrested, Charlie.'

'Nah,' he said, 'they're playing you. They're teaching Amber a lesson. Either that or they're really bored and have nothing better to do.'

At the other end of the square three men and a woman were now playing chess, sipping bright green glasses of créme de menthe and creamy pastis brought out by the waiter.

Charlie said, 'What was the name of the dude, the other dad?'

'Richard Shepherd,' said Julia. 'Why?'

'I'm looking him up,' Charlie replied. Then he laughed. 'He has a website. You can hire him for events, to sing. He still has the porkpie hat.'

'I want to see,' said Julia.

Charlie chortled like he was quite pleased he could and she couldn't. 'Oh and according to Facebook, he is currently on holiday, sunning himself in Noirmoutier. That's quite near you, actually. I went on holiday there once as a kid. Lots of oysters, salt and potatoes. Nice place.'

'Do you think that's where Billy's headed?'

Charlie thought for a second. 'Maybe. I would if I was him.' Then he said, 'What will you do if Amber wants to go after him?'

Julia shook her head. 'I don't know. I've got work on Tuesday.'

'You should go,' he said.

'Why? So I'm not at home?' she asked, half joking, half testing for a response.

Charlie said, 'No, not because of that, because it's an adventure. Better than being here. It's exciting. I'm jealous.'

'You are?'

'A bit,' he said.

Julia's phone beeped to say she was low on battery. 'My phone's running out, that battery pack was a complete swindle.'

'Where did you buy it?'

'Off a market stall.'

Charlie didn't need to reply.

'I need to find a plug. I'd better go.' She stood up, kicking some scraps of tree bark with her foot. 'I'll keep you updated.'

'Yeah, do that,' he said, their tones friendlier. 'If you need any help tracking Billy down let me know.'

'Why, what are you going to do?'

'I have no idea,' Charlie said. 'But it's fun. Like I said, I'm jealous.'

Julia smiled.

She heard Charlie open the fridge then the hiss and crack of a beer can ring-pull. 'Don't forget about the girlfriend. Pandora, is that her name?'

'Why?' Julia frowned.

'Because if this was *Columbo*, she'd be the extra everyone's forgotten about,' Charlie replied. And Julia had a flash of the hours they used to spend curled up watching crap TV at the weekend, wanting to be physically pressed together rather than as separate as could be after too many crossed-wired, badly explained, tired conversations about money and rewiring and debt and the spreadsheet that mapped out their next ten years' income.

'That's very true,' she said.

'Follow her on Instagram,' Charlie said, 'less suspicious than following Billy, she'll never know who you are.'

'You're a genius,' Julia laughed.

'I have my strengths,' he said. 'I may not be Hamish Warrington but—'

Julia cut him off, 'I don't want you to be Hamish Warrington.'

'No?' Charlie laughed like who was she kidding.

'No,' she said. 'I really don't.' And it was the first time it felt like the truth.

CHAPTER SEVENTEEN

Amber went and lay back down on the hard prison bench. Something resembling a cockroach scuttled across the floor. She lifted her feet up. The room was getting stuffier. Sweat beaded on her forehead and trickled down her temples into her hair. Closing her eyes, she thought about when she'd come back home, pregnant and broke, and Lovejoy was in the States, gallivanting with a new beautiful blonde every week according to his mates and then later well-documented on Facebook, and lovely, reliable Ned was there, happy to take care of her, adore her, reliably support her, always having loved her from afar. No questions just acceptance. At the back of her mind though, if she was honest, she'd known a Marcia or similar would come along in the end. Eighteen years she'd lived with the fear. It was almost a relief that the truth was out.

She lay staring at the dark multicolours of her eyelids, thought about how, while Billy was growing up, she had never once brought a man home when Billy was home. She had lived a life of unemotional, anonymous dates the weekends Billy was with Ned. She had lived to make her son happy, to make his life free from the itching, impotent disgust of having a parade of arsehole boyfriends troupe through the shitty living room and demand whatever they wanted from her and her mother.

She hadn't done it for herself.

Her eyes flew open. The cracked tiles of the prison ceiling above her.

Billy was it for Amber. She remembered the first time when, as a little boy, he told her he loved her – it was like a juggernaut, like her heart was laughing at her, '*You wanted love, family, ha ha, well here you go, try this on for size.*' Like everything before that was a game. He was hers. And she wasn't going to jeopardise it. She had found a man good enough for Billy to call a father but weak enough not to encroach on Amber's way of doing things after they'd split. Whether that was morally right or wrong, fine, Amber thought, Julia, have it your way, fight me on that. But she hadn't done any of this for herself.

The strip light flickered.

Amber sat up and found herself staring at the purple-haired woman – the image of her mother. No, I'm not like you, she thought. I put my kid first. No. She shook her head. I didn't tell Lovejoy, I didn't want to get hurt again, WTF, too right, I'd been clobbered by all of you. And yes I'm angry. I'm angry with Dad for dying, and angry with you for being so weak and angry with Lovejoy for leaving and always being completely selfish and I'm angry at myself. I'm not perfect. I made mistakes but I put my kid first. So go! Leave me the hell alone.

She was right forward in her seat, glaring.

The old purple-haired woman looked away.

Amber sat back, surprised at the outburst in her head. Her hands were shaking. Her eyes were welling up with relief.

The young scratching woman sneered. 'Boo hoo, the English crying. Boo hoo,' she said, doing circle fists in front of her eyes.

Amber was crying, she couldn't stop.

But instead of laughing, the old purple-haired woman leant forward and handed her a dirty old handkerchief, causing the young scratching girl to pause. And Amber to realise this woman wasn't at all like her mother either.

An hour later a police officer opened the cell door and beckoned Amber out into the bright white corridor.

The purple-haired woman said a string of something in French that Amber didn't understand but it came with a smile and a little pat on the arm as Amber handed back the handkerchief. She found herself wanting to grip the gnarly old hand tight, instead she smiled back and said, '*Merci.*' The woman tipped her head. The policeman ushered Amber away.

Once out the door, Amber couldn't move fast enough to get away. She scrawled her name on various forms and was reunited with her possessions. As she moved she could smell the disgusting stench of stale sweat and jail ingrained on herself. She rummaged through her bag for her phone to see if there were any more messages from Billy but there was nothing. She saw the Nicorette patches and was surprised that she hadn't thought of them since first being incarcerated. She slapped one on for good measure and stalking out through the waiting area, the green plastic seats, the miserable posters, she marched outside and down the steps, pausing to absorb the view of the little square, the huge leafed trees, the boules players. Swallows swooping in the wide expanse of blue sky. The freedom.

Over on a bench under the plane trees she saw Julia. The sight of her an unexpected relief.

Julia jumped up, she looked tired and hot. 'You're out!' she called.

Amber nodded. She walked over to where Julia was walking towards her. And when they were level, Amber said, 'What a bloody nightmare.' She laughed. Then she said, 'I'm sorry for all the stuff I said.'

Julia shrugged as if it was nothing. 'That's OK.'

'No,' she said, 'it wasn't OK. It was mean. I was upset and I took it out on you.'

Julia seemed quite taken aback by the confession. 'It's OK,' she said again. 'I think most of it was true anyway.'

'No,' Amber shook her head.

Julia rolled her eyes like she knew she was lying.

Amber said, 'Maybe some of it was true, but I shouldn't have said it the way I did.'

Julia looked down at the dusty floor and nodded her head.

'And thank you for the passport thing. I really appreciate it,' Amber added, relishing the feeling of the sun shimmering over her skin, burning down on the parting of her hair.

'I was shitting myself,' said Julia, with an incredulous laugh.

'I'm not surprised,' Amber grinned. 'It was tense! He was an arsehole. But you were bloody marvellous.'

Julia blushed. 'Thanks.'

'I told you she looks like everyone.'

Julia rolled her eyes.

Amber smiled. 'I will be eternally grateful.'

Julia looked away, embarrassed by the attention. 'What happens now?' she asked.

Amber started to walk over towards the bench, 'They've banned me from driving for three months. And I have to come back to go to court at some point.'

Julia looked horrified. 'What are you going to do? What are you going to do with all the stuff?'

Amber shook her head. 'I don't know.' She sat with her arms forward, her elbows resting on her thighs, looking out over at the cafés, the little boutique, the shop selling white china and candles. She felt calmer than she had in years. Finally accepting of what was to come. She reached into her bag and got out her phone. 'Right now all I know is that I have to text Lovejoy.'

Julia's head shot round. 'Really?'

'Yeah,' Amber nodded. 'Really. And then I have to find a shower because I absolutely reek.'

CHAPTER EIGHTEEN

The message Amber sent Lovejoy was short but to the point. Billy could be yours. She didn't call. She wanted to give him the facts, tell him where they were, and then deal with the fallout. It was possibly a cop-out but she hadn't changed that much.

She put the phone back in her bag. From beside her, Julia said, 'There's a gymnasium up the hill, they'll have a shower.'

They walked together past neat flowerbeds wilting in the heat. The air smelling of freshly cut grass.

Amber pushed open the heavy glass doors of the gym and, in no mood to negotiate the price of a shower, paid for one adult to swim, hired a towel and bought a gym branded T-shirt, sports bra and pair of grey tracksuit bottoms from the selection of training wear by the desk.

While Amber was paying, Julia asked the guy behind the desk if he'd plug her phone in to charge and handed it over when he agreed. Then looking back in her bag, said to Amber, 'Oh I forgot, I have a new pair of pants from the pack I bought at the market. Do you want them?' She handed Amber a rolled-up pair of giant baby blue knickers.

Amber laughed when she saw them, 'Blimey, they weren't

what I was expecting.' She held the giant piece of material up for all to see.

Julia swatted it away, cheeks pink, embarrassed. 'I don't normally wear pants like that!'

Amber raised a brow. 'Maybe you should. Might grab Charlie's attention.'

Julia looked even more embarrassed, making Amber grin slyly as she bundled up her pile of clothes and headed for the showers.

Alone in the chlorine-scented changing rooms, Amber found a locker and stripped her dirty clothes off, then stood under the tepid stream of water in the swimming pool shower. She could feel the prison stench start to wash away. Feel the cleansing cool water build her up for what was next.

She reappeared in the baggy grey tracksuit bottoms and matching T-shirt, her hair wet and wavy. Julia was hovering in the reception area, her phone and charger in hand. 'I have to get some clothes,' Amber said as she joined her. Then noticing the slight wildness of Julia's eyes, added, 'Why do you look so nervous?'

Julia swallowed. 'Lovejoy's here.'

Amber flinched. She felt a lurching sickness like a train stopping suddenly. Then she took a deep breath and said, 'Where?'

'Outside.'

Amber took a deep breath in through her nose. 'OK,' she said. 'Here goes.' And stepped out into the blinding sunshine.

He was in her face the moment her foot hit the pavement. 'You should have told me,' Lovejoy hissed, the lines on his face grooved in anger. His eyes furious. 'Eighteen years and you didn't tell me I could be a father?'

'No I didn't,' she said, staring straight up at him.

He looked away, ran his hand through his hair. He huffed and paced. He shook his head, like he couldn't believe what she was saying.

Amber saw Martin perched on the wall of the car park, keeping a safe distance.

Julia was hovering by the gymnasium doors.

'Shall we walk,' said Amber.

Lovejoy joined her for a few paces then stopped at the corner of the gym where it was shaded by an awning. 'I can't believe you kept this from me. I can't believe you let Billy grow up believing that idiot Ned was his father.'

'Ned is not an idiot,' said Amber. 'You can say what you like about me, Lovejoy, but I will not let you slag off Ned.'

Lovejoy scoffed. 'He was always hanging around, all dopey and eager with you. Of course you picked him. He'd do anything you said.'

'That's not fair,' Amber replied sharply. 'He was there for me at a time when I needed him and he's done nothing but be a good father to Billy.'

'Because he was given the bloody chance, Amber,' snapped Lovejoy, turning to rage at the wall. Then looking back at Amber, thumped his hand to his chest and said, 'You didn't give me a chance!'

'You weren't here!' she countered. 'And you'd told everyone you weren't coming back! By the time you were here, what could I do? Billy was settled, happy. There was no way I was going to jeopardise that.'

Lovejoy shot her a furious look. Pacing, hands raking through his hair. To Amber it felt like he was acting a part he'd read in a script rather than showing his true emotions.

'Lovejoy,' she said, a little softer, 'can you honestly look at me and tell me you'd have been there for me if I'd told you?' her eyes beseeching as she studied his reaction.

But Lovejoy wasn't in the mood. 'Don't you turn this round on me, Amber, I am the victim here.'

Amber almost stamped her foot. 'We're all victims, Lovejoy. Can you just imagine for one second what your reaction would have been if I'd told you I was pregnant? If I recall correctly, you'd just flown off to America to make that so-called fortune, telling everyone you weren't coming back till you'd made a million. You were strutting about all full of it, talking about yourself in the third person, "Babe, Lovejoy doesn't do commitment… "' she put on a voice that made Lovejoy wince.

'I didn't say it like that,' Lovejoy muttered.

'Yes you did. Christ,' Amber was getting angry now, ruining her decision to be calm and accepting, 'You were telling everyone how you were going to come back loaded. Now imagine I'd told you. Imagine I'd told you there was a fifty per cent chance the baby was yours. Would you have come back?' She glared at him. 'I needed someone there then.'

He glared back at her. She could see him breathing. He didn't answer.

He raked his hands through his hair. He kicked the wall. Then he said, 'Don't make me out to be the bad one, Amber. You're the one who's made the mistake.'

Amber huffed. 'Yes, I'm a despicable person.'

'Oh you can't just say that and expect to get away with it,' he said, right up close to her now, pointing his finger in her face.

She stepped back. 'I'm not hoping to get away with it. I know what happened, I know what I've done. Yes, I made a mistake, but I did it with the best intentions for my kid in mind,' she said with full confidence. 'But fine, yes, be angry with me, but right now, if you want to be a father, think about Billy not yourself. That's the first step. Think you can do that?'

Lovejoy looked like he wanted to murder her.

Amber went on, 'Hate me, that's fine, but I have to sort this out with Billy. And you have to decide if you're going to be a part of that.'

Lovejoy folded his arms across his chest and glared at her. 'Oh I'm going to be a part of that.'

'Fine,' said Amber glaring back.

CHAPTER NINETEEN

Amber and Lovejoy were at a stand-off, poses mirrored, both furious. The sun was boiling, the air almost misty with heat. Martin was sitting on the wall over by the car park, swinging his leg and scrolling through his phone. Julia was getting a Sprite out of the vending machine. Amber had to remind herself that she was meant to be calm about this. She took a deep breath. She uncrossed her arms.

Lovejoy turned away and kicked the dirt on the floor a couple of times. Then he said, 'So what do we do now?' through gritted teeth.

Amber shook her head and said, 'I don't know. I think we have to find Billy. Talk to him, face to face.'

Lovejoy nodded, face taut.

Then Julia stepped forward and said, 'I think he might be headed to a place called Noirmoutier. It's where your Richard Shepherd is on holiday.

'Noirmoutier?' said Lovejoy. 'Where the hell's that?'

'It's an island off the west coast of France,' she said, coming closer. 'Famous for oysters, potatoes and salt,' she did a little laugh. Martin fell into step with her and smiled too, like they were doing everything they could to lessen the tension.

Amber shielded her eyes from the sun. 'How do you know?'

'I found him on Facebook – well actually Charlie did, while you were in prison.'

Amber said, 'You called Charlie,' surprised, storing the information away as Julia nodded.

'Right well,' said Lovejoy, getting his phone out and googling directions. 'Let's go.'

'I have to buy some clothes first,' said Amber, 'I can't go like this,' she gestured down at her grey tracksuit.

Lovejoy huffed.

'It'll take five minutes and it's on the way,' Amber snapped.

'Fine,' Lovejoy snapped back.

The baking sun seemed to only aggravate the atmosphere between them as they trudged down the hill, past the gardener on the lawn mower and the pansies that spelt out the name of the town.

The silence was obviously too much for Julia because she said, 'I could get some clothes, too. I've worn everything I brought with me.'

'You know, honey, if I can say,' Martin moved in front of Julia as they trudged down the hill, walking backwards so he could face her, 'I don't think the length of that skirt is your friend.'

Surprised by the comment, everyone turned to examine Julia, dressed all in white, in what Amber thought looked like something she'd raided from Lexi Warrington's closet.

'I quite like it,' Lovejoy said, studiously refusing to look anywhere near Amber, like she didn't exist.

Martin shook his head. 'Yes, if she lopped six inches off the bottom. Right now it's not doing her legs any favours.'

Julia looked down as she walked. 'What's it doing to my legs?'

Martin winced. 'It's just. Well. Let's just say it's cutting them off at your most vulnerable point.'

'Are you saying I have fat calves?' Julia asked.

Lovejoy snorted.

'No,' Martin shook his head.

Amber felt herself smiling for the first time since seeing Lovejoy.

Martin was still walking backwards down the hill, gesticulating as he tried to explain himself, suddenly in his element. 'I'm saying you need to think less about fashion and more about your best bits.'

'Well how do I know what my best bits are?' Julia asked.

'Everyone knows their best bits,' said Martin, frowning. 'Like mine is my hair and my shoulders. I have terrible feet and never show my toes. I bet Amber knows her best bits.' He looked at Amber.

'My legs and my arms,' Amber replied without hesitation. 'My hair. My mouth. My eyes. My arse.'

'Everything except her personality,' said Lovejoy.

Amber ran her tongue along her top teeth, refusing to rise to it.

Julia hurried over the tension and said, 'I don't think I have any best bits.'

'Nonsense,' said Martin. 'Everyone has best bits. We just need to find them'

*

There was one clothes shop in the tiny village. The mannequins in the window wore tweed suits and polyester skirts with nude tights and moccasins.

'This looks like our kind of place,' Martin mocked as they pushed open the door to the musty shop, the little bell tinkling above the doorway.

'*Bonjour*,' said a grey-haired woman behind the counter, slightly suspicious of the posse.

'*Bonjour*,' Amber greeted her with a tight smile.

Julia smiled sweetly. Martin waved. Lovejoy nodded his head.

Amber started flicking fast through the rails of brown-striped knitted sweaters and beige slacks then stopped, hands on hips, to state, 'No. There's nothing here I can wear.'

Then the woman behind the counter came over and reeling something off in rapid French that Amber didn't understand, pointed her to a different section of the shop that, while still not being Amber's standard fare, was a hundred per cent better than what she had been looking at. All Breton tops, silk shirts and white Capri pants. Clothes French women might wear on a yacht.

Martin came over as well and feigned a heart attack over a red dress with a white flower print. 'Julia, get over here,' he summoned Julia who was on the other side of the shop holding up pastel ribbed vest tops.

'You really have no clue, do you?' he reprimanded, snatching a baby pink T-shirt from her hands and taking it back to the table saying, 'This is the worst colour for your skin.' Then he held up the red dress. 'This, this is what you should be wearing.' He pointed to the different parts of the design.

'A neat little waist. A length that cuts off just above the knee to lengthen your legs which, while not long,' he lifted up the hem of the white wafty skirt she had on, 'aren't bad. And then a big V here,' he gestured to her chest, 'to show off your bosom.'

Julia chuckled, covering her chest with her arms. 'I don't have a bosom.'

Lovejoy, who was lounging on a comfy chair near the window, said, 'You've got a bosom, kid, believe me.'

Julia flushed beetroot, Amber internally rolled her eyes as she flicked through the rack. She could feel Lovejoy watching her for a reaction and refused to give him the satisfaction of looking back.

After ushering Julia into the changing room, Martin looked at the clothes Amber had picked – a pair of black cigarette pants and a black sleeveless polo-neck. 'Branching out, I see.'

'I like black,' Amber said.

He plucked a canary yellow silk shirt from the rail and handed it to her. 'Go on, I dare you.'

Amber shook her head. 'I'm not your project.'

Martin ignored her, reaching into her changing room and hanging the shirt up. 'Everyone's my project.'

Julia and Amber were side by side in the brown changing rooms. Amber could hear Julia saying, 'Oh I don't know about this, it's very revealing.'

Amber changed out of the tracksuit bottoms to pull on the narrow black cigarette pants, she smiled at the huge knickers Julia had given her, imagining the shock on Julia's husband's face if he ever got to see his wife in them. That'd get him out of the bloody man cave.

As she was doing up the buttons, Amber called over the

changing room partition, 'Did you find anything else on Google, Julia, that Billy might have found? Anything more than that photograph?'

'He has a website,' Julia said. 'He's available for hire. Thin Air broke up, though.'

'That's not surprising,' Amber replied.

'There's a Facebook page with a post about him holidaying in Noirmoutier. I checked Billy's Instagram and he hasn't updated that for a while. So I've found Pandora on Instagram and I've asked permission to follow her. She's got a gazillion followers and I figured she wouldn't have any idea who I was.'

Lovejoy said, 'And this is all to find out exactly where he is?'

Amber felt herself bristle at Lovejoy's involvement. 'Course it is,' she snapped.

'Come on, Julia,' Martin clapped his hands, acting as the peacekeeper, 'don't keep us in suspense!'

Amber heard Julia's changing room curtain open and with a voice all nervous with self-conscious worry Julia said, 'What do you think? I'm just not sure…'

'Oh swoon, swoon, swoon!' cried Martin.

Amber was intrigued. The black polo-neck she'd picked was too small and she couldn't get it on over her head, so she slipped on the yellow shirt Martin had picked in order to go out and see what the fuss was about.

Martin was in the process of buckling a brown leather belt around Julia's surprisingly small waist and when done, he held her hair up as she stood in front of the mirror, tying a ponytail much higher than Amber had ever seen Julia wear.

Over by the window, even Lovejoy was smiling.

Amber could see Julia's reflection, see her face start to split into a grin.

Martin was pointing to her cleavage, her nipped-in waist, her elongated legs. 'See, your best bits.'

The stern shop owner glanced up with an appreciative nod.

Julia looked cautiously at herself, turning from side to side, then she looked at Martin. 'I didn't really know I had any best bits.'

'Well there you have it,' Martin said.

'It looks really good,' Amber agreed. 'The most un-Lexi-Warrington thing I've ever seen you wear.'

Julia blushed.

Amber was about to duck back into the changing room when Martin caught sight of her and dragged her out by the arm. 'Come on, let's see the yellow shirt!'

'No!' Amber tried to get away but he was surprisingly strong. She stood reluctantly in front of the mirror.

They all stared again.

Lovejoy did a double take.

Martin started to say something but then seemed not to know what.

Amber frowned at herself dressed in yellow. The shirt was silky soft and hung loose to where she was tucking it in at the front. The sleeves were too long, so she rolled them up. But it was the colour that seemed to do something to her skin and she couldn't work out if it was good or bad. She had no make-up on and her freshly washed hair was drying in waves. She could see all her wrinkles.

'I look old,' Amber said, squinting disapprovingly at herself.

Martin angled his head as he stared at her. 'You do look a bit older, but not in a bad way.'

Amber gave him a look.

'I don't know what it is,' Martin went on. 'You look sedate.'

'These are not complimentary descriptions.' Amber shook her head.

Julia frowned. 'I think you look really nice.'

'Oh God,' said Amber, starting to unbutton the shirt. 'Old, sedate and nice. Who could ask for more?'

Martin laughed. 'No, she's right, you do look really nice. Very soft.'

Amber caught Lovejoy's eye. He looked away.

She went back into the changing room and stared at herself in front of the mirror. She swallowed. She gave her hair a shake, she stood again. She looked old but she also looked young. And Martin was right, she did look soft. Part of her felt that she looked too normalised, like she would fit in brilliantly on Cedar Lane now. But the other part of her didn't hate it. It felt like what she used to wear. When she'd go to the antiques fairs with her dad dressed in multicoloured Nike high-tops and crazy print leggings. When she wore her hair in plaits or dyed it bright pink. She didn't do anything like that now. Slowly she had lost the colour to walls of black. Like all the darkness, all the secrets, all the anger she'd held tight.

This shirt felt like her, maybe the her she was meant to be.

Opening the changing room curtain, she said nonchalantly, as if it meant nothing, 'I'm going take the shirt, thank you, Martin.'

Martin grinned. 'You're most welcome, Amber. You know it comes in a variety of other shades. I especially like this cobalt blue.' He handed it to her and she took it with a smile.

'Thank you,' she said.

He reached over to the rail of jeans and said, 'These aren't bad either,' and handed her a pale cropped pair.

'No I draw the line at those,' Amber said, turning her nose up.

Martin laughed. 'It was worth a shot.'

All the while, Amber could feel Lovejoy over by the window watching. And to her annoyance she found she wanted him to like her in the shirt.

CHAPTER TWENTY

Everyone was starving hungry. They found a table at a café next to the clothes shop and took their seats. The white plastic tables were shaded by giant orange Aperol umbrellas. Around their feet, pigeons and sparrows pecked at crumbs dropped on the floor. Lovejoy sat on the opposite side of the table to Amber. The sun was still bright but there was the veil of an afternoon haze in the air. Julia was high on the amazement of her own reflection in the clothes shop. She had looked in the mirror how she had never thought she could look – good in her own right, rather than thumbing through clothes rails trying to keep up with Lexi and co.

She felt so good that while they were waiting for the waitress to take their orders, Julia got her phone out and was about to take a selfie for Instagram, but paused before she took it. Who was she taking it for? This was about her, no one else. She didn't need comments and likes to tell her what she already felt.

Instead she sent a text to Charlie updating him on what was going on.

'Good luck!' he wrote back. She wondered what he was doing. She thought how much he would enjoy this. The little tables, the carafe of water, the flickering light of the leaves on the square. He would enjoy the tensions and currents of the group, he'd find it interesting to observe. She also thought he'd quite like her dress.

When the waitress appeared, everyone pounced to order in their hunger, Amber especially who ordered steak frites and salad while the rest of them had simple Croque Monsieur.

Closing his menu, Martin said, 'So what are we doing? Heading to Noirmoutier and waiting on either this Richard character or Pandora to update their social media?'

Amber nodded, handing the waitress her menu.

'And just to clarify,' Martin went on, 'Your van's been impounded so are you going to have to come with us?'

Amber nodded again and Lovejoy did an expression of reluctant agreement.

Martin looked between the pair of them. 'That's going to be a fun journey.' Then he mused for a second. 'What if I don't want to come? Maybe I have burning work appointments at home.'

Lovejoy raised a brow. 'You don't have burning work appointments ever, Martin. And you're so bloody nosy there's no doubt that you want to come, but if it makes you any happier, I'll pay you for the extra day. OK?'

'It does. OK.' Martin grinned, satisfied.

Julia checked her phone to see if Pandora had accepted her Instagram request. Nothing.

The shadows of the plane trees danced over the screen.

The waitress bought the drinks.

Over a sip of cold beer, Lovejoy said, 'Come on then, let's see the picture of this other dude.'

Julia glanced at Amber, who paused for a second, then expressionless got out her phone and the image up of her and Richard Shepherd covered in mud at Glastonbury.

It was weird seeing her in her loose yellow shirt. Her every action looked more vulnerable.

Lovejoy took the phone and zoomed right in on the photo, scrutinising Amber's long blonde grungy hair and Richard Shepherd's porkpie hat and rosary. 'What a joker,' he said, looking up at Amber. 'This is who you were with?'

Amber pursed her lips. 'Yes, Lovejoy,' she said. 'Got a problem with that?'

'No,' Lovejoy replied, amused and defensive in equal measure.

Amber did a curt nod.

Martin clicked his fingers to have a look. Lovejoy held onto the phone for a minute longer, his lip curled in distaste. His dark hooded eyes narrowing. Then he handed it over to Martin.

Julia watched Amber watching.

The food arrived, big plates of gooey toasted sandwiches and a huge plate of sizzling steak frites.

Martin stole one of Amber's chips.

Lovejoy polished half his Croque Monsieur off in two bites, then said, 'So how long were you with him?' feigning disinterest, his attention focused on some activity on the other side of the square – a guy on a motorbike arguing with a ticket inspector.

'Not long,' said Amber, dunking a couple of chips into mayonnaise. 'A month or so.'

Lovejoy took the information in.

Amber started to cut her steak.

Lovejoy went back to his Croque Monsieur.

They ate in silence for a while. Then Martin asked, 'So what was this band he was in?'

As she chewed, Amber said, 'It was kind of grungy, nothing amazing but they were on tour and it was fun. I was a very good groupie.' She smiled.

'I'll bet you were!' said Martin. 'I can just imagine it.'

Amber forked some salad, then sat back. Lovejoy was watching the arguing motorcyclist with great attention. Amber said, 'It was a funny story, actually, how we met. I was abroad buying and I'd just left a bar in the Czech Republic and was heading to the van when this real nasty bastard started coming on to me, you know grabbing me and trying to push me into this alleyway and I was terrified, to be honest.'

Lovejoy looked back to the table.

Amber said, 'I had a sword in the van but I couldn't get it—'

Julia frowned. 'You had a sword!'

Amber nodded as if it were totally ordinary.

'What would you have done with the sword?' Julia asked.

Amber shrugged. 'Killed him probably.'

Julia's eyes widened.

'You wouldn't have killed him.' Lovejoy shook his head. 'At most you'd have stabbed him in the leg or something.'

Amber raised a brow. 'You don't think I could kill someone?'

Lovejoy's lip tilted in a half-smile. 'Oh I have no doubt that you *could* kill someone, Amber. I just don't think you *would* kill someone.' He leant forward a touch. 'You're not half as tough as you make out.'

Amber narrowed her eyes. 'I'll kill you in a minute.'

He smirked and went back to watching the row over the other side of the square.

Martin took a bite of Croque Monsieur, and urged Amber to carry on, 'So you're running from this Czech bloke. And—'

Amber tore her glaring eyes away from Lovejoy and went back to her steak. 'Well then suddenly this absolutely *gorgeous* guy appears,' she really put the emphasis on gorgeous. Julia glanced at Lovejoy and caught an imperceptible, incredulous shake of his head. Amber carried on, 'and he yanks the other guy off me like a real hero and then punches him in the face. The first guy scarpers and Richard, that was who it was who'd hit him, was all shaking his hand like he'd broken it, hopping around the place in agony. Well I couldn't help laughing. And when he'd finally got over the shock of what he'd done he said, "You'd better have a drink with me now!" and well that was that. We had a drink and fell *madly* in love.' She gave Lovejoy a quick there-you-have-it look and popped a chip in her mouth.

Lovejoy was focused on stirring his espresso. He tapped the spoon on the side of his cup, took a sip, put the cup back down, then said, all mock-confused, 'So if it was all so bloody marvellous, how come you're not still with him and, how come he doesn't know about Billy?'

Amber seemed caught off guard by the observation. As if she hadn't thought ahead in her storytelling.

'Are we to presume he found a better groupie?' Lovejoy said dryly, sipping the rest of his tiny coffee.

'Oh piss off,' said Amber, wiping her hands on her napkin and downing her own espresso.

The bill came. Amber said, 'I'll get this.'

'No I will,' said Lovejoy, whipping his wallet out.

'No I will!' said Amber firmly.

'Why don't you split it?' said Martin, calmly.

Amber and Lovejoy threw in equal amounts of euros and they all stood up.

'Thanks,' said Julia as they walked across the square, then immediately put her head down, concentrating on her phone when she saw the officer who had arrested Amber was on the steps of the police station, having a smoke.

It was a sudden stark reminder of her fake passport alter ego and lies to the police. The new dress suddenly felt like a disguise to escape capture.

Amber glared at the police officer leaning against the handrail, perusing the gang as they passed. 'I can't believe he's got my sodding van,' she muttered. 'That's all my Emerald House stuff.'

'So it is,' mused Lovejoy.

The policeman lifted his hand in an amused wave as they passed. Julia felt Amber bristle. She felt his eyes following them. Felt her nerves start to simmer.

Then just as they were almost out of sight, Julia heard him shout, 'Madame! In the red.'

She stopped up short. Her breath caught. She turned. Pointed to herself.

The officer nodded, flicking the fag butt away, ripping open a pack of gum like he had all the time in the world.

The others stopped walking. 'What does he want?' Julia asked.

'I don't know,' Amber said.

The officer beckoned for her to come over.

Julia was sweating now. Her heart thumping around like a crazed bull. She was going to jail for passport fraud. Holy shit. 'Remember the passport, Amber? Should you come too?'

Amber exhaled, as if she couldn't handle another problem. 'I think that would be suspicious. Why would I go anywhere near him? You should just go casually and see what he wants. It'll be nothing,' she said, trying but failing to sound reassuring.

Martin crossed his arms. 'Go on. It's never good to keep the police waiting.'

Julia wanted to ring Charlie. But no, she was on her own.

She walked back across the road trying to ignore her shaky legs. The officer watched her with bright blue eyes. She had visions of her parents hiring the best lawyers for the court case, not quite able to fathom why she'd done what she'd done. Or on the other hand, not done it slightly better and got away with it.

She imagined the glee with which Lexi, Alicia and Nicky would discuss the news on their spin-off, Cedar Lane Blondes, WhatsApp group.

The officer chewed his gum.

Julia stopped in front of him. '*Oui?*' she said, voice a touch higher than normal.

She saw him glance down at her shaking hand. She moved it behind her back.

He smiled, taking his time, enjoying himself.

Julia was on the cusp of confessing. Anything to lessen her sentence. She was not someone who played it cool. She was the good one. The one who was never late at school, who never missed a deadline. She would be hopeless in jail.

The officer glanced briefly behind her at Amber, then, on a lazy chew of his gum, said, 'If you want, *you* can get the van out.'

Julia felt her brows raise to the middle of her forehead. 'I'm sorry?'

He chewed, long and slow. 'The van. Her van,' he pointed at Amber, '*You* – not her – can get it out, if you can drive.'

'I can drive,' said Julia.

He shrugged like there you go.

She felt a smile spread through her.

He made a face like he wasn't all bad-guy.

An overwhelming euphoria rose up through Julia's body – she wasn't going to jail. She could get the van out. It would all work out OK. Then she realised that this man thought she was someone else. She was the woman in the fake passport. She couldn't get the van out because Christine Miller didn't have a driver's licence. Julia paused. Christine Miller probably did have a driver's licence somewhere in Amber's bag but it would mean Julia having to imitate her once again under the terrifying eyes of the law.

The officer said, 'You can thank me, if you like.'

Julia nodded. 'Thank you,' she said. Distracted. Then she repeated it, snapping back to attention, remembering who she was talking to, 'Thank you.' Then she turned and hurried back to where Amber was standing, watching.

'Well?' said Amber.

Julia said, 'He says *I* can get the van out.'

'No way!' Amber laughed, she clapped her hands together.

'But, Amber, he thinks I'm Christine Miller.'

Amber stopped clapping. 'Oh shit.'

'What's going on?' Lovejoy asked.

Amber reluctantly explained.

'Oh Jesus, Amber,' Lovejoy exhaled, expression like she was a walking disaster.

Julia felt he was definitely enjoying being on his high horse. Using the situation to vent his own annoyance at Amber. So she jumped in and said, 'I can do it. I don't mind.'

Lovejoy scoffed. 'Do you know the penalty for passport fraud?'

Julia shook her head.

'Well neither do I,' said Lovejoy, 'but it's not going to be good.' He looked at Amber. 'And you'd let her do it, I take it?'

'No, of course I wouldn't,' snapped Amber, although it was questionable whether she'd have given it a shot.

They all stood where they were. The police officer still watching.

Julia said, 'He's wondering why we're not doing anything. I don't want him to get suspicious.'

'Well someone's got to get the van out,' said Amber.

Julia thought of all the antiques in the back for Emerald House, all their work.

Martin looked a little sheepish and said, 'I would but I actually don't have my driver's licence on me.'

'But you've been driving here.' Julia frowned. 'Don't you have to have it with you? Isn't that illegal?'

Martin nodded. 'Probably.'

These people were so not Julia's people. She'd once stolen a pot plant by mistake, her mother had handed it to her in the garden centre and she'd walked out absent-mindedly still holding it when they left. Her mother had made her go back in and apologise to the manager.

It occurred to her how narrow her world was. How safe. How filtered her opinions, how firm she saw the line between right and wrong. Not that she thought it was good Martin didn't have his driver's licence, just that he wasn't living in fear that he'd forgotten it.

She thought of the people on Cedar Lane – all in their couples with their two kids, their extensions, their Honda Accords – all the ones at Lexi's party anyway. All the normal ones. The weird guy who carried an empty Co-op plastic bag everywhere hadn't been invited, nor had the renters with the four kids who you could hear arguing when you walked past their open window, or the students who didn't pick up their dog's poo, or the trendy hipster couple Lexi had ostracised as full of themselves after they'd politely declined to sign her petition against Sainsbury's. It was a cherry-picked selection. An echo chamber of like-minded lifestyles and beliefs. Julia had never deemed herself narrow-minded before but suddenly she felt like she lived in a bubble. Her aspirations filtered constantly through the beliefs of a tight little section of the world that perceived itself normal.

'I really will do it,' Julia said, more defiant this time. 'It's fine. I don't mind.'

Amber shook her head. 'No you won't,' she said firmly.

They all stood in the street. The late sun filtering through the trees. Martin tapped his foot. Amber was looking over at the police garage, obviously trying to work out a way round things. Julia checked her phone.

Then Lovejoy sighed and said, 'Come on then, I'll get the

van out,' tone quietly smug, like he was the reluctant hero saving the day.

'No,' Amber shook her head, 'I don't want you to get it out.'

Lovejoy crossed his arms across his chest. 'I'm getting the van out,' he stated.

'No,' said Amber.

'Why not?'

'Because I don't want you to. Because you're doing it to be superior, to teach me a lesson.'

'No I'm not, I'm doing it because I'm a nice person.'

'Oh please!' Amber rolled her eyes, walking a few paces away. 'You're doing it to get back at me.'

Lovejoy made a show of looking confused. 'How can doing you a favour be getting back at you.'

Amber glared at him. 'You know.'

Lovejoy raised his hands. 'Clearly I don't.'

'Pandora's accepted my follow request,' Julia cut in.

Amber immediately came over and took the phone. 'Where are they?'

Julia took the phone back and clicked on the Instagram profile, on the latest picture, of Pandora walking down a narrow street lined with white houses and at the end an oyster shack, she was glancing over her shoulder, grinning all straight white teeth, like a movie star. 'The hashtag is #lovingNoirmoutier.'

Julia showed Amber.

Amber studied the Instagram picture, then clicked on another on Pandora's profile – one of Pandora and Billy on the plane, heads touching in a joint selfie.

She handed the phone back. Then she inhaled a deep breath

through her nose and exhaled. She looked down at the pavement for a moment then back up. 'Lovejoy,' she said. 'Could you please get my van out of the police station?'

They stared at each other.

Julia found she was holding her breath.

'Yes, Amber,' he said. 'I can.'

CHAPTER TWENTY-ONE

The police had done a half-hearted search of the van making the whole thing seem more, as Charlie had suggested, to teach Amber a lesson than anything else. They'd taken the passenger-side door panel off, clearly rifled through the glove compartment and had a cursory flick through their luggage. Some of the antiques had been dragged out and lay haphazardly strewn on the tarmac.

Julia watched as Amber repacked the boxes in the back, stacked up the mirrors she'd bought and tended to the taxidermy fox who'd taken a bit of a battering. 'Arseholes,' Amber muttered, stroking its fur.

Lovejoy stood watching, hands on his hips. 'Next time just pay the fine.'

Amber glared at him.

'So,' he said, having a stretch then smoothing down his T-shirt, 'It's a two-hour drive to Noirmoutier. Shall we get a move on?'

'Are you sure you want to come?' Amber said, holding the keys, eyeing him warily. 'Are you sure this is what you want because if you're going to back out at any point—'

'Amber,' said Lovejoy, with a huff of exasperated annoyance, 'you don't get to call the shots anymore. I'm coming.'

Amber nodded, chastened. She chucked Julia the keys. 'You're safe to drive now, just avoid the police station on the way out. I'll insure you on the way.'

Julia got in without a quibble. She felt a burst of adrenaline sitting behind the big steering wheel, high up, foot pressing down on the heavy pedals. There was fear as well, she'd never driven anything bigger than a Vauxhall Corsa.

Amber climbed in next to her, slamming the door hard.

As Julia was getting herself familiar with the gears and repositioning the rear-view mirror which she noticed with some trepidation was half obscured by antiques and reflected back just a grinning fox, Martin called from Lovejoy's van, 'It'll be late when we get there. Where are we going to sleep?'

Amber rolled her head his way, and said laconically, 'In the van.'

Martin made a face. 'I'm not sleeping in the van.' Then he thought for a second. 'Don't worry, I'll sort something out.'

Amber warned, 'Martin—' but couldn't finish because Lovejoy drove away, Martin with his phone in one hand, grinning and waving.

Amber huffed. 'Right let's go!' to Julia.

And Julia immediately stalled the van.

Amber said, 'It's OK, take your time.'

Julia tried again, slower this time, and the van trundled out of the parking lot in the direction of the motorway.

They drove in silence. Amber clearly hated being driven. Being out of control.

As Julia kept safely in the slow lane, Amber said with antsy impatience, 'Can you overtake this caravan, please?'

When Julia hesitantly pulled out. Amber muttered, 'Drop it down. You need to drop it down a gear to get some speed.'

Julia gritted her teeth and tried to ignore her but after two more similar orders she suddenly pulled into a truck stop at the side of the road and slammed the brakes on. 'Stop it,' she said. 'Stop it.'

Amber sat up with surprise.

'I'm trying. Just don't shout at me.' Julia gripped the steering wheel.

Amber looked visibly startled. She shuffled herself back in her seat, readjusting her position and said, 'Fine, sorry. I apologise.'

Julia did a nod. She rolled her shoulders back, flicked her hair off her face and indicated to pull out. And this time she found herself driving with more confidence. Pushing her foot down, overtaking a car that had overtaken her and then slowing down as soon as it got in front. She reached over and put the radio on. It was some terrible French pop song. Amber turned it up.

At the toll booth, Amber had to stretch out the window almost to her waist to get the ticket, 'Can you get a little closer next time,' she gently mocked.

They drove past patchwork fields and telephone pylons. The sun pale white on the horizon.

It was a comfortable silence between them. Amber had borrowed Julia's phone and was doing a deep dive on Pandora's Instagram feed. Zooming in on the photos of her and Billy together. Looking at what they'd been up to on their travels before he'd discovered the news about his dad.

Julia glanced over, looked at Amber's obsessive study of

the minutiae of each picture. It was a pose that seemed so achingly familiar. 'You were right, you know,' Julia said.

'About what?' Amber replied, not looking up from the phone.

'I do spend my time looking at Lexi's Instagram,' Julia said. 'I do think her life is perfect and mine doesn't match up.'

Amber sat back in her seat, chucking the phone into the cup-holder. She thought for a second, then she turned her head in Julia's direction and said, 'Do you know why they had their first summer party?'

Julia didn't know. 'Because it was a nice thing to do?' she offered. 'To show off their amazing house?'

Amber shook her head. 'No. Because he had an affair.'

'He didn't?' said Julia, aghast.

Amber nodded. 'He did. It was with a woman called Eleanor from the tennis club – really slutty looking, nothing like Lexi. Everyone knew. There was a big showdown in the street. He was an idiot. Got found out because he parked his car outside her house every Wednesday.

Julia frowned. 'That can't be true.'

'Oh it is,' Amber replied. 'Did you know the major giveaway of an affair, just for future reference, is suspicious car parking? Especially when it's such a cliché of a car like a black Porsche 911 like Hamish drives. The party was a big show to everyone that they weren't splitting up. Still is, I think.'

Julia was stunned. 'I can't believe it.'

Amber said, 'There you go. Not quite so perfect.'

'How did I not know?' Julia asked.

'Because she's the greatest PR of her own life.'

'God.' Julia drove on, stunned. She gazed out at the traffic ahead, the low bridges, the signs to historic French towns thinking about all the stuff she'd done to impress Lexi and her gang. All the gloss she'd believed hook, line and sinker. There had been no moment when she'd considered what was on the screen or on show when she popped round wasn't completely real. 'I totally fell for it.'

Amber shrugged. 'Yes you did.'

They carried on, Julia running through endless times she'd peered through her window at the goings on at Lexi's house. Taken a screenshot and zoomed in on her Instagram stories to see what they were watching on TV and watch it herself. The conversations she had listened to about the best nurseries in the area, getting panicked about enrolment for a kid she didn't even have. She had got so frantic. So embroiled in the myth. Then she remembered looking through her own Instagram feed, seeing the early photos of her and Charlie, naïve and fun. Relaxed and happy. She glanced across at Amber and said, 'I think I've really lost myself,' as they trundled along the motorway. The signs started pointing to Nantes as the sun began to blur in the late afternoon and rows of clouds like sausages filled the sky.

Amber looked away from the road to Julia. 'Why?'

'I don't know. I've got so caught up in what I should be, I think, what I should be doing. Listening to Lexi. Trying to be better. To be somebody. All I think about now is having a more exciting life, better holidays, a swanky extension and— God everything like that. It's so stupid.'

'What did you used to think about?' Amber asked.

'I don't know. Nothing. What I was going to have for dinner,' she laughed. 'I always wanted to be successful and

I'd think about pensions and money and the future, but I think I thought of other stuff too. I think Charlie always used to really help me do that, to see the other side of life. The fun bits, the odd bits. And I've stopped listening to him in favour of people like Lexi. God, I'm so stupid.'

Amber sat up straight. 'Don't be so hard on yourself. Christ, I don't even have a pension.'

Julia slowed the van. 'You don't have a pension?' she said, incredulous.

Amber laughed. 'No.'

'You should have a pension,' Julia urged.

Amber waved a hand. 'Oh who cares. It's fine. Anyway I got shares in Fever-Tree on the recommendation of your dad. They're probably as good in the long run.'

'Not you as well,' Julia sighed. 'We were meant to get them and I never did.'

'Well you have a pension so it's OK,' Amber said as if it didn't matter. Then she turned to look Julia's way. 'You can't have everything. You can't beat yourself up about having one thing and not the other. No one manages to do everything.'

Julia looked ahead at the open road. 'Some people do.'

'Julia, you have a house and a nice husband and a good job, what more do you want?' Amber asked, rummaging in the plastic bag of supplies for a Coke.

Julia thought for a while as she drove. She clutched the steering wheel as she pondered the question. 'I suppose I feel that it's me, that I'm not good enough. That I've lost myself somewhere, trying to fit in with Lexi, trying to make my parents proud...'

Amber took a swig of Coke and then put the can in the

cup-holder. 'Your parents are proud,' she said. 'They're so proud.'

'They think I could do better.'

Amber shrugged. 'So what. Who cares.' She threw her hands into the air. 'They're a different generation with different values and different ideas. They can't change and you're never going to change them, it's a physical impossibility.' She picked up the Coke and proffered the can to Julia, 'You want some?' she asked.

Julia shook her head.

Amber went on, 'And the thing is with Lexi and her lot – they're so busy trying to impress each other, trying to summon up whatever gossip they can to create some excitement in their lives, that they'll never really give a shit about you. Unless you send texts about her husband,' Amber added with a laugh.

Julia shook her head in despair. The embarrassment still stung. But then she thought about what Amber had said – about her parents, about Lexi and her pals. There was liberation in the idea of not caring. Of not buying in.

Amber put her feet up on the dashboard. 'All that Cedar Lane lot, they're all as bored as anyone. Christ, how boring must it be being a below-average Instagram influencer? Taking a million photos of yourself for not that many likes. And underneath it all, all the gloss, there's nothing. Don't you see that, Julia? There's no kindness, no compassion.' The afternoon sun flickered through rows of forest trees. They drove past fields of cows and little houses. Amber sipped her Coke. 'What you have to change is the way you react to them. To everyone in fact. What they say has to mean less.' She paused, turned her head to look at Julia. 'You have to care less. Take me for example, I don't care what anyone thinks, except Billy, but he's my son and that's my job. But I don't want him to worry about what I think about him. I want him to be free, to enjoy his life. I'd be horrified if I found out he wasn't happy because he was trying to please me. Are you sure you don't want a Coke?'

'I'll have some water,' said Julia.

'Water coming up,' said Amber, rummaging through the plastic bag. 'And a packet of Monster Munch?'

'OK,' Julia laughed.

Amber opened the crisps and handed them to Julia. Then she opened her own bag. With her mouth full of Monster Munch she added, 'I think you need to start focusing on your own opinion, Julia. Block out their noise. Pick what works for you. Like your dad's knowledge of share prices. That Fever-Tree stock, wow! You did miss out. But you didn't get any because clearly you were too busy panicking to see the good bits.' Amber popped another Monster Munch into her mouth with a grin.

Julia considered it and nodded slowly.

Amber said, 'What does your opinion say now?'

'I don't know,' said Julia.

Amber laughed.

Julia smiled.

'OK,' said Amber, rearranging how she was sitting, getting comfy, straightening out her yellow shirt and tucking her legs up underneath her. 'Tell me what's good about you.'

'Oh I couldn't do that,' said Julia quickly. 'I told you it was a nightmare on the management away-day. I couldn't do it. My mind literally goes blank. I don't know.'

'Well think.'

Julia thought and came up with nothing. 'It's impossible.'

On the road signs, the name Noirmoutier started to appear.

'Just one thing,' urged Amber.

Julia thought then said, reluctantly, 'I'm organised.'

'OK, and...?'

Julia shook her head. 'You said one thing!'

'And now I'm asking for another,' said Amber.

Julia thought again. 'I'm quite clever, maybe.'

'You're very clever,' said Amber, emphatic. 'You're kind,' she went on, 'you were especially kind to Billy. You're patient. You care about other people.'

'I sound really boring,' Julia said with a laugh. 'I want to be brave and cool and love taking risks. Like you.'

Amber rolled her eyes. 'You don't want to be like me, I promise.' Then she added, 'I think you're brave.'

'I'm not brave.'

'What about all that at the police station. You impersonated Christine Miller, for God's sake.' Amber raised a brow. 'You're not only brave, Julia, you're a bona fide criminal. If that's not cool, I don't know what is.'

Julia considered it.

Amber said, 'And you're funny.'

'I don't think I'm funny.'

'Tell me a joke.' Amber smiled as she swigged her Coke.

'I don't know any jokes,' said Julia.

'Everyone knows one joke,' Amber replied. 'Come on.'

Julia racked her brains, then she remembered one she'd heard someone tell at the office Christmas party that had made her laugh. 'What's a three-legged donkey called?'

Amber raised a brow, 'I don't know Julia, what is a three-legged donkey called?'

'A wonky,' Julia said with a chortle.

Amber gave a wry smile. 'See, you're marginally amusing.'

Julia shook her head. 'That *was* funny!'

'There you go then, you're funny.' Amber laughed, eyes creasing at the sides. 'And you've got great tits!'

'Stop it,' Julia thwacked her on the thigh. 'I'm blushing.'

Amber grinned and sat back, eating her crisps and picking up Julia's phone to go back to scrolling through Pandora's Instagram.

Julia turned off the motorway, they passed an industrial estate and went through a little village with a tabac and boulangerie, and people sitting outside cafés enjoying the evening sun.

Julia was mulling through everything they'd said. As she looked out at the café tables with people enjoying a vin blanc or a last espresso of the day, she said, 'So what do I do about Charlie?'

Amber put the phone down again. 'What do you want to do about Charlie?' she asked.

Julia circled a roundabout with a palm tree and a statue of a man with a hunting dog. 'I want to sort things out. I want things to go back to how they were – before everything got in the way.' Then she paused and said, 'When we were good for each other. When we worked as a team, I suppose, but that sounds so clichéd.'

Amber shook her head. 'It sounds fine to me. I think you've just got to do it. Tell him. Be...' she paused for emphasis, '*honest*,' she said in a tone that conjured up their past conversation in the van. Mocking, like it was the word of the day.

Julia smiled and nodded.

Amber rolled her window right down and breathed in the smell of the sea as it appeared on the horizon, then she added, 'And I always think, when one is away, a bit of phone sex never does any harm.'

'Oh my God,' Julia blushed scarlet, making a face. She giggled to herself at the idea. Then she thought about it a bit more and said, 'Really? No. I couldn't.'

'Just a quick sext then.' Amber sat back, feet up on the dash, and grinned, 'You're brave, remember. And you may as well put those giant pants to good use!' She added, cracking herself up.

Julia blushed even more.

When they came to the Passage du Gois, the four-kilometre causeway that joined Noirmoutier to the mainland, outside it was dusk, the outlines of the trees fading.

There was a sign with a picture of a car underwater that said, 'Risk of drowning.' Julia looked hesitantly at Amber, who just shrugged. Then there was another sign that said, 'Danger Route Submersible' with pictures of cars being slowly flooded as the tide came in till they eventually disappeared under water.

'Amber, is this safe?' Julia asked, feeling her palms start to sweat on the wheel.

'It's fine,' Amber said. 'Pull over so I can read that board.'

Julia pulled over. In front of them was a giant noticeboard lit up with numbers and times and lots of stuff in French.

An old, toothless fisherman was ambling past with his red

bucket in one hand and the stub of a cigarette in the other. Julia watched as he and Amber struck up conversation. They laughed. He even proffered Amber the cigarette which she waved away. Then she came striding back to the van.

'You can cross up to an hour and a half after low tide,' she said, doing up her seat belt.

'And what are we now?' asked Julia.

'An hour and twenty minutes.'

'So we can't cross?' she said.

Amber looked at her. 'He reckons we'll make it.'

'Him?' Julia frowned at the ancient fisherman.

'He looks like he knows his stuff,' she said, holding in a smile. 'And anyway, there are towers along the way in case we get stuck.'

'Amber! We could drown.'

Amber rolled her eyes. 'We're not going to drown. Well not if you get a move on, anyway. Come on.'

A text beeped on Amber's phone. 'It's from Martin,' she said. '"*Booked us into an Airbnb – we're here and it's effing fabulous!*" Bollocks, they're already there. Let's go, come on. I don't want them running into Billy without me.'

'Amber, it's a whole island, they're not going to run into Billy. What's the other option, if we don't drive this road?' Julia asked, creeping the van forward to the start of the causeway. The evening light fading. It felt stupid and reckless.

'We wait twelve hours for the next low tide.' Amber clicked her fingers. 'Come on, it'll be fine. You just said you wanted to be less risk-averse.'

Julia blew out a breath. 'Shit.' She stared out at the crossing. 'OK.'

They edged forward. The road was covered with seaweed. Julia had to hold tight to the wheel. 'I'm slipping, Amber.'

'No you're not, you're alright,' Amber said, using a tone that seemed perfected on Billy.

Julia could feel her breathing get shallow. They passed one of the rescue towers. 'The water is really high.'

'It's fine,' said Amber.

Julia checked her mirrors. 'There's no one behind us.'

The sea was dark with tiny flicks of white water on the surface. The blue of the sky seemed mockingly jolly in comparison.

Amber peered out the window. 'Well obviously no one else wants to come to Noirmoutier.'

'It's four kilometres, yeah? And ten minutes. That's four hundred metres a minute. That's doable, isn't it?' Julia said, needing the validation. The tyres losing grip as they skidded over bright green seaweed.

'Well, eight minutes now actually. So you'd better speed up.'

'Shit, Amber.' Julia could feel her panic rise with the water. 'We should have waited.'

'Where would the fun be in that?' Amber laughed.

'Where's the fun in this?' Julia asked, peering right forward, clutching the wheel.

'This is fun, it's exciting.' Amber leant out the window again to look down at the water. 'It is rising very fast.'

'Shut up, Amber.'

She laughed again.

'You're doing this on purpose to wind me up.'

'No I'm not.' Amber sat back again. 'It seriously is coming up fast, so if you don't want to sit in that tower for the night you really had better put your foot down.'

'Shit, shit, shit.' Julia wiped the sweat off her forehead. 'Oh my God, I'm going to die.'

'Stop whining and just drive. Faster!' said Amber.

It felt like driving into an abyss. Water everywhere. Their little scrap of road disappearing into the distance.

'Why did we do this?'

Amber leant across to look at the speedometer. 'You're halfway. Just keep going.'

Julia checked the mirror again. 'Oh God, Amber, behind us some of the road is actually submerged.' She really thought she might cry.

Amber had a look. 'Bit faster then?'

It was the first time Julia had sensed any sign of panic in Amber's voice. She put her foot down. The car skidded on the seaweed.

'Careful,' warned Amber. 'Focus. Breathe.'

Julia breathed.

'You're doing well,' Amber said.

Water was just starting to lap the edge of the road ahead, running in rivulets on the tarmac.

'Just keep breathing, Julia.'

Julia nodded.

'Enjoy it,' Amber added.

Julia didn't take her eyes off the slowly sinking road. 'How can I bloody enjoy it? I'm going to die.'

Amber snorted. 'You're not going to die.'

Julia laughed slightly manically.

Water sprayed from their tyres.

They passed another tower. 'Last kilometre, Julia. Hold your nerve.'

The tide was coming in fast now. Julia could barely see anything but water behind her. Ahead it was getting harder to see where the road was. 'Do you promise we're not going to die?'

'Julia,' Amber looked at her, 'I promise, we're not going to die.' She paused, then added, 'As long as you drive a hell of a lot faster.'

Julia floored the van. Tyres slipping. Arms cramping on the wheel. Teeth clenched. Eyes wide staring at the disappearing tarmac. 'I hate you,' she said to Amber.

'I thought you wanted to be like me,' Amber laughed.

'I take it back.'

Amber laughed again, unexpectedly cracked up. Julia smiled.

The water was mid-tyre height. The resistance tugging heavy at the van. Julia's body ached.

'OK, I can see land,' Amber said, pointing at the windscreen, rising out of her seat. 'You've got about two fifty metres. Go! Go! Go, Julia!'

Julia was panting with exertion. Foot to the floor. She could see the end but she could barely see the road any more. It was stupid and dangerous and they shouldn't be doing it. But it was the most alive she had felt in possibly her whole life. The most in the moment. The most afraid and focused and relied upon.

Amber was going, 'Come on, come on, you can go faster than that.' Then when Julia did speed up, she'd say, 'Watch out, keep it steady.' Julia could tell she was itching to be behind the wheel herself.

The last stretch was almost the equivalent of driving straight out into the sea. No road behind them, nothing ahead. Just a quiet plea that there was something beneath their wheels.

And then finally they were on dry land. And Julia screeched to a halt, put her hand on her heart and bent her head over, gulping in air. 'Oh my God. Oh my God, I am never doing that again. I really seriously hate you.'

But Amber was beaming. 'That's was brilliant!'

'It was not brilliant,' Julia said, turning the engine off and getting out of the van, just to give herself a moment. She stood with her hand on the door, deep breathing. Amber opened her door and sat with her legs dangling out of the van.

As Julia stood getting her breath back she watched a man in a fluorescent yellow vest approach Amber. He looked annoyed and said something in French as he got closer.

Amber said, 'Sorry, I'm English. *Non comprends pas*?'

The man shook his head. 'It's dangerous,' he said louder, this time so Julia could hear, gesturing to the causeway. 'Next time, you take the bridge. *Oui*?'

Julia narrowed her eyes. 'The bridge?' she said.

'The bridge.' He pointed into the distance.

Julia swallowed. Then she nodded. Then she got back into the van. 'There's a bridge?' she said to Amber, incredulous. 'Did you know there was a bridge?'

She watched as Amber tried her best to suppress her smile. 'No.'

'You liar!' Julia gasped. 'You did know.'

Amber shrugged. 'So what if I knew? You wouldn't have done it if I'd told you there was a bridge.'

'We could have died.'

'We were never going to die. It was an adventure.'

Julia slammed the door of the van and sat for a moment in fuming silence.

She felt Amber watching her. 'Tell me you didn't enjoy it just a little bit.'

'I didn't enjoy it just a little bit,' said Julia flatly as she started the engine.

Amber's mouth twitched. 'See! You're funny.'

Julia started driving again in silence, staring hard at the road ahead. Had she enjoyed it? No. But she felt strangely high now. Like she had a story under her belt. The kind that kept people listening in the pub. The kind that wasn't safe or reliable. That had required heart-thumping courage and made her feel alive. And now invincible. It made her think that maybe Amber was right on another count, maybe she was brave. She glanced over at her, trying not to smile, 'I maybe enjoyed it a tiny bit. But only this much' – Julia held her finger and thumb a millimetre apart.

'Well see,' said Amber, bare feet up on the dash, 'that's better than nothing.'

CHAPTER TWENTY-TWO

They followed the directions Martin had WhatsApped, and arrived out the front of a gothic mansion positioned off the Bois de la Chaise, a shady promenade surrounded by oaks and pine trees with a view of the sea at the very far end. It had dipped into evening, the sky threaded with navy. Clouds like mountains. The last of the sun a dazzling orange slice at the end of the road. The air through the open windows smelt of salt and tree sap, cicadas and crickets buzzed in the heat and they could hear the roll of the surf in the distance.

Lovejoy's van was parked in the driveway. Martin was standing on the front step, as if he'd been waiting for them to arrive, arms outstretched to emphasise the glory of the building. 'Better than sleeping in the van?' he shouted.

Amber got out, peering over the top of her sunglasses. 'How the hell have you wangled this?'

Julia stared up at the house in awe. There were tall French windows on every room with peeling white shutters that shadowed stripes on the brickwork in the late sun. Two little balconied attic windows poked out of the slate barn roof. The house was painted white, the colour fading to grey where it needed a refresh. There was a brick path leading to a dark wood front door beside which were two giant rhododendron bushes hot pink with flowers.

Martin trotted over. 'I have a killer eye for an Airbnb.'

'Where's Lovejoy?' Amber asked, hauling her case out of the boot of the van.

'Gone for a brooding walk,' said Martin.

Amber laughed despite herself.

'Come on,' Martin beckoned them up the red-brick path and in through the big front door. 'I'll show you the rooms, it's bloody marvellous.'

Inside it was immediately cool. The ground-floor rooms all opened onto the big hexagonal hallway where they stood, blue and gold tiles underfoot. The plasterwork was cracked and giant oil paintings in elaborate gold frames half-covered peeling wallpaper.

'I call it, dilapidated faded glory,' said Martin with a flourish. 'There's bread and cheese in the kitchen and some wine,' he gestured towards the huge kitchen table just visible through one of the doors. Then beckoning them towards the living room, he said, 'Let me give you the tour.'

'I love it already,' said Amber, entranced.

Julia's eyes opened wide as they walked round the house. Amazed at the grand disrepair. The bare plaster wall in the dining room reminded her of their kitchen at home but here it had been made a feature, draped with hanging plants and fairy lights to give it character. Here, the mismatched chairs looked quirky and off-beat. The living room was all white with bare floorboards, a Persian rug worn with splodges of damp and a threadbare sofa. But despite being faded, everything was beautifully, artfully arranged. There was a bold poster from a modern art exhibition heroed above the fireplace and a giant, oversized vase on a side table. All the papers and magazines were stored in a couple of old wooden wine boxes. And in the centre of the room hung a prized crystal chandelier, twinkling in rainbow prisms.

They followed behind Martin, up the stairs that were bare of carpet, sanded and white washed. Julia looked at them thinking, I could do that with ours. Tendrils of houseplants escaped over every surface, even winding down the bannister, and on the landing was a huge stuffed swan wearing a crown.

It was impossible not to appreciate the majesty of the place, however shabby and old it was.

'This is my room,' said Martin, pushing open a bright turquoise door. 'That's Lovejoy's,' he added, pointing to a giant room with black walls and a bare wooden floor. 'That one's the bathroom,' he said, pointing to doors as he walked down the corridor. 'There are two more on this floor and three on the top. So unless you want to be upstairs on your own, it's between these two.' Martin gestured to the two doors side by side.

Julia poked her nose into the first one. On the dark red wall behind the bed was a collection of deer skulls ranging in size from the tiny to the gigantic. She made a face. Amber laughed. 'I'll have this one.'

'Yeah,' Martin nodded, 'The other one's much more up Julia's street.'

Julia just crossed her fingers for no skulls or taxidermy as she turned the door handle. Like the living room, it was painted all white, even the floorboards. There was an old wooden French bed with a white throw and a chintzy flowered sofa. Shabby cream velvet curtains looped over floor-to-ceiling windows with glass so old it made the view wobble. The furnishings reminded her of half the stuff they had boxed up in the attic left behind by the previous owner and ready for the charity shop. But here, what Julia would have considered a dreadful ornament of a white horse galloping looked suddenly covetable on its own on a side table with a plain metal lamp. Even the ceiling, cracked like a spider's web, looked artful here simply because it was embraced – the problem reframed from a crisis to a celebration.

'It's perfect,' she said.

Martin looked suitably thrilled.

They explored the rest of the house, then outside where the last of the sun was flickering through the branches of giant firs onto a rotting Wendy house and a long picnic table.

Amber said she was knackered and went off to her room. Martin got his phone out and started taking selfies with his hair loose against a backdrop of the bright yellow mimosas. Julia stood in the kitchen watching through the big glass doors, picking at the bread, her body still tingling with adrenaline from the causeway drive. Her limbs restless. She had to do something.

She tapped her fingers to her lips. She watched Martin a bit more. Then she slowly backed away till she got to the hallway and then skidded up the stairs two at a time. She was going to attempt the phone sex. Courage, she thought. She had courage.

Going into her bedroom, Julia locked the door and closed the curtain. Then she perched on the edge of her bed, psyching herself up with a deep, steadying, you-can-do-this breath before she undid her belt and unzipped her dress, pulling it off so she was sitting just in her underwear. She wasn't quite sure what to do next so decided to start with a simple photo – ease herself in gently.

Looking down though, all she could see were the little rolls of her stomach. She crossed her arms around her waist. It was so embarrassing. She went to stand in front of the cracked wardrobe mirror. Standing up, her stomach looked better. The pants were so huge they somehow accentuated her waist. She'd been wearing the yellow striped bikini top as a bra, and knew she should take it off but she couldn't bring herself to go topless.

Silently cringing, she held up her phone and took a snap.

Awful.

She exhaled.

She tied her hair up and went to the dresser to put some blusher on. She put a bit on her front, then a bit on her thighs.

She took another snap.

Equally awful.

She sat on the side of her neatly made bed. She couldn't do it. She felt stupid and self-conscious. She wasn't cut out for this kind of thing.

Then she thought about Amber. Her bed in the hotel room had been immediately dishevelled, the sheets all mussed up, her suitcase had lain spilling its contents on the floor. She had seen her getting dressed, her underwear was all black lace, her perfume heady and dark, her tops scraps of silk. That was what sexy meant. Amber had no trouble being naked. She probably enjoyed it.

Julia went back to her make-up bag and put on a bit

more mascara and some lip gloss. She sprayed herself with some perfume to get in the mood, then she took down her hair, messing it up as best she could, and pulling back the bed covers, lay herself down draping one corner of the sheet over her thighs.

She took another photo.

Better.

Although she'd maybe gone a bit over the top with the bird's nest hair. Smoothing it down and repositioning herself she took thirty-five more shots until finally she found one she was happy with – eyes a little sultry, stomach sucked in flat, hair almost tousled. It wasn't Kate Moss but it would do.

She WhatsApped it to Charlie and waited. Lying back on the white sheets staring up with trepidation at the cracks in the ceiling.

Her phone rang. She answered with her best sultry, 'Hello.'

'I'm assuming you meant to send that to me,' Charlie's voice said.

Julia frowned. 'Yes, of course I did.'

'OK, good, just checking,' he half-laughed.

Julia didn't want it to get all jokey. Trying to maintain the mood, she said all husky, 'Did you like it?'

There was a pause while Charlie was clearly looking at the photograph again. 'Yes it's very nice. Where are you?'

'In an Airbnb in Noirmoutier,' Julia said. Then rolling onto her side said, 'Tell me what you're wearing.'

Charlie snorted a laugh. 'Come off it, Julia.'

'I'm serious,' she snapped. 'This is a moment.'

Charlie paused, then said, 'My Gap jeans and the blue

T-shirt with the hole under the armpit. And...' he paused again, 'my grey stripy boxers.'

Julia knew those pants. She'd washed them a million times.

'Julia,' Charlie said, 'this isn't really my thing.'

She felt herself tense, despondent. 'Well maybe it needs to be your thing,' she said, pulling the sheet up over herself, feeling like a fool for baring herself.

'It's just not me,' he sighed. 'Not us. I don't know what I'd say.'

Julia didn't reply. She wasn't a hundred per cent sure what she was going to say either.

'Whose idea was this?'

'Mine,' she said.

He waited.

'Amber's,' she admitted. 'To get us back on track. To spice things up.'

'I don't think spicing things up is the problem,' said Charlie. 'Or not this way anyway. Look, Julia, to be honest, I'm not even sure where we are at the moment. With our marriage, with you, with everything, it's all over the place.'

'I know,' said Julia, pulling the sheet up tighter.

Charlie exhaled slowly. 'Well, why don't we talk rather than spice?'

Julia nodded. 'OK.'

There was a pause.

Julia stared up at the old chandelier hanging precariously from a chipped ceiling rose, half the lightbulbs missing. 'What do you want to talk about?' she asked, hesitant. Suddenly a bit apprehensive.

'I don't know,' Charlie replied, maybe nervous, too. 'What do you want to talk about?'

'I asked first.'

'Technically, I did.'

There was another pause.

Julia looked across at the strip of dusty light peeking through a gap in the curtain, a sliver of the old mottled glass of the French windows was just visible. 'What's your weather like?'

'Boiling,' Charlie replied. 'What's yours like?'

'Pretty warm,' Julia said, folding the sheet with her fingers.

Charlie said, 'I'm nodding, by the way.'

There was another pause. They were like awkward teenagers. Julia racked her brains for something good to say, trying to come up with something to rival the abandoned phone sex. It felt so important but her mind was blank.

Then Charlie said, 'Lexi came round with a casserole for me.'

Julia sat up. 'She didn't?'

'She did.' Charlie laughed. 'I think they all think I'm destitute. My wife's run away and I've been left cuckolded.'

Julia rolled her eyes. 'You haven't been cuckolded.' She could just imagine Lexi standing all big doe-eyes on her doorstep with her vegan lasagne.

'No I know. Well I have kind of, but it was meant to be a joke,' Charlie replied, tone frustrated with himself for having to explain.

'Oh.'

'Not a very funny one,' he admitted.

'It was funny,' Julia urged, not wanting him to feel bad. 'Now I know it was a joke.' She did a little laugh to emphasise the fact.

'Don't give me a pity laugh.'

Julia laughed properly. 'I wasn't.'

'You were!'

She sat back against the pillows, smiling. She heard the creak of a chair at Charlie's end as he sat down. Then she said, 'D'you know, I was remembering our first date earlier. Do you remember it?'

'I do, Julia,' Charlie said, voice more relaxed. 'The premier seats of Cineworld with a large sweet and salty popcorn and a Diet Coke to share. Even though I hate Diet Coke.'

'Such chivalry,' she laughed.

'That's me,' he said and she could imagine him grinning, pleased with himself. Then a few seconds later he asked, 'Why were you thinking about our first date?'

'I was thinking about all of it. You know, about us,' she said, watching the slivers of light cast shadows on the creases in the sheet.

And he said, 'Go on… '

So she told him everything she'd thought sitting on the bench after Amber's arrest. All the things she'd discussed with Amber in the van. And when she finished, she added, 'I think we've lost our way. Well I know I have. And I know you're so unhappy at work and… Well instead of helping each other, I think we've retreated to our own corners. You especially,' she said.

Charlie thought for a while then said, 'If someone makes you feel you're not good enough, you tend to retreat.'

'I know,' said Julia, looking up and catching the reflection of herself in the wardrobe mirror at the end of the bed, thinking of how she was with her parents and her brother.

How she was with her neighbours. With everything. How so often she felt not quite up to par. But as Amber had said, she needed to start focusing on her own opinion because, after all, whether one is good enough surely depends who's defining good. 'I think I lost sight of what I had.'

'Yeah,' he agreed, then added, 'Because I am pretty awesome.'

Julia laughed. Charlie chuckled. There was a silence. Then Julia said, softly, 'I'm sorry, Charlie.'

'That's OK,' he said. 'I'm sorry, too.'

After a pause, Julia added, 'I don't want you to feel like you're not good enough.'

Charlie didn't reply.

'Charlie?' she said.

'Sorry, I was just having another look at those huge pants in the picture you sent… ' he said. 'Those babies are a hell of a pair of knickers.'

Cringing, Julia lifted up the covers to have a look at her giant pants.

'I've never seen them before have I?' he checked, suddenly doubting himself.

'No,' she replied. 'I got them at the market.'

'Sexy,' he laughed.

Julia blushed.

Then they talked. Julia lying on her side on the bed, looking at the galloping horse ornament and the fraying rug. Laughing. Chatting. Smiling. She gave him a tour of the room with her phone camera. She showed him the cracks in the ceiling. 'I think we should make ours a feature,' she said.

Charlie didn't disagree.

'How are your tomatoes?' Julia asked.

'Very well actually, thanks for asking,' Charlie replied. And Julia suddenly appreciated the comfort of normality. How covetable her life felt from afar. 'D'you know Old Harry popped round today to give me some advice,' Charlie went on. 'He's really knowledgeable on planting. I know it's not your thing but he's helped me loads. We had a cup of tea and he'd made a sponge cake. Can you believe it? It was fun. Good cake too, not as good as yours. He likes to bake though. I told him you were a baker.'

'Oh God, Charlie, you didn't?' Julia put her hand to her forehead, imagining the chats she'd have to have with weird Old Harry now in the Costcutter queue.

'Why not? It's good. You can be friends. He's interesting. Did you know he used to live in Bulgaria?'

'I didn't know that,' she said, remembering suddenly her thoughts on the echo chamber, the curated, exclusive views of Lexi and Alicia that had narrowed her own world. Maybe chatting to Old Harry wouldn't be so bad. 'OK,' she said. 'That sounds good.'

There was a pause.

'What are you doing?' Julia asked.

'I'm smiling,' said Charlie.

Julia was smiling too when she hung up the phone.

She stared at it for a moment, then pushing the sheet away, she got up and opened the curtain, letting the dusky evening light in. Then she went to stand in front of the wardrobe mirror and reached behind her back to unhook her bra. When she looked down at herself now, instead of noticing the rolls, she saw just the light tan from the French sunshine.

She studied herself in the mirror. She did have good boobs, she thought. Then she tentatively stepped out of her giant pants, resisting the urge to reach for something to cover up with. She forced herself to stand completely naked in front of the mirror, unflinching. To stare at herself. She put her shoulders back, she pushed her chest out a little, she angled her hips, she laughed. Then she raised her phone and took one selfie. Smiling, confident.

But she didn't send this one to anyone. She kept it for herself.

CHAPTER TWENTY-THREE

Amber didn't sleep well, tossing and turning half the night. She was too hot, the bed was too soft, the birds too loud. And she was nervous about seeing Billy. Nervous about what was going to happen and what she was going to say. She had lain awake staring at all the skulls mounted on the wall above the bed, an ominous reminder that things had the potential to go quite badly.

As she got dressed, her hand shook so much doing her eyeliner that she had to give up, relying instead on a couple more lashings of mascara. She wore the bright blue shirt she had bought from the boutique. She wondered what Billy would think when he saw it.

She wondered how Lovejoy was feeling.

It was early, she was awake before anyone else. Downstairs she had some bread and jam and sat in the dawn quiet on the veranda drinking thick black coffee and watching blue tits peck the dead ivy on the side of the house for bugs. She watched the sun rise high in the bright pale sky. The thump of her heart echoing the sound of the sea as the nerves rose and fell.

Julia appeared, barefoot, yawning. 'I just called in sick to work for tomorrow. You can put very bad liar on my list of things about me. I couldn't stop rambling into the answer machine. I told them all the gory details of my supposed chronic gastroenteritis. They're going to think I'm insane.' She flopped down on the other chair.

Amber said, 'Here have a coffee,' and poured Julia a cup from the cafetière she'd made earlier. 'It's a bit cold.'

'Thanks,' said Julia, taking a slurp. 'It is cold.' She put the cup down. 'Shirt looks nice, by the way,' she added, gesturing to Amber's blue top.

Amber waved the compliment away. 'So does your dress,' she said, pointing to Julia's new red dress. Then she leant back in her chair and stared out at the lush green garden, at the towering pines and the jagged palms. 'So did you brave the phone sex?'

'I did,' said Julia looking out at the garden.

'Wow,' Amber was surprised. 'How did it go?'

'Terribly,' said Julia, raising a brow as she glanced her way.

'Oh no,' Amber couldn't hold in her snigger.

Julia smiled, leaning forward, hands wrapped round her cold cup of coffee, surveying the wide expanse of overgrown garden. 'No, it was good. Not the phone sex bit but the conversation. It broke the ice.' She turned back to look at Amber. 'I'm not sure we're phone sex people.'

Amber looked her up and down, contemplating. 'No, possibly not.'

Julia sat back and laughed. 'Thanks for the advice though.'

Amber rolled her head to meet her gaze. 'That's OK. What are friends for?'

Julia's eyes widened a fraction. 'Am I your friend?'

Amber felt a little perplexed at the pleasure on Julia's face. She couldn't quite believe that her friendship could mean so much to a person. 'Yes, course you are,' she said.

And Julia sat back with a grin, hair all askew from sleep, dress a bit crumpled, sipping her coffee and closing her eyes to absorb the heat of the sun on her face. 'You're my friend, too,' she said after a second.

Amber laughed, completely thrown by how good it felt to hear, amazed that those words could give her the much-needed shot of confidence that she had needed to face the day. 'Thank you,' she said.

Julia opened one eye, rolled her head to look at her. 'You're welcome.'

The shutters of one of the upstairs rooms flew open. 'Morning!' said Martin, stretching his arms wide to the view. 'I feel like a Disney princess.'

Amber laughed. Then the shutters on the window next door opened and Lovejoy looked out, his face tired and emotionless. His hair all askew and eyes hooded. They hadn't spoken last night. 'What's the plan?' he said.

Julia got her phone out. 'I need to check on Pandora.'

Martin yawned and rested his elbows on the windowsill, chin cupped in his hands as he watched. 'She's probably still asleep,' he said. 'Great shirt, Amber, I did do well.'

Amber gave him a warning look.

Martin grinned back.

Julia said, 'She's not asleep, she's doing yoga on the beach.'

'Really?' Amber looked across at Julia's screen. There was a photo of Pandora in a striped bikini doing some complicated upside-down pose with a backdrop of white beach huts.

Lovejoy appeared on the veranda next to them, dressed in grey jeans and a black T-shirt. 'Bloody hell, that's impressive,' he said, looking at Pandora's yoga pose.

Amber ignored him. 'Do you know which beach it is?'

This time the photo was tagged with a location pin. 'It's called Plage Rouge.' Julia clicked on the pin. All the other tagged images were of the same rows of beautiful little beach huts, white sand and a lighthouse peeping out of pine trees.

Martin came outside, phone in hand, already tapping in directions. He was dressed in double denim with his cut-offs and shirt, with camouflage pool sliders on his feet. 'It's over there,' he pointed out past the giant fir trees.

'Well let's go,' said Lovejoy, turning and heading back into the house to get his stuff to go out. Martin followed.

Julia stood up and began to walk away.

Amber stayed where she was for a second. The nerves suddenly rising again, clogging her throat, immobilising her. She wasn't used to being out of control. She wasn't used to not being the one directing events. For the first time, she was stepping into a situation and would have to wait and see how it played out. Whether it would at any point work in her favour. And that faintly terrified her.

Julia paused and came back to stand next to her. 'Are you coming?' she said softly.

Amber breathed in deep through her nose to steal herself. 'Yes.'

Martin tracked the route on his phone. Leading them halfway down the road before pointing towards a small forest path.

'You sure this is right?' asked Amber as they tripped over tree roots and through spider's webs.

'Google never lies,' he said.

It made Amber think of bloody I-work-at-Google Marcia. What she'd think of this debacle now. Lovejoy stalking silently beside her through the cool darkness of the towering trees. Her smugness level would be off the charts. She'd be all honesty-is-the-best-policy, we aim for complete transparency at Google.

As she tramped next to Lovejoy, Amber had to begrudgingly admit that honesty probably was the best policy. An end of the lies. She'd never tell Marcia that though.

She stole a quick glance at Lovejoy's rigid expression, the tiredness of his eyes. He never looked her way. It would be weird when this was all over.

When Lovejoy had first come back from the States she'd kept him at arm's length. Watching him swagger into fairs and auctions she was at. Any guilt she felt at her lie was easily quashed when she watched him work his way through various girlfriends, leave them sobbing in the pub or brag about some complicated web of two-timing he had going on that he was barely able to keep up with. But over time the bantering friendship of their teenage years had gradually returned, Lovejoy always acting the underdog, Amber always out of reach. Him with his cocky, knowing glint in his eye as he sidled up next to her at six a.m. at a fair, smelling of dust, dirt and the same Persil washing powder his mum always used, and cracked some inappropriate joke, her eye-rollingly impervious. Now it was about to be taken away, she realised she was not completely immune.

She glanced at him again, his dark eyes fixed on the forest floor ahead of him. She would miss what they had.

Christ, she thought, Marcia would have a field day with that.

'Urgh, I've walked through a spider's web!' Ahead of them, Martin did a little dance trying to rid himself of a possible arachnid.

Lovejoy chuckled. Then he accidentally caught Amber's eye, and immediately stopped smiling.

Martin kept swiping at invisible spiders. Lovejoy dropped a pace behind. Julia was at the back. The path turned to grey rocks that they clambered over to get to an earthy clearing. The tangy sharpness of the pine now mixed heavy with the salt of the sea. Through the tree branches were lapping waves and ahead of them a set of steps down to the beach.

'Here we go,' said Martin, leading the way. 'Plage Rouge.'

The beach was clear blue water and white sand. A tiny arc of white beach huts with shutters and red roofs. The lighthouse watched through the trees.

Amber saw Billy immediately. Right out at sea by the rocks, on a paddleboard. His back to them, with waifish blonde Pandora. She'd recognise him anywhere. Her heart squeezed.

The only other people on the beach were a family all set up with picnic rug and umbrella. There were loads of kids in trunks and frilly swimsuits and a frazzled-looking woman in a kaftan who was trying to grab them and rub lotion into their miniature limbs, while a man with a long ponytail ignored them as he tried to meditate, legs crossed, eyes closed.

Once they hit the sand, the others didn't seem to know what to do. Julia and Martin stood looking a bit awkward, Lovejoy immediately hung back and let Amber lead the charge.

Billy hadn't seen them.

Amber took her shoes off and started to walk across the sand towards him. She was maybe two metres away when the meditating man opened his eyes and said, 'Amber Beddington! Well look at you.'

She narrowed her eyes to study the man, his long dyed-black hair, his rimless glasses, his trendy deep-V-necked T-shirt and natty thin scarf looped round his neck. He even had the rosary on. 'Richard?'

He stood up. 'Amber!' he said, arm outstretched. Smile showing a row of capped teeth and an unmoving, botoxed forehead.

'You look exactly the same,' she said, because she couldn't think of anything else to say. And he did almost look the same, embarrassingly so.

He absorbed the compliment with a satisfied, 'Thanks.' Then said, 'I believe I have something of yours,' gesturing out towards the water.

They both turned to look at Billy, laughing and splashing with Pandora.

'Yes,' she said. 'I'm sorry about that. Him turning up like that, it must have been a shock.'

Richard said. 'It was a bit of a shock to be honest, yes.'

The others, Martin, Julia and Lovejoy, had sidled closer.

Richard waved a hand in greeting. Then he gestured, almost as an afterthought, to the woman in the kaftan trying to lotion-up the kids. 'This is my wife, Wendy.'

Amber raised a hand. The frazzled-looking woman smiled.

Richard went on, 'Billy emailed and told me he wanted to do an interview on Thin Air.' He laughed. 'Appealed to my ego, embarrassingly. I do get some requests nowadays. There was talk of us doing one of those concerts, you know, "Back to the Nineties" but I'd rather do something more serious.'

Amber smiled. As he spoke, she took in his set-up, the wife scurrying round doing all the work, while Richard seemed to float off in a world of his own. She thought about when she'd met him, all those years ago, how alone she'd been, how desperate she'd been for love. She wondered if she had been desperate enough to stay with him and end up like poor, harassed Wendy on the tartan picnic rug. Amber remembered the morning she'd woken up in Richard's trailer alone, only to step outside and find him lying on the patch of grass next to where they were parked, a willowy new groupie wrapped tight around him. They had both looked up when Amber opened the trailer door, then unceremoniously got back to it. That had marked the end of Amber's stint as his number one fan. She suddenly thanked God for, rather than abjectly resented, that willowy new groupie.

On the beach, Richard turned to look at Amber. 'He's not mine, Amber.'

'He might be,' she said.

Richard shook his head. 'No he can't be. I can't have children, unfortunately.'

Amber frowned. 'What about all these?' she pointed to the swarming mass of small kids dotted about them.

'Adopted, all of them. Wendy's a saint.'

Wendy, on the rug, rolled her eyes.

'I haven't told him – Billy,' Richard continued. 'Couldn't bring myself to. Didn't want to hurt his feelings.' He shaded his eyes to look out at the paddle-boarders. 'Oh, I think they've seen us.'

Amber turned to look at Billy, paddling faster now into shore.

At that point, Lovejoy stepped forward. 'Can I just clarify, did you just say, he couldn't be yours?'

Richard peered over his glasses at Lovejoy. 'I did indeed.'

Lovejoy swallowed. He tried to speak but no words came out. Amber watched as he struggled to process what had been said. She watched as he took a step back, then another. Billy was getting closer. Amber frowned. Lovejoy turned away. She was about to say something, call him back, but then Billy's paddleboard hit the shore. 'Mum! What are you doing here?'

CHAPTER TWENTY-FOUR

Lovejoy had stopped at the bottom on the beach steps, one hand on the bannister, head hung low, eyes focused on the sandy wooden slats. Amber kept half on eye on him to check that he wasn't about to scarper. In front of her, Richard stood, awkward. Like he didn't deal well with difficult situations. Amber knew he wasn't going to be the one to tell Billy he wasn't his father. The same as once he hadn't been the one to tell Amber she was no longer his girlfriend.

Billy was standing, awkward, unsure, wearing the board-shorts Amber had bought him last summer. Behind his skinny white back and slightly pink shoulders, the sun glinted on the calm ripples of the sea.

No one was moving.

Pandora was tying her white-blonde hair into a bun right on top of her head. She wore a retro blue and white striped bikini comprising of waist-high shorts and a buttoned-up-the-front bra top. Her sunglasses were shaped like red hearts.

'We need to talk, Billy,' said Amber.

Billy glanced from her to Richard and then to Pandora, who nodded like that was a good idea.

Billy then looked at Amber, his hair all wet, his expression young and hurt. 'OK,' he shrugged and started to walk off down the beach in the direction of the rocks.

Amber followed. It was boiling hot. The sand burnt her feet. The blue shirt stuck to her skin. Her jeans were too heavy. She had to psych herself up as she walked, this was no time for her own emotions and fears. No wobbling worries about the outcome. This was her son, upset and confused, and she had to do whatever she could to make that better.

She started to jog to catch up with him. Something she hadn't been able to do a couple of months ago – she'd have been wheezing to a standstill. It felt good to be free. At the rocks, she caught up with him. He sat down, quiet. Amber had to pause for a second and catch her breath. 'I've given up smoking,' she panted. 'Down to one patch a day.' She pointed to her arm.

'Good,' said Billy, half pleased, half mad at her.

Amber sat down, her lung capacity had improved but it was nowhere near perfect. 'Yeah,' she breathed, resting on the shiny grey rocks next to a patch of limpets and a rock pool.

Billy scuffed the sand with his toe.

Amber felt her heart rate finally regain some normality. She looked up at Billy, shielding her eyes from the sun and said, 'Billy, Richard's not your dad.'

'Yes he is.'

'No,' Amber shook her head, 'he's not.'

Neither of them spoke.

Billy looked confused.

Amber chewed on her lip. This was as hard as she imagined it would be. 'He can't have kids, Billy. Those are all adopted,' she said, nodding towards his bouncing brood. 'He just told me, I didn't know.'

Billy stared down at the sand, mulling it over, jaw rigid. The waves rolled gently on the shore. The sun flickered silver on the sea. Finally, he looked at her and asked, 'Who is then?'

Amber nodded towards the figure who was standing separate from the others over by the steps and the beach huts, hands on his hips, deep in thought. She crossed her fingers he wasn't getting ready to flee. 'Lovejoy,' she said.

'What?' Billy frowned. 'But you said he wasn't.'

Amber tipped her head. 'I know... I just—' she started. 'It was all too complicated.'

Billy stared over at Lovejoy's figure. Then he hung his head. 'That's who I thought it was,' he said, 'but I was hoping it wasn't.'

Amber looked up surprised. 'What's wrong with Lovejoy?'

'Well it's Lovejoy,' said Billy, who'd known him since he was a kid. Who'd been around him and his string of various different fake-boobed blondes. Seen as he'd had drinks poured over him and his face slapped. Billy had seen the cliché. He slumped down on the rock next to Amber. 'It's, I don't know... disappointing.'

'No hang on,' said Amber, suddenly defensive, thinking about the friendship she'd had with Lovejoy, his presence in her life. It was so complex. She had thought him too unreliable and selfish to be a father but, now his integrity was being questioned, it made her think of qualities she liked in him. 'Lovejoy's OK. He can be a pain but he has a good heart.'

Billy made a face.

Amber looked at where Lovejoy was pacing. 'He's fun to be around. He's a good dealer. He'll make you laugh.'

Billy turned his head her way, his hair flopping back again.

'So if he's so great, why didn't you tell me he was my father then?'

At that Amber realised she'd dug herself into a bit of a hole. 'Because,' she said, 'it's complicated. At the time you were born, he wouldn't have been such a good father. And he wasn't there, and Ned was and he promised he'd give you everything you'd ever need. By the time Lovejoy came back we were settled. We had our life. I didn't want anything to disturb that. Ned looked after you so well.' She leant back against the smooth grey rocks. 'But what I'm saying is just because Lovejoy would have been useless then doesn't mean he'd be useless now.' She looked at Billy, his puckered forehead and confusion. 'You've got him at his best,' she half-laughed.

Billy snorted. He rested his elbows on his knees and hung his head low. 'I just can't really work out what I feel. I love Dad – Ned. And I'm glad he was my dad.'

Amber nodded.

Billy looked at her. 'But it's like everything's turned upside down. And you lied all these years,' he sighed, disappointed.

Amber nodded, making sure she didn't turn away, that she held his gaze despite the fact she wanted to stand up and exhale. 'Yes,' she said. 'I did.'

They were silent for a while. The waves lapped. The sun scorched down. Amber pulled at her blue shirt to fan herself.

'What's that shirt?' Billy asked.

'It's new,' Amber said. 'I got arrested and needed to get some stuff after jail.'

'Oh Mum, you didn't get arrested again?' Billy rolled his eyes.

Amber shrugged. 'It was OK. Nothing I couldn't handle.' She looked down at her blue shirt. 'Do you like it?'

'Yeah it's cool,' he said. 'Colourful.'

She agreed.

They were silent again.

He toyed with the rock pool, dipping his finger in and trailing it through the water.

Amber crossed her legs and folded her arms, turning slightly his way. 'Listen, Billy, I can't sit here and say that I did everything right. Because clearly, I didn't. But at the time I just wanted to do what I thought was best for you. And Ned was the most reliable of the men I knew then. I knew he'd stick around. And that seemed the most important thing because… I had no one else.' Amber looked momentarily out at the wide lapping blue sea, then back to Billy's profile, his attention on the rock pool, his thick, brown salt-crusted hair. 'I thought I was doing what was best at the time. And I was really young – I was your age. I'd lost my dad, my mum had left, I was a bit of a mess to be honest.' She paused at the memory of herself. Thought about the moment when she'd thrown up at a Belgian flea market, right in the middle of the main square. Alone after she'd split up with Richard, she was back to doing to what she did best – buying and selling. She'd put the vomiting down to bad mussels for dinner but when she'd been unable to get up in the morning for sickness she'd realised it was more than that. She was sleeping in a car park at the time and had barely enough money for petrol but she'd bought the pregnancy test, taken it in the public loo, then sat for what seemed like hours, staring at the Belgian graffiti, terrified about what to do next. Fortuitously, Ned had sent her a text right at that moment, showing her the picture of the new car he'd just bought with his bonus. And

Amber's brain had clicked into gear. She'd left the public toilets, jumped in the van and driven non-stop to the ferry port, arriving on Ned's doorstep the next morning, tired, vulnerable and barely able to speak for morning sickness. And he had looked so completely delighted to see her that she had almost burst into tears.

On the beach, Amber had to swallow down a lump of self-pity before she could speak. 'But Billy, even if it wasn't right what I did, I did it because I love you. Everything from the moment you were born, I've done because I love you. And, yes, this will take some time to process, and yes you should be really mad at me for a while – or as long as you like – but whatever happens, however you feel,' she waved a hand, emphatic, 'I will always love you and I will always be here for you.'

Billy stared down at the sand.

Amber leant back against the rock, the smooth stone warm against her shirt.

Seagulls swooped and dived on the water as little shoals of fish jumped. Further up the beach, Lovejoy was now sitting on the steps of a weather-beaten beach hut, Richard Shepherd was talking to Julia. Martin and Pandora were playing with the little kids while Wendy took a moment to flick through a magazine. The gentle surf rolled onto the sand.

Then suddenly Lovejoy stood up and started to walk towards them. Amber didn't know what to do, whether to nudge Billy so he'd notice or wait and let it play out. She felt her heart rate rise as to what he'd say. How mad he would get, how the blame would play out. She watched him walk with eyes narrowed against the sun, messy hair half falling over his eyes, dark stubble on his chin.

As he approached and his shadow fell over them, Billy looked up.

Lovejoy gave him a nod. 'Alright, mate?'

'Yeah,' said Billy.

Lovejoy gestured to the rock beside him. 'Can I sit down?'

Billy nodded.

The tiny waves rustled on the sand, churning up shells and tiny pebbles.

Lovejoy sat down, leaning forward, elbows on his knees, exactly as Billy had been sitting, head low. Then he turned and looked across at Billy, who was picking at a limpet on the rock. 'Don't be mad at your mum,' he said.

Amber's eyes widened in shock. Of all the things she expected him to say, that was not one of them.

Billy didn't say anything.

Lovejoy licked his bottom lip, pushed his hair back from his face.

Amber watched, intrigued as to what he was going to say next.

'Thing is,' Lovejoy said, 'we were all deadbeats. All of us, him,' he nodded at Richard, 'Me. Half the other guys.' He exhaled, long and slow. Then he sat up taller. 'Your mum said to me yesterday that if I'd known about you I wouldn't have stuck around. And at the time, I was furious. But I've had to think about it. And I hate to say – it shames me to say it – but she was right. I wouldn't have been there. I would have been a shit dad.' He shook his head. 'To be honest, I'm pretty terrified now.'

Amber looked at Lovejoy's face as she listened. Saw how

much older he looked than when they were kids. How much gentler. How much more relaxed.

Lovejoy twisted round so he was better positioned to look at Billy and the barnacles he was now picking off the limpet. 'You know they're alive?' Lovejoy said about the barnacles.

Billy stopped picking.

'If you want to look at it another way,' Lovejoy went on, 'your mum had to put up with living with boring old Ned for you, that's the ultimate sacrifice!' He laughed. Billy didn't. Amber shook her head, despairing. Lovejoy stopped laughing. 'Sorry. That wasn't funny. Ned's a good bloke. And a great dad. Clearly better than me. I'm nervous.' Lovejoy paused, rubbed the back of his neck as he thought. 'I suppose what I'm trying to say, and it's hard to admit, but I think she might be the least selfish of all of us. And you're lucky to have her. And I like to think that I'm less of a dick than I was back then. Although I've possibly just proved that's not the case. Sorry.' He exhaled. Shook his head like he was an idiot. Then he said, 'Billy, what I can say, is there is no other kid I would be more proud to find out was mine, God's honest truth.'

Amber found herself welling up. She couldn't believe it. She had to turn away and surreptitiously dab at her eyes.

Billy looked at Lovejoy momentarily, assessing.

Lovejoy took a deep breath before he added, 'Maybe when we get home I can take you for a drink and we can see how it goes from there. Hang out, you know. Only if you want.'

All eyes were on Billy.

Amber said, 'You want that, Billy?'

At first he didn't do anything and Amber thought it was all a lost cause. Then very softly, he nodded. 'Yeah,' he said to Lovejoy. 'Yeah OK.' Then he looked across at Amber and said, 'Will you come too?'

She half-smiled in absolute relief. 'Yes,' she said, putting her hand over her son's where it rested on the rock. 'Absolutely.'

Then she looked up and found Lovejoy watching, the bright blue sea and cloudless sky behind him. 'Thanks,' she mouthed and he gave a quiet nod in return.

CHAPTER TWENTY-FIVE

They didn't stay long at the beach. Billy and Pandora picked up their luggage and came to stay with them at the big gothic house. Richard Shepherd went back to his holiday with his wife and family.

While Amber fell into an exhausted sleep in the afternoon, Julia went with the others to explore the island on rickety bikes they found in the garage. It was scorching hot. The air smelt of the wide planes of salt marshes stretching out on either side of them as they cycled. They went past fields dotted with flocks of white herons, tiny roadside restaurants and white houses with battered palm trees in their gardens until they reached the sea and the rows of oyster beds. Fishermen shouted as they hauled in black crates of shellfish while a tractor launched a boat down the slipway into the water.

Julia paused to watch for a second, wishing Charlie was there, knowing he'd love this, before cycling to join the others who had stopped at a shack selling oysters.

Martin counted through everyone who would eat them. 'I will,' he said, 'And Amber will, won't she?'

Billy nodded. 'Yeah and I will. Panda?' he looked at Pandora who went over and inspected the shellfish.

'Are they ethically sourced?' she asked the tough-looking fisherwoman behind the makeshift counter.

The woman looked Pandora up and down, in her broderie anglaise smock, heart-shaped glasses and white-blonde top knot. 'They are from the sea,' she said, bluntly. 'There.' She turned and pointed towards the beds of oysters just behind them.

Pandora peered towards the water. 'OK,' she said, the answer appearing acceptable to her. 'I'll have a dozen.'

'Yeah, me too,' said Lovejoy, picking one up and giving it a sniff. 'Love an oyster. Julia, are you having any?' he asked.

Julia had been trying to avoid the question. She couldn't think of anything more revolting – just the texture made her shudder – but she didn't want to be the loser who said no. 'OK,' she said, voice clearly unsure.

Martin laughed. 'I'll eat yours if you hate them.'

When they cycled home, Pandora went rummaging through the house and came out with the big gold candelabra from the living room and sat it majestically on the long wooden garden table along with some paraffin lanterns that she hung from the tree branches.

Lovejoy found two tennis racquets and a dog-chewed ball and tentatively offered one to Billy. 'Fancy a game, mate?'

Billy looked at the racquet. Julia saw Pandora pause while hanging a lantern to give Billy big-eyes, encouraging him to accept.

Billy put his glasses on and stood up, swiping his hair from his eyes. 'OK but I'm not very good.'

Lovejoy held his arms wide and said, 'Believe me, I'm no champion.'

Billy cracked a small smile.

Julia set the table and took orders from Martin to slice the lemons, wash samphire that they'd bought from the beach shack, and mix the gin and tonic, while Martin got busy shucking the oysters. Pandora dusted off an old record player and as the sun began to dim, loud French opera filled the garden.

Amber appeared in the doorway, bleary from sleep. She saw the gin and tonics and said, 'Perfect. Just a dash of tonic in mine, please.' Then settled herself down in one of the big armchairs out the back.

Julia came to sit next to her with the drinks. They watched the terrible game of tennis happening on the lawn. 'They're enjoying themselves,' Julia said about Lovejoy and Billy.

'Yes I hope so,' said Amber, watching intrigued.

The peace was interrupted by the sound of Julia's phone ringing.

Amber yawned. 'Who's that? Is that Charlie?' she asked as Julia looked at who was calling.

Julia shook her head, staring at the name on the screen. She could feel her courage diminish. 'It's my mother,' Julia said.

'Don't answer,' Amber suggested.

'I have to, otherwise she'll ring and ring. And then call Charlie.'

'Oh,' Amber made a face. 'Just remember you're in control,' she said, picking up her gin and tonic, 'and just because they're your family,' she added, 'it doesn't make them right. Unless of course it's to do with share prices.' Then slipping on her sunglasses, she went over to stand on the sidelines of the tennis.

Julia took a deep breath. 'Hi, Mum,' she said brightly.

'Are you still in France?' said her mum without any hello.

'Yes,' Julia replied. Watching the tennis back and forth.

'So what are you doing about the application for the promotion?' her mother asked. 'Your father was chatting to, oh I can't remember his name, at the golf club and he said he hadn't heard anything from you. Today's the deadline, apparently. Can you do it from France? What's that music?'

Julia turned away from the tennis. She moved into the hallway away from Pandora's opera music, Billy's shouts of triumph and Martin's loud swearing at the oysters that wouldn't shuck. 'Hang on a minute, Mum. I'm just moving.'

Julia went into the living room. It was dark, huge curtains obscuring half the windows, the walls painted deep red. She stood by the mantelpiece, on it was a glass dome underneath which was a flight of tiny stuffed birds, none of them bigger than the palm of her hand. She took a deep breath and said, 'I'm not going for the promotion.'

'Why not?' her mother asked surprised. 'You must. Hold on, your father's saying something.' Julia heard her dad's voice in the background. 'Wait a sec. No, darling,' her mum called to her dad, 'She says she's not applying.' There was a pause, then she said to Julia, 'He wants to know why not.'

Julia stared at the colourful little stuffed birds under the dome, their wings spread wide, their bodies pinned into place, all of them trapped forever mid-flight. And she said, 'Because I'm OK as I am. I like my job and I'm good at it. I don't want a promotion. If anything, Mum, I want less time at work, not more.'

Her mum was silent for a moment, then she said, 'But what about the money for the house?'

'I don't know,' said Julia, almost with a laugh, the freedom of having no idea intoxicating.

'Oh Julia, don't be silly. I don't know what's happening with Charlie but don't lose your head over this.'

'I haven't lost my head,' said Julia, smiling at herself in the huge mirror.

Then her dad came on the phone; they'd evidently put her on speakerphone. 'Is everything alright, Julia,' he asked concerned. 'Should we be worried about you off in France alone?'

'No,' she said. 'You don't need to worry about me. Don't worry about me at all.' She paused. 'Just know that I am a grown woman and I can totally make the right decisions for my life. OK?' It was such a simple sentence but it felt like it had taken a lifetime to say. The relief of hearing the words left her hands shaking.

They were both quiet for a second. 'What does Charlie have to say about it?' asked her mum.

Julia said, 'It's not about Charlie. It's about me,' surprised at how confident her voice sounded.

'You're not getting a divorce are you, Julia? Because I was talking to Suzy Maynard just this morning at the gym and she says that the holiday in the Canaries was a bust and now they're getting divorced and it's all getting *very* nasty.'

'No, Mum,' Julia smiled again, 'No I hope I'm not getting a divorce.'

'Thank God for that,' said her mother.

Julia walked away from the little birds under the dome

and over to the window, looked out at the low sun feathering the garden, saw a tennis ball shoot into the flowerbed, saw Pandora pirouetting on the patio, Amber going to the kitchen to refill her drink, and Martin carrying a tray of oysters aloft.

'Well, it is a shame,' her mother went on, 'about the promotion. But if you think you know what you're doing... '

'I know I know what I'm doing, Mum,' said Julia firmly.

'Fine,' her mum replied, a little short. 'Right, good.'

Everyone was silent for a moment. Then her dad said, 'You really should get a Santander 1,2,3 card though, Julia. Those cash machines abroad are daylight robbery.'

And Julia had to suppress a laugh as she said, 'OK, Dad, I will,' because it felt suddenly easier to concede on the small things.

Her mum said, 'Well, we must dash, Julia, we're off to Waitrose.'

'OK, bye,' Julia replied, thinking how insignificant the chat was to them, yet how monumental to her.

Life really did just tick on, unchanging.

She was staring at her phone in proud awe of herself when she heard the creak of a floorboard and the heavy scent of Chanel. Turning, she saw that Amber had come to stand next to her.

She was looking out at the garden, hands behind her back. 'Alright?' said Amber.

'I'm shaking,' Julia said looking at her hands. 'Time for a very large gin and tonic, I think.'

But, instead of heading into the kitchen, to Julia's surprise, Amber reached over and put her arm round her shoulders, drawing her close. 'Well done,' she said. 'I'm proud of you.'

Julia glanced across at Amber's profile. 'Thanks,' she said. 'Don't mention it,' Amber replied.

They stood, side by side, both staring out the window at Billy and Lovejoy's tennis game that was down to its last ball, all the others over the fence or stuck in the guttering.

Julia took a risk and, putting her arm round Amber's waist, said, 'I'm proud of you, too,' gesturing towards the laughing tennis players.

Amber laughed, deep and throaty. 'Well thank you very much,' she said. 'I appreciate that.'

And Julia grinned.

Then they went outside and Julia ate her first and only ever oyster. Geckos sat poised for moths on the white walls, and the music drifted softly on a gentle breeze. The oyster was as disgusting as she thought it would be. But she'd tried it at least.

CHAPTER TWENTY-SIX

The huge wide sky was dotted with a million stars. Bats circled round the tops of the trees. With the music down low they could hear the sound of the sea breaking in the distance. Amber was exhausted. She sat in her chair happily contented, full of oysters and gin and feeling the tightness in her chest that had followed her for eighteen years starting to lose its grip.

They stayed in the garden long into the darkness. Pandora, who Amber was beginning to realise had boundless energy and enthusiasm, decided to try and teach everyone some yoga. Julia, Martin and Billy were keen enough and Lovejoy, who would have flat out refused in the past, joined in out of a new-found fatherly attempt at bonding with Billy. That made Amber smile to herself as she stayed in her chair. She had absolutely no intention of doing yoga but would happily pass judgement on the others' failed contortions.

As she was reaching for her drink she saw a message flash up on Julia's phone. It was from Charlie.

She was about to call to Julia when she saw what it said: I'm here. It was meant to be a surprise but I can't find a bloody doorbell. Could you answer the door, please?

Amber snorted a laugh. Then she looked at the message, biting down on her lip thinking about poor Charlie trying to make a grand gesture but getting stuck on the doorstep. How did everything always seem to go wrong for them. She felt a bubble of excitement for Julia at the fact he was here, that he'd left his tomatoes and hopped on a plane. The idea thrilled her. It made her want to do something for Julia, who was currently all tangled up in one of Pandora's poses. To make it special. So she got up out her chair and sloped away to the hallway as quietly as possible to let Charlie in.

But pulling open the front door, Amber was confronted with Charlie Fletcher standing stark naked on the doorstep.

'Oh Jesus Christ!' Amber said in shock.

'Shit,' yelped Charlie.

They faced each other for a second, Charlie blushing redder and redder, hands clutched to his crotch, Amber frozen with surprise laughter. The next minute, Charlie dashed to the right to hide in the rhododendron bush by the door.

Amber put her hand over her mouth, hardly able to contain her amusement. 'Oh God, I'm so sorry, Charlie. I thought you were stuck out here.'

Charlie's voice was resigned with mortification, 'Don't worry, that was, you know, part of the plan.'

Amber struggled to keep a straight face. 'Yes,' she said. 'Yes I see that now.'

There were footsteps in the hallway. 'What's going on?' asked Martin, appearing next to Amber.

Then Julia said, 'Is there someone at the door?'

Lovejoy peered out, 'Who is it?'

They were all there, looking out into the darkness.

Amber said, 'It's someone for Julia.'

'Who?' Julia looked confused. 'Where?'

'Hi Julia,' said Charlie's voice from the rhododendron bush.

'Charlie?' Julia peered in through the leaves. 'What are you doing in the—' then she clocked his lack of apparel. 'Oh.'

'Surprise!' he said, with less enthusiasm than he might have done had Amber not opened the door.

Everyone else peered in. 'Oh!' they said in unison. Pandora squealed. Lovejoy glanced back at Amber and winked, delighted by the turn of events.

Amber was trying to hold in a grin. 'I think I somewhat ruined the surprise. Sorry. Come on, everyone, let's leave them to it.'

CHAPTER TWENTY-SEVEN

Julia stood alone on the doorstep. She could feel the smile on her face. 'You can come out now, Charlie, they've all gone.'

There was a pause. The leaves on the rhododendron shook a little as he moved. 'I don't think I can now, Julia. The moment's been er... well, I've kind of lost my nerve.'

Julia bit down on her lip. 'I can't believe you came here and took all your clothes off on the doorstep.'

'No,' he said, 'neither can I, it seemed a good idea at the time. I felt the situation deserved a grand gesture.'

Julia felt her chest swell. 'Oh Charlie.'

'It didn't turn out very well though did it? Do you think you could pass me a towel or something?'

Julia nipped to the living room and came back with one of the blankets on the sofa. 'Here.' She handed it through the branches. 'I think it's perfect,' she said, with a giggle. 'It's exactly our kind of grand gesture.' She had a sudden vision of all the guests at Emerald House having their breakfast in their dressing gowns. She knew her and Charlie would have shuffled self-consciously along the corridor in their dressing gowns and slippers wondering why the hell they hadn't just got dressed. But that was who they were, she finally acknowledged, who she was meant to be. And who wanted to have breakfast in their dressing gown with a load of strangers anyway?

'Thanks!' Charlie said, taking the striped Tibetan blanket with relief. Then he appeared out of the rhododendron bush with it tied round his waist, his hair all messed up. 'That's better.'

Julia looked at his face, all the familiar lines of him, the tiny creases at the corners of his eyes, the slight wonkiness of his nose. 'It's so nice to see you.'

'Yeah?' he asked.

She nodded.

'Good,' he said, quite chuffed. 'It's pretty nice to see you, too.'

They looked at each other on the doorstep. Pleased but a bit shy. Julia opened her mouth to speak but Charlie cut her off, 'So have you got those giant pants on?'

Julia tipped her head. 'Maybe.'

Charlie grinned. There was a lightness to him that she hadn't seen for ages. His hair all mussed up and a glint in his eyes.

Before she could say anything else he stepped forward and looping his arms under her legs and round he back he hoisted her up in the air. 'Right then,' he said.

'Charlie, what are you doing?' she struggled, completely caught off guard.

'Another big romantic gesture,' he said, stalking forward a few paces. 'Oh shit, my blanket's falling down. Hang on.' He stopped, put her down and retied the Tibetan blanket tight round his waist. 'OK, let's try again.' He lifted her up again. 'Oh God, that really hurt my back.'

'Are you OK?' she asked.

'Yes,' he said, wincing. 'Yeah, I'm fine. I just pulled something at home doing the ceiling and that must have aggravated it. Have you got any Nurofen with you?'

'No,' she laughed.

'That's OK,' Charlie nodded, serious. Then he crossed the hallway and concentrated on taking the stairs. 'There's a lot of stairs,' he said, clearly daunted.

Julia said, 'Do you want to put me down?'

'No, no, I can do it,' he huffed forward one step at a time.

Julia tried to suppress a laugh.

Three quarters of the way up the stairs Charlie stopped and put her down, rubbing his lower back. 'I think that's probably enough of a gesture.'

Julia's smile widened. 'It was a great gesture.'

'Hamish Warrington would probably have slung you over his shoulder,' Charlie said.

'I don't want to be slung over Hamish's shoulder. I want to be slung over your shoulder.'

'Christ,' said Charlie. 'I could try but probably best to do it when we're up on the landing. Might not be that safe on the stairs.'

'I didn't mean it literally,' Julia laughed. 'I don't want to be slung over anyone's shoulder.'

'Sure?'

'Sure.'

Charlie looked down at her and grinned again. 'Good.'

Then, almost taking in his surroundings for the first time, said, 'Is that a dead swan wearing a crown on the landing?'

'It is.' Julia nodded.

'Interesting,' said Charlie. 'Very interesting. Right,' he looked around. 'Which way to the boudoir?'

Julia was lying drifting off to sleep with Charlie's arms wrapped around her, the moonlight streaming through the wobbly glass when he sat up suddenly and said, 'Shall we just leave everything behind and move to France? We could get a farmhouse or some old chateau. Do glamping or yurts or something and live completely off-grid. Wouldn't that be good?'

Julia rolled over so she was facing his wide-eyes. 'No, Charlie. Maybe it would at some point but right now we don't have the money and we'd lose too much selling our house.'

Charlie's face fell a bit, despondent. 'Yeah, you're right.' He wiggled back down the bed, pulling the sheet up over them both. 'And I've never really liked yurts. I always think they look a bit hot. And there's only one room.'

Julia leant up on her elbow. 'We can move to France one day, Charlie, that's totally fine by me, but right now I think we just need to change some small things.' She reached up and touched his face. 'We need to change the way we look at what we have.'

Charlie looked uncertain. 'Please don't make me say I'm grateful for things.'

Julia laughed. 'I won't, I promise.'

'OK, go on then,' said Charlie.

'Well,' Julia thought for a second. 'The first thing we need to sort out is your job that you hate.'

'Agreed,' said Charlie. 'Yes, we definitely need to do that. Or I need to do that.'

'I can help,' she said. 'And then we need to work out how to sort the house without spending any more money. Just so that we can live for a bit, and enjoy ourselves again.'

'Agreed again.' He ran his hand up her arm, stroking her skin. 'But I'm not really sure how we do that.'

'Well look at this place,' Julia gestured to the walls and the cracked ceiling. 'I think the answer is to paint it white. All of it. Just to cover all the stuff we hate and make it like a blank canvas.'

'Shit loads of white paint,' he laughed. 'I like it.'

Julia sat up, cross-legged on the bed, sheet tight around her, getting into her stride. 'And we can make a feature out of the shabby walls in the kitchen and all the odd chairs. Here they've taken all the doors off the kitchen cupboards and just don't have any. It works really well. We could do that, easily. And we can go to some exhibitions – which would be a nice day out – and buy some posters – there's one downstairs which adds loads of colour. And then, I was thinking, we could get lots of indoor plants. Put them everywhere. You like plants, and they look good.'

'I do like plants,' he said dryly, intrigued by her enthusiasm.

'And all the stuff in the attic,' she went on. 'I think we should get it down, have a look at it again. I think maybe there's some stuff we could use, you know, to put on the mantelpiece or on the bookshelves.'

'Blimey, you have changed,' he said, a smile spreading

across his face. 'No more hankering after a neon light like Lexi's then.'

'No,' she shook her head. 'No more hankering after any-thing of Lexi's.'

'Thank God for that,' he laughed. Then he kissed the top of her head and said, 'It all sounds good. And cheap. And like it'll give us a bit of space.'

Julia nodded, pleased with his reaction. 'And I'm not going for the promotion. And I don't want an extension. And I don't really like bi-folding doors.'

'What have bi-folding doors got to do with anything?' Charlie frowned, unaware of the complete list of wants that had been escalating in Julia's head.

'Nothing,' she said, holding in a smile. Then she reached out and held onto his hand. 'Charlie, you know we were talking on the phone about being good enough and stuff?'

'Ye-ah?' said Charlie, somewhat wary. 'This sounds like it might be getting dangerously close to being grateful.'

Julia bashed him on the arm. 'No I wasn't going to say anything about being grateful. I was just going to say, I think you're absolutely good enough. I think you're great.'

Charlie looked at her and smiled. 'I think you're great too,' he said softly.

Then the noise of Julia's phone ringing cut into the moment.

Charlie peered over to see who it was. 'It's your mother, you'd better get it.'

But Julia shook her head. Instead she reached over, silenced the call and wrote a quick text, Super busy at the mo, can't talk. Will ring later. x

Charlie watched impressed. 'Blimey.'

Julia shrugged, 'That's the way I roll now.'

'I like it,' he said. Then reaching for her phone said, 'Shall we look up what else we could do with the house?'

'No,' said Julia, taking the phone off him and chucking it towards her bag. 'Let's just lie here for a bit.'

CHAPTER TWENTY-EIGHT

A cloying still heat closed in as night fell making it impossible to sleep. Amber was lying in bed, staring up at the deer skulls lit by the moonlight when there was a knock at her door. 'Hang on,' she said, reaching down to the floor to find her vest and pull it on. Then hoicing the sheet up over her, called, 'Come in.'

Lovejoy stuck his head in. 'I think my room is haunted.'

Amber sat up, holding the sheet to her chest. 'You were fine last night.'

'I think maybe the ghost was busy last night. But it's definitely haunted now. Can I come in?' he asked, standing expectant, hair all ruffled, eyes hooded.

Amber rolled her eyes. 'I'm not going to have sex with you, Lovejoy.'

He looked at her, affronted. 'I don't want to have sex with you.'

She scoffed. 'Lovejoy, you want to have sex with anyone.'

'That is so not true. I'm insulted.' He came into the room, dressed in navy boxers and a white T-shirt. 'It's not my fault the ghost chose me to haunt.'

Amber raised a brow.

Lovejoy walked over to the bed and lay down next to her. The mattress dipped. All the little hairs on her body could suddenly sense him, smell the Persil on his T-shirt. Amber shifted away an inch. Lovejoy made himself comfortable, lying on his back. 'Look at all those skulls,' he said, staring up.

Amber lay on her back next to him, looking up at the hollow-eyed skulls.

Neither of them said anything for a bit. Through the half-closed curtains the moon cast a shadow straight across them on the bed.

Lovejoy said, 'I think it went as well as can be expected today, don't you think?'

Amber nodded. 'I think so.'

'I like Billy,' he said.

'Me too,' said Amber.

They were silent again. Amber could feel that her hand rested near his on the sheet. It all felt suddenly so familiar.

Lovejoy said, 'He's starting to look like your dad.'

Amber paused, thought about it. 'I suppose he is.'

Lovejoy rolled his head to look at her, eyes bright in the moonlight. 'I can still see it, you know, the day he collapsed. You all calm like you knew what you were doing giving him mouth to mouth. Fuck I was terrified.'

Amber stared up at the skulls. 'Me too,' she said. 'I was terrified.'

'You didn't look terrified,' Lovejoy said, rolling onto his side and looking at her profile.

She shrugged. Didn't look at him.

Lovejoy paused. Then he said, 'I think quite a lot that I could have handled that time better.'

Amber laughed, glancing his way. 'You don't think it quite a lot.'

Lovejoy grinned. 'OK, thinking about it now, I've thought that I could have handled it better. Been better to you.'

'We were teenagers,' she said. 'What did we know about handling things?'

Lovejoy shrugged. 'Yeah but maybe I could have stayed. I didn't have to go to the States straight away. I was being selfish and I knew it. You could have come and lived with me and my mum and then you wouldn't have been on your own and you wouldn't have gone off. You wouldn't have met that other guy. I maybe wouldn't have been like I was.'

'You were always going to be like you were!' Amber laughed. Then she ran her hand over her mouth, thinking. Outside lines of cloud slid over the light. She rolled onto her side to look at him. 'We would have been the same whatever,' she said. 'I think we end up in the same place no matter what.'

Lovejoy looked like he wasn't so sure.

Amber said, 'Can you imagine what it would have been like, us living together. We'd have been a nightmare.'

He laughed. '*You* would have been a nightmare.'

Amber bashed him on the arm. '*You* would have been a nightmare.'

They lay looking at each other.

Then Amber took a breath and said, 'In the spirit of being honest, which I'm trying to be,' she paused, 'although it's very difficult. I just want to say that back then, I did have feelings for you, I loved you I think, and when you left it really hurt me.'

Lovejoy looked down at the sheet.

Amber swallowed before carrying on, tone much lighter. 'I don't anymore, of course.'

'Of course,' said Lovejoy, all jokey but clearly a little uncomfortable so when there was suddenly a rattling sound out the window, he sat bolt upright and said, nervously, 'What's that noise? See it's haunted in here as well.'

'It's rain, Lovejoy,' Amber replied, dryly.

'Oh.' He lay back down. Amber rolled onto her back again. Through the open window they could hear the rain shaking the leaves on the trees. Lovejoy said, 'I am sorry about back then, you know, not being ready and all that.'

Amber looked over at him. 'Thanks,' she said. She wasn't very good at apologies and had to take a steeling breath before she replied, 'I'm sorry I didn't tell you. That, well, I didn't give you a chance.' She paused. 'Even though I know you would have proved me right.'

Lovejoy laughed, incredulous. 'You can't help yourself can you?'

'What? It's true.'

'Can't even handle a simple apology.'

Amber laughed. The sound of the rain outside got louder, splashing off the canopy of leaves. 'OK, I'm sorry.'

Lovejoy tipped his head. 'Thank you.'

They listened to the rain in silence for a second, then Amber said, 'You still would have proved me—'

'Amber!' he held up a hand in warning.

She laughed.

The rain really started to pour, crashing down through the trees.

'Do you think you should close the window?' Lovejoy asked.

'No, I like it,' said Amber.

They watched the downpour, the backs of their hands almost touching.

Then Lovejoy moved his away to scratch his chin as he said, 'Back to work tomorrow. Emerald House. Enemies again.'

Amber nodded. 'Yes. Enemies again.'

CHAPTER TWENTY-NINE

Lovejoy and Amber fell asleep side by side. Amber slept with a calm peace she hadn't felt for weeks, months, years. And woke as the morning sun beamed through her open window.

She looked at the bed next to her.

Lovejoy was gone.

She rubbed her eyes and sat up, drawing the sheet up over her knees, the room cool from the night of rain. She looked again at the space next to her on the bed and narrowed her eyes, thinking.

Then she got out of bed and went to look out the window. Lovejoy's van was gone.

Amber jogged out into the corridor and flinging open the doors saw Martin and Lovejoy's rooms were empty.

'Julia, wake up!' she shouted, banging on Julia's door. 'Get up, we have to go! Billy,' she yelled up the stairs. 'We're going!'

Julia appeared all bleary-eyed at the door. 'What's going on?'

'The bastard's left. Lovejoy's gone. He's on his way to Emerald House. He's got a head start. We have to go.'

Billy appeared from the attic room. 'How could he do that? I knew I shouldn't have trusted him,' he said.

'Don't be ridiculous, Billy,' Amber snapped. 'If I'd thought about it, I'd have done exactly the same thing.' And while she knew that was true, and that this was a competition and she would do everything she could to beat Lovejoy, she hated the feeling that part of her had hoped to wake up with him there. She strode back to her room to start packing. 'Come on, everyone, we need to get going!'

Downstairs there was a loud bash and some swearing.

They went to peer over the bannister and saw Pandora, in a huge white Adidas T-shirt and tiny stretch red hot pants, nursing her ankle, having come in the front door and tripped over a silver drinks trolley. 'What's this doing in front of the door?' she asked.

'My trolley!' gasped Julia, running down the stairs. 'He's given it back,' she said, 'I can't believe he's given it back.' She looked back up at Amber with a grin as she ran her hands over the silverwork. Then she picked up the note that had fluttered to the floor and read, *'Didn't want to leave without returning everything to its rightful owner. See you there. Good luck! LJ.'*

'That's nice of him,' said Charlie.

Julia looked up from the hallway, 'That is actually quite nice of him,' she said to Amber.

Amber stared down at the sparkling trolley. It was nice of him. It was a really good piece. Julia had done well to spot it. She would never have expected Lovejoy to give it back out of fairness. It was more likely he was just trying to absolve himself of any wrongdoing so nothing marred his victory. Amber harrumphed. Then turning back to her room said, 'Everyone, pack up we're leaving, this second. We cannot let him win.'

As Amber was packing she could hear Charlie through the wall say to Julia, 'This is all very exciting.'

And Julia reply, a little giddy, 'I know.'

That at least made her smile as she threw all her stuff into her bag, showering and dressing in record time, refusing to let her mind focus on anything else other than the task of winning her Emerald House contract back.

The rain had broken the heat. Outside the air was fresh and crisp, there was a sea mist that clung to their skin in a layer of sparkling moisture. With the house locked up and everyone dressed and ready, Julia, Charlie, Billy and Pandora all stood in a line by the van, possessions at their feet, no one saying anything as Amber tried for the umpteenth time to start the van.

'You'll flood the engine, Mum.'

'Thank you, Billy,' she said, without looking, just concentrating on turning the key and listening to the throaty rumble that wouldn't tick over.

Charlie said, 'If the worst comes to it, I could probably give you a tow.'

They all turned to look at the tiny Fiat 500 Charlie had hired.

'Maybe not,' Charlie added.

'Shit!' Amber bashed the steering wheel. Then she got out and opened the bonnet, staring at a mass of wires and blackened bits of machinery that she knew nothing about. 'Anyone know anything about cars?' she asked, knowing full well that none of them had a clue.

Pandora's hand shot up. 'I do!'

Everyone turned to look at her.

'You do,' Amber said, surprised.

Pandora trotted over. 'Oh yes,' she said with a chuffed little flick of her hair. 'I went to a very progressive boarding school.'

Billy grinned. Amber watched her with a new-found respect. Her white-blonde hair flowing as she leaned herself under the bonnet to diagnose the issue.

Amber was just getting her toolkit out the back of the van when a giant blue Cadillac eased its way round the corner of the drive and stopped right in the middle, blocking them all in.

'Oh Jesus Christ,' said Amber, hand to her forehead in disbelief. 'What now?'

An old man in a tweed suit with long wispy hair and a pipe unfolded himself from the ancient car and walked round to open the door for his wife, a woman in a turquoise twin set with a necklace made of dolls' heads the size of quails' eggs.

'*Bonjour*,' the old lady smiled.

Amber stepped forward, introducing herself the best she could with her limited French.

But it was Julia who came into her own. As Amber struggled, she stepped forward and chatted with a tumble of A-level French.

Amber happily stopped speaking and let Julia take the lead. She turned to see Charlie beaming with pride. 'She's good, isn't she?' he said.

Julia and the old couple had a really long, convoluted chat with lots of big laughs and clapped hands. Amber had no idea what she was waffling on about but she was starting to get antsy, time was of the essence.

Suddenly behind her the van's engine sprang to life and Pandora jumped down from the driver's seat, wiping her hands on a rag, saying, 'All done.'

'Amazing,' said Amber. 'Julia, can you tell them we loved staying at their house but we're sorry we're in a hurry and have to go—'

Julia held up a hand, indicating for Amber to wait a sec. The old woman was talking, big gesticulations with her hands. Julia was nodding. Amber was practically hopping from foot to foot with impatience, 'Come on, Julia,' she muttered.

But the old woman was giving a long explanation about something. Julia said, '*Mais oui,*' and started to smile. Then she gestured that she'd like to talk to Amber.

The old woman held her hands wide, '*Bien sûr, bien sûr.*'

Julia was almost giddy as she spoke. 'She says that the house, all its contents, it's for sale.'

'Excuse me?' Amber was hardly able to believe what she was hearing. 'Are they serious?'

Julia nodded. 'Yeah, definitely. They're downsizing,' Julia said with a grin. 'Moving back to Paris. The whole lot has to go. She's asking if you want to pick anything? It's all a very reasonable price.'

The old couple were watching, waiting, eager little faces.

'Do I want to pick anything?' Amber's face split into a grin. '*Oui. Oui,*' she said, nodding at the couple. 'Definitely *oui*!'

Together they all trotted back up the steps to the house. Amber with visions of chandeliers and age-speckled mirrors.

'You should text Lovejoy,' Julia said, coming up beside her.

'Tell him what's happened. Remind him that when you leave you miss out,' she added.

Amber glanced across at her. 'I should,' she said with a nod. But she didn't because the notion was a little too bittersweet. Instead she turned to Charlie and said, 'I hope there's room in your tiny car for a taxidermy swan.'

CHAPTER THIRTY

An hour and a half later, they left the Noirmoutier house laden down. Billy had been up on the van roof like a little chimpanzee tying on chairs and a small wardrobe with intricate knots and binds. Charlie helped him from the ground, sweat beading on his forehead, while Julia crammed as much as she could into the Fiat 500. Amber's van was so full they had to bungee the back doors together. She'd bought practically everything she could lay her hands on, much to the old French couple's delight. Pandora had bought for herself a vintage satin nightdress and was wafting about in it, smelling a bit musty.

With both vehicles bursting at the seams it was time to go. They left to much kissing and gesticulating with the old couple and then they were off. Charlie, Julia and the swan in the Fiat. Amber, Billy and Pandora in the van.

Halfway out the gates, the van in front, Julia suddenly shouted out the window of the Fiat. 'Amber! You're not allowed to drive.'

'Shit.' Amber braked hard. Behind her, Charlie had to do an emergency stop, the swan head tipping forward between them from the back seat. Billy and Amber changed places.

Julia presumed with Billy at the wheel, they'd all be travelling at a more sedate pace but as soon as they pulled out onto the quiet tree-lined avenue the van shot off.

'Bloody hell!' said Charlie. 'He's got half a house on the roof. He can't drive that fast! Surely she'll tell him to slow down.'

Julia shook her head. 'I think we're just going to have to speed up.'

'Blimey,' said Charlie, pressing tentatively on the accelerator – there would be no sixty-seven miles per hour cruise control today. 'It really is an adventure.'

She reached forward and put the radio on. Loud French DJ chat blared out. Charlie winced. 'Really?'

'Really,' she said.

And after a second or two, he started nodding to the music. 'I used to like a bit of French rap.'

Julia rolled her head to look at him. 'You did not.'

'I did!' he said. 'You don't know everything about me, Julia. I have very diverse music tastes.'

She snorted a laugh. 'Since when?'

'Since right this second,' he said, slipping his sunglasses on, still nodding his head to the beat while cruising along in the fast lane, clearly really enjoying himself. 'The light's really different in France, isn't it?'

'What?' Julia couldn't believe what she was hearing. 'When I said that years ago, you said that was rubbish.'

'I never said that,' said Charlie, shaking his head.

'You did!'

He laughed. 'Maybe I did. It sounds like something I'd say.' He shrugged. 'I'm clearly an idiot.'

Julia put her bare feet up on the dash. Smiling. She looked out the window at the sun pooling outwards on the horizon, the patchwork fields with brown cows, the looming big telephone pylons and thought how completely happy she was. How completely content with where she was right at that exact moment.

The French rap booming out of the speakers almost blocked out the fact that her phone was beeping with new WhatsApp messages.

She picked it up and had a look.

Lexi Warrington created group "Emerald House"
Lexi Warrington added Alicia
Lexi Warrington added Nicky
Lexi Warrington added You.

Lexi: Julia! How are you? Hope you weren't too hungover after the party. God, wasn't it crazy? Soz if things got a bit out of control #toomuchprosecco!! I've just heard from Harry next door you're in France with AMBER. Random!? Didn't realise you were so close. Can't believe Harry knew and I didn't! I'm offended, LOL xxx

Alicia: We saw you get in the van but had no idea you were going on holiday TOGETHER. So cool!!!

Nicky: Sounds really fun! France is fab this time of year.

Lexi: So do you think Amber can get you membership to Emerald House? Would love to come if you're taking guests!! ☺

Charlie turned down the radio and looking across at her asked, 'Who is it?'

Julia looked up from the phone. 'Lexi Warrington asking whether I can take her to Emerald House with me.'

'No way?' Charlie snorted a laugh. 'She is unbelievable.'

Julia looked at the messages. She looked at the name of the group: *Cedar Lane Friends*.

This was all she'd ever wanted.

At the top of the screen it said *Lexi is typing…*

Julia realised, with a flutter of pleasure, that she had no interest in what Lexi was about to say.

And with a touch of the screen, Julia left the group.

She put her phone back in her bag and as she did, saw that the little fluffy pompom that hung from the strap had fallen off. But she didn't bother to look for it. Instead she went back to looking at the landscape. The towering trees, the arched bridges, the sun radiant on the hot tarmac.

Pandora called to tell them that, clearly under Amber's instruction, she had managed to get them all booked onto a Eurotunnel that cut timing to the wire.

Charlie glanced at the satnav, the blue line marking the long journey ahead of them. 'There's no chance we'll get that.'

Julia grinned. 'You wanna bet?'

CHAPTER THIRTY-ONE

They arrived at the new Emerald House flagship hotel just off Russell Square at twenty past three. A giant turreted red-brick building with stained-glass windows and rows of flag poles all sporting flags with the Emerald House crest. Amber swung the van into the deliveries entrance and Charlie followed suit with the Fiat. It was sweltering hot. The air smelt heavily of London traffic.

Lovejoy's van was already parked.

Amber pulled up on the other side of the lot, Charlie drew up next to her, and they all piled out.

'I'm going to find Olga,' Amber said, 'let her know we're here. This is the room plan,' she handed Julia the drawing she'd done in the van in her notebook.

'This is great,' said Julia.

Amber made a face like of course it was.

Julia stifled a smile.

'If you could get these pieces out first and have them ready, we'll start taking them through to the room when I get back. OK?'

They nodded in unison.

Amber gave them all a quick nod then she went off towards

the door with a sign that read 'Office' and an arrow pointing forward. She paused for a second, glanced over her shoulder at them all standing there, watching, and said, 'Thanks, you know, for all this.'

They smiled back. It felt nice to have them all behind her, all part of her team.

Amber headed down the corridor, luxurious with its dark green linen wallpaper and big gold lights.

The door to Olga Lupé's office was open. Olga was on the phone, her back to the door, she was looking out the window. Her hair hung loose down her back almost to her bum. She was dressed in her trademark wide-legged trouser suit, this time it was lilac. When she turned around and saw Amber standing in the doorway she did a smile that resembled a wince. Amber had always thought Olga had a funny face, she should have been stunning but all her features were just slightly askew. Her slim nose was a bit too pointy, her cheekbones too razor sharp.

'I have to go,' Olga said to whoever was on the phone and hung up. 'Amber,' she said, still wincing, organising some papers on her desk as she spoke, not willing to give Amber her full attention.

'Olga.'

'Lovejoy's already here,' she said, glancing up from her paper shuffling.

'I know,' Amber said.

Olga nodded. 'For a minute I thought maybe you weren't coming. You're so hard to pin down.' She pursed her lips. 'I always appreciate it if someone rings to let me know they're on their way.'

Amber had to force herself to nod. 'Sorry,' she said. 'In the past Henri has always trusted me to get the job done.'

Olga winced again. 'Well,' she said, matter-of-fact, closing the file of papers, 'Different styles.' Then she sat down in her white leather chair. 'Lovejoy's room is looking fab. You should take a peek,' she said, then as if remembering she should make some effort, added all saccharine, 'I can't wait to see what you've come up with. Exciting stuff!'

Amber forced herself to smile in agreement.

But Olga's attention was elsewhere now, her phone was beeping with notifications. 'You know where the room is, don't you? Don't let me keep you,' she said, without looking up from the screen.

Amber had to physically bite her tongue as she walked away. She stomped back down to the deliveries entrance, fuming.

The others had started unloading furniture out of the van. Charlie, Julia and Billy were lifting and dragging the huge, speckled-mirrored armoire off the roof. Pandora was struggling with a knot of French wingback chairs and a crystal chandelier.

Just as Amber walked in, from a different door came Lovejoy and Martin, looking sweaty and exhausted.

Lovejoy stopped up short when he saw them. Martin looked immediately guilty and couldn't meet Amber's eye.

'Afternoon,' said Lovejoy.

'Hi,' said Amber curtly, stalking over to the Fiat 500 to try and manoeuvre the taxidermy swan out the back.

When Lovejoy saw it he said, 'What are you doing with that?' clearly recognising the swan. Then suddenly clocking the other gems from the house, he strode over, frowning. 'How did you get all this?'

Amber folded her arms across her chest. 'The owners turned up, sold us anything we wanted.'

Lovejoy paled.

'You should have stuck around a bit longer,' she said, brow raised. Then she laughed, 'Oh yeah, I forgot, that's not your style.'

Lovejoy swallowed, pretending to ignore the sarcasm. Then he shook his head. 'I can't believe you got all this,' he said, hand trailing over one of the French chairs.

Amber tilted her head in a satisfied grin. 'Bit less confident now, are you?'

He ran his hand through his hair. He exchanged a look with Martin, who shrugged as if in defeat. Martin looked like all he wanted to do was swap sides and have a natter about what had happened after they'd left.

But Lovejoy wouldn't give Amber the satisfaction. He walked past her to unlock his van and said, 'I'm actually very confident. The room's had the seal of Olga's approval and we're not even finished.'

Amber rolled her eyes. 'Whatever.'

Amber, Julia, Charlie, Billy and Pandora worked on the room till the sun started to fade out the window and daytime noises turned to sounds of evening commuters and clinking glasses in sprawling pubs. They had hauled various pieces of furniture into lifts and up staircases, climbed ladders, banged fingers with nails. They were sweaty, exhausted, dirty and calloused by the time Amber said, 'It's done.'

Everyone stood back to admire. It was a feast for the eyes. The cream curtains draped in luxurious folds as they had in Noirmoutier and the chandelier glass sparkled where it hung temporarily on a hook in the ceiling, waiting for the electrician. All the little touches came together – the fox in the hallway by the coat peg, the china dog from the fair peeking out from under a vintage writing desk above which hung one of the many mirrors they'd taken from the old house. In the corner was Julia's silver drinks trolley, dressed with etched French champagne flutes and the glass-domed songbirds, and next to it, majestic in its new home, was the swan.

'It looks amazing,' said Julia. 'So completely amazing.'

Amber took it all in, pride thumping in her chest. 'It does,' she exhaled, relieved, reaching up to straighten a piece of chandelier glass. 'I wonder what Lovejoy's looks like.'

Pandora nudged Billy and said, 'Shall we go and have a look?'

'No, no,' said Amber. 'He'll see you.'

'I'm very subtle,' said Pandora, and she dragged Billy off without waiting for a reply.

Amber paced the room, restless. Julia and Charlie sat in the French chairs.

Pandora and Billy came back a few minutes later and Amber hated how much she wanted to know what they had to say.

Billy came to stand next to her in the centre of the room. 'It's good,' he said. 'More clean lines than this, but that's his style. But it's just nowhere near as good as this, Mum. Like, nowhere near.' He gave her a squeeze round the shoulders.

Pandora nodded, then said, all thin gesticulating arms, 'You know, it's like at the end of *Bake-Off* and one is really good but the other is just like, oh my God, outstanding.' She gave Amber big wide-eyes. 'Well, it's like that,' she said, emphatic. 'You've got it in the bag.'

'Thanks.' Amber laughed. She could feel her nerves. She caught a glimpse of herself in the speckled armoire mirror. 'Oh God, look at me, I can't see Olga looking like this,' she said. 'I look a wreck.' She was madly trying to flatten out her hair when she felt the others stiffen in the doorway.

Olga's voice said, 'Oh look what you've done in here,' as she sashayed into the room, all swishing lilac trousers and a cloud of bespoke perfume. 'How cute,' she scrunched up her nose at the swan. It was an expression that didn't suit her.

Amber tried to stand as calm and friendly as she could. Julia beckoned for the others to leave the room.

'This is just great,' Olga drawled, circling the floor space. Amber knew it was, she could feel it fizzing through her body, she'd never done anything better. 'Oh, and look at that chandelier, I might nab that for my house,' Olga laughed, as if she and Amber were great gal pals.

Amber tried to smile. 'Take it if you want.'

'I wouldn't dare, Amber,' Olga replied, all faux-wide-eyed, running a hand along the cream curtains, straightening the folds.

'Is Henri coming?' Amber asked, presuming he'd be along any minute to give a second opinion.

Olga glanced over her shoulder. 'Not today.'

Amber nodded. She wanted to pick the phone up and order Henri here. But she stood, silent, hating that she was waiting for Olga's approval.

Olga looked some more, she picked things up and put them down, she knelt to pat the china dog under the desk, then she did another circuit of the room, face expressionless.

In the end, Amber couldn't stand it any longer. 'So what do you think?' she asked.

Olga paused by the bed. 'I think it's fabulous,' she said.

Amber felt her whole body relax. 'Yeah?' she couldn't hide the smile.

'Of course.' Olga smiled, sitting down, giving the mattress a quick test as a side-thought, her long legs crossed, arms resting languid over her knees. 'But the thing is, for me, Amber, taking everything into account, it's just not quite right.'

'What?' Amber frowned, unsure she'd heard correctly.

'There are other factors to consider as well as just good room design,' said Olga, removing a speck of lint from the bedspread.

'What more could you want than good room design?' Amber asked, confused, feeling her hand start to tremble.

Olga tilted her head. 'I have to look for a partnership that works for me, Amber. And, while the room is fabulous, and thank you for all your hard work, this isn't the partnership for me.' She was clearly trying to make her eyes look sad as she said, 'I'm sorry. I think your time with Emerald House has come to an end.'

CHAPTER THIRTY-TWO

Amber stepped out into the corridor, the trademark dark emerald linen wallpaper so familiar to her. The doors to each room were black lacquered and low white globe lights hung at regular intervals illuminating her steps, it felt like heading into an endless passage. At the far end the others were waiting nervously. Amber could barely look at their hopeful smiles.

'We have to leave,' she said, voice catching as she marched past them.

'Mum?' Billy jogged to catch up with her. 'What happened?'

'They fired me.'

'What?' Julia stopped, horrified. 'Why?'

Amber pressed the button for the elevator, bashing it over and over trying to get it to come quicker. 'Because she hates me. Because she doesn't think we can work together. Because she just wants someone at her beck and call.' The lift wasn't coming. Amber stopped pressing the button and just stood, she let her shoulders sag. 'I had a feeling it would happen,' she said. 'You can't change people's opinions of you, can you? I just hoped that the work would speak for itself. That I'd done enough—'

'You did enough, Mum,' said Billy. 'You've always done enough.'

Julia was standing hands on hips, staring down the corridor they'd just come from. 'What a complete bitch.'

Caught off guard, Amber laughed.

'She's a cow-bag,' Pandora added with glee.

The gold doors of the lift pinged open.

'That's it then,' said Amber.

Just as they were sloping in, Charlie paused, holding the doors open, and said, 'Amber, have they paid you for the goods you've delivered to the room?'

Amber frowned. 'No,' she said, 'not till I invoice them. Why?'

The lift doors tried to shut but Charlie held them back. 'Well if they've fired you,' he said, a sly grin starting to spread on his face, 'why leave them with all your best stuff?'

Amber suddenly understood what he was driving at. 'Oh Charlie,' she said, striding out of the lift. 'You're a genius.' She cupped his face with her hand. 'I'm so pleased we've dragged you out of your man cave!'

Charlie flushed beetroot.

Julia gave him a wink.

And then they all walked as fast as they could back to the room.

'Billy you take the fox,' said Amber. 'Pandora, that mirror next to the bed and if you can carry it get the other one as well. Julia—'

But Julia was already wheeling the drinks trolley out of the room complete with vintage champagne flutes and glass-domed songbirds.

'Wow.' Amber was amazed.

'What else do you want?' Charlie asked.

'We can't really take the curtains can we?' Amber said, hands on her hips, looking at the fabric she'd just spent ages hanging.

'Why the bloody hell not?' asked Charlie, jumping up on a vintage chair to start unhooking the little hooks. 'Damn, there's hundreds of them!' he muttered.

From the doorway, Pandora said, 'Someone's coming.'

'Well get going,' Amber chivvied, running to the corner of the room to grab the swan. 'Charlie, leave the curtains, it's fine.'

'No!' he called. 'I'm nearly done.' He undid the last hook and the curtain pooled down on his head. Scrambling to get out of the material, he bundled it up onto the vintage chair and started lugging the whole lot out of the room. At the doorway he paused. 'Amber, the chandelier!'

'Leave it!' she called back.

'Absolutely not!' he shouted, putting down the chair to do a running leap onto the bed to grab the chandelier off its temporary hook.

Amber paused to watch, impressed.

'Got it!' Charlie cheered as he jumped down from the bed, all the crystal pieces clinking like wind-chimes.

'Let's go,' Julia called. 'Come on.'

Together they ran out of the room, just as one of the doors along the corridor opened and Olga appeared, barring the way to the lift.

Amber stopped, frozen, holding the swan tight round its belly.

'What's going on?' Olga asked, forehead puckered. 'What the hell are you doing?'

It was Julia who spoke, 'We are taking what is ours!'

Olga strode forward. 'Put it all back right now, these are goods commissioned by Emerald House.' Her cool eyes narrowed as she said, 'Amber, may I remind you, we have a contract. Take these things and you will never work for us again in any capacity. You'll never work for anyone.'

Amber looked from Olga to her swan and back again. Word would spread about this. It would certainly be career-limiting. But then she looked at Julia, all riled up and practically hopping from foot to foot, and Billy and Pandora clutching their goods and Charlie with his vintage French chair loaded with curtains and a chandelier. All of them on her side. All of them there to support her. She looked back at Olga. 'I don't have a contract actually,' she said.

'I think you do,' said Olga, tone patronising as if Amber hadn't the first clue of business.

'No,' said Amber. 'No, I've never signed anything. I don't really like being tied into things. And Henri was always fine with that.' She tilted her head, looking at Olga's face, like a Picasso, all the sharp angles of her, the control in her eyes. 'That's the thing about friendship, Olga.' Amber smiled, gesturing to her own little team. 'It's amazing what people will do for you simply because they want to.'

Olga rolled her eyes, and scoffed like it was all beneath her. 'Put the things back in the room, Amber.'

'No!' again, it was Julia who cut in. Stepping forward and pointing a finger at Olga she declared, 'No we will not. You have failed to see the value of what you had. You're despicable.'

Olga raised a brow, arms crossed watching them, then looking to Amber, pointedly challenging her to defy the order.

But by that stage, Amber didn't have a choice because Julia had grabbed her arm and, wheeling her trolley round, ordered, 'We are too good for you! Turn around, everyone, to the service elevator!'

And they all turned and fast-walked back down the corridor, Julia having to stretch her arm over the trolley to hold her glass-domed birds and champagne glasses in place. Pandora struggling with the mirrors, Amber almost waddling under the weight of the swan.

Julia said, 'God, I feel quite invigorated. She was terrifying.'

'You were great,' said Charlie.

Amber suddenly found herself laughing.

Julia said, 'What?'

'*You're despicable!*' Amber repeated, mimicking Julia's voice all prim and righteous.

'Well,' said Julia, with a little snigger at herself, jogging along behind her trolley, 'I could hardly call her a bitch and cow-bag, could I?'

CHAPTER THIRTY-THREE

They ended up in a tiny drawing room pub with mottled glass in the windows that served tankards of ale and pork scratchings – which no one ate after Pandora gave a big spiel about some hideous animal cruelty video she'd seen on YouTube.

They sat huddled round a velvet booth table, brass sconces above them and black and white pictures of Victorian London on the walls. They chatted about everything that had happened that day. They laughed about running from Olga, recounting the story over and over.

Then Julia said to Amber, 'How do you feel?'

Amber took a sip of her Guinness. 'Furious,' she said. Then she shrugged. 'I don't know. I'm so angry that it can just be taken away. But, well, working with Olga wouldn't have been ideal, would it?' She had to pause before she said anything because she could feel herself on the unexpected verge of tears. She dabbed at her eye with a napkin. 'God, look what I've become.'

Billy said, 'But you'll be able to find something else, won't you, Mum?' face all concern.

'Yes of course I will,' said Amber, emphatic, blowing her

nose. 'It's just, well… This is all I've known. And I liked it. I loved it. Before bloody Olga.' She swept her hair out of her eyes. 'It looks a bit blank ahead.'

An awkward silence followed. Billy staring nervously at his mum.

'I'll be OK. It'll be fine,' Amber said, with as much conviction as she could muster. 'Honestly.'

To change the subject, Charlie suggested they play the *Who Wants to Be a Millionaire* quiz machine, and he and Julia mesmerised them all with their collective trivia knowledge. They won sixty quid and were just about to buy more drinks with it when the door to the pub opened and Lovejoy and Martin walked in.

'Oh here we go,' Amber sighed.

Billy narrowed his eyes.

Lovejoy came over to the table, looking worn out but buoyant, his black T-shirt all dusty, his face smudged. 'Alright?'

'Peachy,' said Amber dryly.

Lovejoy sat down on the stool next to her. Martin went over to the bar where Charlie was getting a round.

'So,' said Amber, 'she offered you the job.'

'Uh-huh,' Lovejoy nodded.

Billy scowled.

Amber finished off her drink. She tried her hardest not to look jealous. Not to be a sore loser but she could see her face in the mirror opposite and it wasn't working.

'Didn't take it though,' said Lovejoy, eyes glinting.

Amber's head shot round to face him. She narrowed her eyes. 'What?' She felt a tingling run over her skin and tried to ignore it. 'Why not? You idiot, you should have taken it.'

Lovejoy looked confused. 'I thought you'd be pleased,' he said, running his hands through his hair and holding it back off his face.

'Why?' Amber looked at him like he was an idiot. Part of her was braced, waiting for something – the punchline, the news he'd been offered something even better – the other part of her started wondering if he'd done it for her, but then she scolded herself, she knew Lovejoy better than that. 'It's a great job.'

Lovejoy held his hands wide. 'But it's your job. I didn't want to take your job. I thought about it and it made me feel bad.'

'I don't believe you,' Amber said, leaning back against the velvet booth, eyes wary.

'It's true! You're meant to be pleased!' Lovejoy huffed. 'I did it for you.'

'Why?' Amber muttered, untrusting. She couldn't believe he would pass up this opportunity.

Charlie and Martin hovered awkwardly with the new drinks.

'For God's sake, Amber,' Lovejoy said, voice raised, end of his tether. 'I was doing the room and it just didn't feel right. I didn't like myself. And when she offered me the job I knew I couldn't take it. I did it for you and Billy to show you that I've changed. That—' he pointed to himself, 'I'm a good person.' He ran his hand over his jaw and shrugged before saying, 'It's just it took me a while to get there, you know, old habits and all that.'

Amber didn't say anything. She felt Julia kick her under the table. She looked up to see her grinning, Amber looked away. Charlie and Martin put the drinks down on the table and sat down.

Billy said, 'I understand, Lovejoy.'

'Thank you, Billy,' Lovejoy replied.

Amber sat silent, refusing to look at anyone. Her brain was having trouble processing the information. No one was fitting into their usual roles. 'So you're not taking the job?' she had to clarify. 'You're not working for Emerald House.'

'No,' said Lovejoy.

Amber nodded. He'd done it for Billy. And for her – she had to file that one away to think about properly later.

After a moment, Lovejoy gave her a nudge on the arm. 'Admit you're pleased I didn't take it.'

Amber could feel everyone watching her. She took a sip of her drink. Inside she'd started to feel a fizz of pleasure that he hadn't taken it, but there was no way she was showing him how much it meant to her. Still held back by that little bit of fear. So when she put her glass back on the table she held her hand up, an infinitesimal gap between her finger and thumb, and said, 'Maybe I'm this much pleased.'

Lovejoy grinned.

Julia did a wry smile.

Over the other side of the table, Charlie took a sip of the frothy foam of his Guinness and said, 'All that furniture and antiques, you two should start your own hotel chain.'

'You should!' Billy cut in. 'That would be so cool.'

Amber rolled her eyes. 'We couldn't work together.'

Next to Charlie, Martin nodded in agreement, tying his hair up in a bun. 'It would be a disaster.'

Lovejoy frowned. 'I don't think it would be a disaster—'

Amber shook her head at the idea.

'I'm serious,' said Lovejoy. 'It could be good.'

Martin raised his eyebrows. 'Okaaay!' he said, just to appease him, and taking his drink went to stand by Charlie who had been lured back by the *Who Wants to Be a Millionaire* game.

Charlie got stuck on a geography question which Martin scoffed at the idea of knowing himself when Charlie looked at him for an answer, so they called Julia over. Then there was something about *Love Island* which Pandora knew the answer to and went to stand by the machine. Billy joined when it transpired Pandora wasn't a hundred per cent sure what the answer was and was stuck between two possibilities.

It left Lovejoy and Amber alone at the table.

Lovejoy leant forward, elbows resting on the table. 'I have something to tell you,' he said.

Amber glanced up. 'Yeah?'

Lovejoy nodded. 'In the spirit of honesty and all that,' he said, pausing to sip his drink, 'I think I might have loved you too, back then.'

Amber laughed, 'Oh thanks! You think.'

Lovejoy grinned. 'Well I can't be sure because I was young and a twat.'

Amber smiled down at the table.

'But,' Lovejoy toyed with the beer mat, 'you're the only one who stayed, you know, in my head, so...'

Amber glanced up.

'I reckon that was love,' he said, peeling the corner off the beer mat and then chucking it back on the table.

'Stayed eh?' Amber said, leaning back, surveying him. His glinting eyes, dirty T-shirt and arrow tattoo. 'So I'm still there?' she teased.

Lovejoy sat back, caught off guard. 'I didn't say that.'

306

'Yeah you did,' she laughed. 'That means you love me,' she said, as if they were taunting each other in the playground.

'Don't be ridiculous,' Lovejoy dismissed the suggestion, stretching his arms up, 'if anyone loves anyone, it's you who loves me. You admitted it.'

'*Loved*, Lovejoy. Loved being the operative word,' Amber clarified.

Lovejoy took another sip of his pint, looking across at her over the rim. 'So you don't love me?'

'Do *you* not love me?' she asked, bantering, but suddenly sweaty-palmed.

'I asked first,' said Lovejoy.

'I asked second,' she replied, her voice hitching imperceptibly.

He raised a brow.

Amber was suddenly caught by the silence around them and looked up to see everyone standing by the *Who Wants to Be a Millionaire* machine watching. Eyes wide. Listening.

'We don't love each other,' Amber said quickly, reassuring the group.

Pandora made a sad face.

Julia smiled down at the floor.

Lovejoy sat back, hands behind his head, grinning.

Amber rolled her eyes. She'd had enough of the joking around, she was tired. She got up and went to the loo. 'Get on with the game,' she told the others, tapping the quiz machine.

In the ladies, she stared at herself in the mirror. She looked as tired and messy as Lovejoy did. She even had a vague mascara streak down her face from when she'd welled up that no one had told her about. How embarrassing.

The door opened as she was wiping it away.

307

She looked up. 'Lovejoy,' she said, surprised to see him striding in with absolutely no concern for the fact it was the ladies. 'You're not allowed in here.'

He shrugged. 'Yeah I know,' he said, leaning against the wall.

'Well leave,' she said, nodding towards the door.

'Hang on a minute.' He held up a hand. His lips were half-smiling. His eyes were all hooded and knowing, Amber didn't want to look at them so she focused on the arrow tattoo on his arm. 'Listen,' he said. 'It strikes me that some shit has happened between us in the last couple of days and we need to talk about it, which we have and we will, but, I don't know, it's kind of made me remember what it was like – us.' He pushed off from the wall to move forward, dark eyes still fixed on her. 'Hasn't it you?'

Amber shrugged, the room seemed to be shrinking. 'A bit,' she said, awkward as to the direction of the conversation. Unsure. She was unpractised at talking about feelings. She took a step back, it set the hand-dryer off. 'Shit,' she said, trying to get it to stop.

The noise bellowed.

Lovejoy reached over and turned it off at the wall. His arm trapping her between the hand-dryer and the sink. She could feel him looking down at her, she stared at his chest, at the flecks of dust on his T-shirt. She could smell the familiar scent of him.

'What if,' he said, 'this is our time?'

She shook her head. 'It's not our time.'

'Why not?'

She couldn't keep her eyes off his T-shirt.

With his free hand he reached down and tilted up her chin. 'It might be,' he said.

'Seduced in the ladies' toilet,' she half-laughed. Her hands were shaking a little. 'Lovejoy, I don't think I can do this,' she said.

'Why not?'

'Because there's too much history.'

'History might be a good thing,' he said. 'Saves us having to get to know each other. It's a bloody nightmare having to chat to all these people on Tinder.'

'You said it was great,' she challenged.

'I was lying,' he said, flatly.

'Well that's not very romantic, is it? Let's do it because it's easier than doing it with someone else.'

Lovejoy shook his head. 'That's not what I was saying. I was saying, let's maybe do it because we like each other.'

Amber swallowed.

Lovejoy sensed a weakening. 'And we both admit we did once love each other.'

Amber glanced away, at the mirror, saw them both older and wiser and more lined than their teenage selves. But she felt as juvenile, as desperate not to show him her weakness. And she wondered suddenly why. What she was trying to prove. Surely, if she'd learnt anything it was that honesty wasn't a bad thing. She wondered whether, if she *had* told him in the past, perhaps it *would* have been different. Perhaps it might not have changed things, but it would have opened up the possibility. It wouldn't have been a lifetime of what if.

She looked back, and this time looked up to meet his eyes. 'We did admit that,' she said.

Lovejoy reached up and brushed her hair out of her eye, tucking it behind her ear. 'Well how about it then? How about we see if we might maybe quite like each other in the present?'

Amber made herself hold his gaze, forced herself not to look away. 'OK,' she said. And when she saw him smile, she felt herself smile.

CHAPTER THIRTY-FOUR

THE CEDAR LANE WHATSAPP GROUP

Lexi Warrington: This is UNACCEPTABLE! Amber, I'm sorry to have to say this, but if you were selling to a developer you SHOULD have let us know! It's common decency. Our quiet little street will be RUINED with lorries, dust and building work. It's OUTRAGEOUS. I've seen the plans, they've called it an eco-house which we know is code for giant MONSTROSITY with a tuft of grass on the roof. Complaints MUST be made ASAP. Remember, it'll be your house the lorries park in front of!!!

Also Amber, as you are leaving the street, I'm removing you from this WhatsApp group. Nothing personal! ;-)

Julia Fletcher: Hi Lexi, speaking of removing/adding to the Cedar Lane WhatsApp group, I've noticed a number of people who live on the street aren't currently included. I know this must have been an oversight, so I've spoken to all those not yet invited and will forward their numbers on so you can add them ASAP. We need to make sure the whole street is represented!

Re the eco-house, I think the plans look incredible. Would move in myself if I could! ☺ And on the subject of plans. I'm 100% in favour of the new Sainsbury's, especially as they've proposed a Saturday farmer's market in the car park. And Amber wants me to add that their boil in the bag mussels are fab! Julia x

Hazel from number twenty-two: Oh yes, I completely agree about the mussels! ☺

Lexi Warrington is typing...

Then Julia sent fourteen phone numbers of Cedar Lane residents not currently included on the WhatsApp group, one after the other, drowning out whatever passive-aggressive response Lexi was getting ready to reply. Then she muted the group for a week, now fully aware that what was on there today would soon be completely irrelevant. Old news. Tomorrow's fish and chip paper, if, as Amber pointed out, fish and chips didn't come in natty little cardboard boxes nowadays. And so the thread rolled on regardless...

Linda from number eighty-seven: Heads up, John Lewis sale starts tomorrow, guys! Yay!

CHAPTER THIRTY-FIVE

One year later

'No, Charlie, it's this way, that's a one-way street.' Julia rang the bell on her bike to stop him.

Charlie stopped, lifted up his sunglasses. 'Oh so it is,' he said, noticing the sign. 'This looks like a nice café,' he added, pointing to the tables laid out on the pavement, the waiter bringing out trays of little beers and glasses of pastis to tourists soaking up the sunshine.

Julia beckoned for him to stop stopping and follow her down the side street. She was excited.

'OK, OK, I'm coming,' he said, cycling up to meet her.

Up ahead was the Hotel Croissant, the giant gold croissant that swung from the signpost sparkling as the sun hit it. The hotel had been freshly painted a Farrow & Ball-esque pale grey, looking even better than it did on the Instagram renovation shots.

Julia and Charlie locked up their bikes out front. Charlie was in yellow shorts and his faded green T-shirt, Julia was in a skirt and plunging red V-neck that followed the specifications of Martin's fashion advice to the letter. They'd spent the last ten days cycling round France, tanned and relaxed.

Sleeping in their tent at various different campsites, eating bread and cheese and drinking cheap wine. Going to sleep soon after the sun set and waking up at dawn. Completely unglamorous but totally them.

And now they were on the last leg of their holiday. Staying at the Hotel Croissant.

Julia pushed open the door. Inside, there were gold tiles on the wall of the entrance hall and reclaimed wooden floorboards. The front desk was an old glass-fronted haberdashery counter with hundreds of tiny drawers and a big gold service bell. In the far corner was a white taxidermy swan with a crown on its head and behind the counter stood a very tanned Amber Beddington.

'You're here!' Amber smiled, looking up from a swanky new iMac. She was wearing her yellow shirt and a pair of denim shorts. Her hair was jet black and hung longer than it had in Cedar Lane, skimming her shoulders. Sunglasses pushed her fringe from her forehead.

'We made it,' said Julia, walking forward, gazing around the place. 'It looks amazing.'

'Do you think?' Amber asked, clearly proud of the job she'd done, running her hand along the polished counter.

'It's phenomenal,' Julia replied going to peer into a lounge room off to the left. 'Emerald House, eat your heart out.'

Just then Lovejoy appeared from a door to the back, as sun-kissed as Amber, dressed in a black shirt and jeans. His hair too was longer and his face effortlessly relaxed. 'Hello, hello!' he said, arms wide in greeting. 'Welcome. What do you think?' he asked.

Julia grinned, still loving seeing them together, Lovejoy's

arm draped casually over Amber's shoulders. Amber trying to pretend she was cool with it all but her grin shining bright from within. Julia tipped her head back and looked all the way up the staircase, she saw just a treasure trove of elegant luxury spiralling round to the crystal chandelier at the very top. 'I love it,' she said. 'I really love it.'

Lovejoy gave Amber's shoulder a squeeze. Then he came round the counter and, picking up their bags, said to Charlie, 'Let me give you the tour, mate, and I'll show you your room. Best in the house,' he added.

As they disappeared up the stairs, Julia went to stand with Amber. 'It really is so, so great,' she said.

'I like it,' said Amber, looking round, surveying her abode. 'It's been pretty hard work but it's nice, you know, having complete control. And I can usually convince Lovejoy that my way of doing things is the best.'

'I'll bet you can,' Julia laughed. Then she leant against the counter and asked, more serious, 'And how's it all going, you know, with the two of you?'

'It's good,' Amber said, coyly. 'It's fun.'

Julia raised a brow. 'You still like him.'

Amber closed her eyes, blushing. 'Yes, I like him. We like each other. We can admit it now.'

Julia clapped her hands with joy. 'It's so lovely.'

'How's Lexi Warrington?' Amber asked, clearly keen to change the subject. 'Still getting her knickers in a twist about the build?'

'Oh yes,' Julia nodded. 'She's forever sticking notes on the builder's van to stop them parking in front of her house. I watch them every morning just peel it off and scrunch it up.'

Amber smiled, eyes narrowed with delight. 'And do you see her a lot?'

'No,' Julia shook her head. 'Not really. I'm too busy. And I just figure, if someone doesn't make you feel good about yourself, why go after it. I'm nice to her and everything but I'm less "Hi Lexi",' she did a manic smile-and-wave impression of herself.

Amber nodded. 'Good.' Then opening the door behind her said, 'Shall we go and sit outside?' She beckoned Julia out of the back room and through to the garden. It was all over-grown and ramshackle with wild flowers, in the corner there was a small plunge pool with some lounger chairs around it and then behind that a broken fence that led to a tangle of scrubland. 'We haven't got round to doing this, yet,' Amber said, pulling out one of the rusted chairs for Julia to sit down on. 'I'm hoping it'll be a breakfast terrace for guests but at the moment we just get distracted lounging in the pool. I'm telling myself it's good to have a break.'

'Absolutely,' said Julia. 'You've been working hard!'

'That's exactly what I tell myself.'

Julia looked around at the wilderness, at the falling holly-hocks and cascades of vibrant bougainvillaea. Around the edge of the patio were terracotta pots filled with white geraniums and a rusted bench. 'It's a really lovely space. I can't believe it's here, I didn't see it when we stayed for the antiques fair.'

'I know,' Amber took a seat, 'it was all closed up, we prised open the door and discovered it, what a good day that was!' Stretching her long tanned legs out under the table, she added, 'So tell me, why are you so busy?'

'Well,' Julia tucked her seat in under the table and rested

Through the back door, Lovejoy and Charlie appeared, back from the tour. They pulled over the broken old bench to sit down on.

Lovejoy put his face up to the sun.

Charlie said, 'It looks brilliant, Amber. All incredible.'

'Thank you, Charlie,' Amber replied, as if his compliment really meant the world to her. 'And tell me, what are you up to? Got a new job?'

'I have actually, thanks for asking,' Charlie said, making himself at home on the bench.

'He has a van,' Julia cut in.

'Intriguing,' Amber replied.

Lovejoy sat forward, gesticulating excitedly with his hands as he spoke, keen to impart news that he knew and Amber didn't. 'He's working for one of those veg box companies, Amber. You know the ones who always put the flyers through the door.'

'Yeah, yeah. I'm a franchisee. I've got the whole town signed up!' Charlie's face lit up as he talked about it. 'The pay's shit but it's really good. And I still work at my old job but as a contractor now, so it's less money but more freedom. And anytime we get stuck for money we Airbnb out one of the rooms in the house, or the whole place, and go and stay with friends or Julia's parents.'

'They think we're really enterprising,' Julia laughed. 'It's something my dad can talk about at the club. None of his friends understand Airbnb, so it makes him feel clued-up.'

Charlie said, 'Ideally I'd like to set something up on my own but for now it's just learning all the logistics of the business.'

'Sounds great,' said Amber. 'Well done.'

'Thanks.' Charlie's cheeks pinked a little with pride.

Lovejoy added, clearly having heard all about it on the tour, 'He wants to move to the country, sell veg to fancy restaurants.' Then he turned to Charlie and said, 'I told Amber we should turn this patch into a veg garden but she's having none of it.'

Charlie gave the scrubby patio a once-over. 'It's an ideal space for vegetables,' he said, gesturing to the sun-drenched plants. 'You could maybe make a couple of small beds for some carrots and tomatoes and stuff over there.'

Amber waved her hand. 'Ignore him, Charlie, he's never going to do it.'

Lovejoy frowned with affront. 'I'd do it!'

'Please!' Amber rolled her eyes. 'There is no way you're going to grow vegetables. You'd get bored and they'd all die.'

Lovejoy sat up straight, expression aghast. 'You're so unsupportive.'

'I'm supportive,' Amber countered. 'Just not of things that I know you're never going to do.'

'That's unsupportive!' he replied, arms raised in frustration.

Amber made a face, mimicking his chat.

Julia laughed.

'Don't encourage her,' Lovejoy said.

Amber nudged Julia with her foot. 'Do you want to move to the country?'

Julia shrugged, toying with a bit of rusty paint on the table. 'I wouldn't rule it out. I don't know. Maybe.' She laughed at her own indecision. 'But Charlie wants pigs and I don't want pigs because they're ugly and smelly.'

Lovejoy chuckled.

Amber said, 'I thought the whole thing was that pigs didn't smell.'

'Yes, thank you,' said Charlie, hands held wide. 'They're very clean animals.'

Julia shook her head. 'All people who say they don't smell don't have pigs.'

Charlie was about to counter when a window from the kitchen opened and Pandora's white-blonde head stuck out, 'Hi, Julia! Hi, Charlie! How are you? Do you want a drink?'

'Oh my God, you gave me such a shock!' Julia held her hand to her chest.

'Oops, sorry.' Pandora made a guilty face. She was wearing a red bandana in her hair and a huge white shirt, the sleeve rolled up to reveal tan-freckled arms. Her make-up was perfectly contoured and her eyebrows drawn on thick. She said, 'Does anyone want a cup of tea? Or a beer? Wine?'

Charlie said, 'I wouldn't say no to a beer.'

Julia nodded. 'Wine would be lovely, thanks.'

'OK!' Pandora smiled brightly and disappeared back into the kitchen, pulling the shutters closed behind her.

Julia looked questioningly at Amber. 'What's Pandora doing here?'

Amber shook her head, despairing. 'She's on a gap year, she did a ski season over the winter and was meant to be staying on for the summer but they fired her for, I think, being generally quite shit at being a chalet girl and just going skiing all the time. So she's here,' Amber gestured to the kitchen, 'being a hotel maid.'

'And what's she like?' Julia asked.

Amber shook her head. 'She's so bad.'

Everyone laughed.

It was warm in the garden, a little haven of bees buzzing around the hollyhocks and lavender. There was a lemon tree in the far corner fat and heavy with ripe fruits. And a fig tree opposite that filled the air with sticky sweetness. The sun glinted invitingly on the turquoise pool water. The filter hummed and the odd swallow swooped to skim the surface for a drink.

Pandora came out carrying a tray of wine glasses and beer and a bottle in a cooler and sat herself down in one of the other chairs. 'I'm taking a break, Amber.'

'OK,' Amber nodded, resigned.

Then a voice said, 'Julia! Charlie! You've arrived!' and she turned to see Martin coming down the stairs. He strutted over, dressed in his kilt and a bright yellow T-shirt. He'd had all his hair lopped off really short.

Julia stood up. 'Martin, I didn't realise you were here, too. And look at your hair.'

'Don't it's dreadful. The worst mistake of my life,' he said, coming over and holding Julia's shoulders, air-kissing her on both cheeks. Then doing the same to Charlie. He pulled out a chair and poured himself a glass of wine. 'I'm just here on a bit of a holiday.'

Amber said, 'I'm not sure ten months is a bit of a holiday, Martin.'

Martin shrugged. 'An extended visit,' he corrected. 'The Channel 5 job fell through. Which really is fine because no one watches Channel 5. I'm actually going back soon to audition for *Shipwrecked*.'

'I hope you get it,' said Pandora, all serious. 'You really would be amazing on that.'

'I think so,' Martin agreed. 'I just need my hair to grow back,' he added, running his hand over his shorn off locks. 'I'm like Samson, all my powers have gone. That's why I'm hiding out here,' he joked.

Amber raised a brow. 'I thought you were just enjoying the free holiday.'

Martin made a face of affront. 'Er, excuse me, I've been very useful. I decorated two of the rooms.'

Amber scoffed.

'I did!' Martin said, defensive. 'And I've given you all my extensive style knowledge free of charge.'

Amber shook her head. Martin settled himself down satisfied he'd won the argument.

Pandora poured everyone's drinks and handed them round. Lovejoy said, 'I think it's getting hotter,' and wiped the sweat from his brow. Julia watched as Amber got up and opened a big white sun parasol, granting him some welcome shade. The gesture made her smile. Amber noticed and rolled her eyes but then had to hold in a bashful smile herself.

Julia sipped her wine, enjoying the shade from the parasol and the sweet perfume of the fig. She glanced around the group – Lovejoy chatting with Charlie, both of them swigging from their beer cans, Pandora re-plaiting her hair as she talked *Shipwrecked* tactics with Martin, Amber listening to what Lovejoy and Charlie were saying and interjecting – then she said, 'I can't believe we're all here! We're only missing one person, aren't we? How's Billy getting on at uni?'

'Ask him yourself,' Amber replied. 'Billy! Get out here!' she hollered and a couple of minutes later, Billy sloped out, yawning, fumbling with his glasses, looking like he'd just got out of bed. 'It's the holidays and he decided his were best spent in France,' she said it slightly exasperated but it was clear she was delighted to have him there.

Billy sat down on the arm of Pandora's chair. 'Well everyone else was here,' he yawned. 'It was unfair otherwise. And we're meant to live with our parents, aren't we? We're the boomerang generation.'

'I think that's actually us,' said Charlie, correcting him. 'Millennials are the boomerang generation.'

'But you don't live at home?' said Pandora, puzzled.

'No, Pandora, because it's not the law,' Amber said. She turned to Julia, despairing. 'Look at what I have to put up with. And do you know, I was actually worried we might be lonely out here.'

Julia shook her head. 'No, I think it's fantastic. Maybe we'll move in, too.'

Charlie looked quite taken with the idea. 'Or at least up the road, we passed some good-looking land on the way in.'

Lovejoy raised a glass. 'Do it. The more the merrier,' he said. 'You could buy that land there… ' he indicated towards the wild scrub at the end of their garden.

Charlie gave Julia a nudge. 'Maybe we should.'

'Maybe.' Julia tipped her head, not completely against the idea. As she took a sip of her wine, a little white dog trotted out and sat at Billy's bare feet. 'Who's this?' Julia asked.

'Alfonso,' said Billy, leaning down to hoic the dog up onto his lap.

Amber said, 'Ned's dog,' with a knowing raise of her brow.

'Oh.' Julia was intrigued. 'How is Ned?'

'Ask Billy,' Amber replied. 'He went to Canada for Christmas. Billy, how was Canada?' Amber gave him a nudge.

Billy shrugged, scratching the dog's ears. 'Alright. Bit boring. And the baby cried *all the time*!' he added with clear exasperation.

Beside him Amber looked smug. Then she leant forward and raised her glass. 'Well isn't this lovely. Everyone here. I would like to make a toast to the lovely developer who bought my house so I could buy the Hotel Croissant!'

'Hear, hear!' agreed Lovejoy.

Pandora leaned in and, with a sweep of her hair, said, 'I'd like to make a toast to Martin getting on *Shipwrecked*.'

'Oh good one,' said Martin, grinning, 'Cheers to that!'

'Once you're on one reality show you can be on them all,' Pandora added with absolute certainty.

Billy yawned again, rubbing his hand over his face to try and wake himself up. 'I think we should toast to that Olga woman for making you lose your job.'

Amber made a face. 'I wouldn't go that far. Let's just stick with the developer and the hotel.'

Everyone reached their glasses forward and clinked. 'To Hotel Croissant.'

They sat for a while, enjoying the sunshine, the calm hum of the bees and the stillness of the garden. Then Lovejoy finished his beer and said, 'Right then, who's ready for a dip in the pool?'

'Oh me, me!' Pandora jumped up.

'Don't you have rooms to do?' Amber asked.

Pandora rolled her eyes, 'Really?'

'Yes, really!' said Amber emphatic.

Billy stood up with a yawn. 'I'll help you.'

Pandora beamed. 'Oh thanks, Billy.' And they trotted off together, the white dog in tow.

Lovejoy strode over to the plunge pool, yanking his T-shirt off over his head. 'I am sweltering. You coming, Charlie?'

Charlie downed the rest of his beer and followed suit. Pulling off his green T-shirt, his shorts doubling as swimming trunks. Clearly relaxed in this company, Julia noticed. No hot tub-esque tantrums.

Martin stood up and said, 'Me too, I need to work on my tan, no one wants to be the pasty one on *Shipwrecked*.'

Julia looked at Amber. 'You getting in?'

'Christ no, I'm quite happy sitting here,' she said, head tipped back, all glossy dark hair, eyes closed absorbing the sun.

So they sat side by side, sipping chilled white wine, bees buzzing in the lavender, the guys joking in the pool, through the upstairs window came the sound of Pandora singing out-of-tune as she made the beds and Billy correcting her when she got the words wrong.

Amber rolled her head to look at Julia, opening one eye, she said, 'We should probably make a toast to Lexi Warrington.'

Julia made a face. 'Why?'

'Well,' said Amber, sitting up a bit straighter, 'without her posting the messages you sent, you wouldn't have come to France, we wouldn't have gone to get Billy, you and Charlie wouldn't have, me and Lovejoy wouldn't have, yadda, yadda, yadda.'

Julia thought about it. 'I'm not sure I want to toast Lexi.'

'No,' Amber shook her head, 'me neither.' Then she said, 'You could toast me then, instead.'

Julia laughed. 'OK. To Amber,' she said, lifting her glass, 'without whom I wouldn't have gone to France.'

Amber clinked her glass, and took a sip, then settled back down.

Julia frowned. 'Aren't you going to toast me?'

'No.'

'Oh.'

'Just kidding.' Amber grinned. Then she sat up and, raising her glass aloft, the azure water of the plunge pool glinting in the sunlight, the air filled with the sound of everyone enjoying themselves, the wine crisp, the sun warming their skin, said, 'To my good friend Julia. I'm very glad you chose me to run away with.'

Newport Community
Learning & Libraries